“Into the Hood: Pierre & Anneka”

Ms. T. Nicole

Text **Treasured** to **444999**

To subscribe to our Mailing List.

Interested in becoming a part of the Treasured Publications family?

Submit manuscripts to

Info@Treasuredpub.com

Into the Hood: Pierre & Anneka

Ms. T. Nicole

Thank you for taking the time to read my work.

Follow me on my social media to find out about upcoming projects and work

Twitter: Tomeika_Diva

Facebook: https://www.facebook.com/MsTNicole/?fref=ts

Instagram: @creativediva12

YouTube: www.youtube.com/creativediva12

Into the Hood: Pierre & Anneka

Acknowledgements

This book is intended to entertain and is recommended for ages sixteen and up. This is a book based on urban fiction, so please be advised that it will contain explicit language and adult content.

I truly want to thank God for giving me the gift to entertain through my words and twisted mind. When others thought and said that I was crazy, I used those words and picked up a pen. The day that happened was the day that changed my life. No matter what happens in my life, I want to truly take the time to say thank you to the family members and close friends who always stand by me and support me. No matter what I pen, you all are always pushing me to do more and make me feel as if I could one day be great.

Mom, you are amazing; you never once allowed me to believe that failure was an option. Alexandria, you may not be able to read any of my books, but just know that Mommy loves you and will always do whatever I can to show you the same love and support, just as your grandma has done with me. I love you, baby doll.

I want to thank my siblings for always being an ear and shoulder for me. No matter what I faced in life, and Lord knows the last six months have been trying, you all have been there for me, and I love you and can't thank you enough. When I wanted to give up and throw in the towel, you all wouldn't allow me to do that, so for that, I'm saying thank you.

My promise to you all is that I will continue to use this gift and allow my gift to make room for me. Let's get to the top. ☺ Love you all -MiMi

Into the Hood: Pierre & Anneka
"Into the Hood: Pierre & Anneka"

Synopsis

A beautiful, eighteen-year-old young lady—Anneka Snow—is on a journey after the tragic death of her mom. After she runs away from the only man that is supposed to always love and protect her, Anneka finds herself on a journey, trying to fight to survive.

On her quest, she's met by seven different men, each with their own purpose, but her naïve spirit, enchanted beauty, and lack of life experience may be the reason her life might be spared.

The men grow to love Anneka. She cleans, cooks, loves apples, and has a nurturing spirit that causes everyone in her path to fall deep into her spell.

While on this journey, Anneka is faced with the changes of her new life. Trying to keep her head above water and making it out alive, Anneka is forced to adapt to her new situation while making the best of her circumstances. While staring death in the eyes, a new love interest may be her only means of survival. The hunt began for this spoiled princess, and nothing will stop the citizens of New York from finding her. Will Anneka have her happily ever after?

Find out now in *Into the Hood: Pierre & Anneka*

Into the Hood: Pierre & Anneka

Prologue

Being raised by a politician, I watched how men of power lied, cheated, and manipulated others to get what they wanted, my father included. My father was a mean and powerful man—a senator here in New York. I wished I could brag about being a spoiled little Daddy's girl, but that was the furthest thing from the truth. The way that man treated me and my mom was nothing more than disgusting. I couldn't wait until the day that I'd be able to walk away from his ass and never look back. I was supposed to be learning how I should be treated by this man, and at this rate, I was seeing a really bad example.

I'd like to think of myself as the fairest of them all. I'd always tried to see the good in people, but the more I tried, the angrier I would become as I watched the reality of my so-called perfect life. People were good, but one bad apple could surely spoil the bunch, and my father was the epitome of the meaning 'bad apple'.

A little over a year ago, something happened to me that forever changed my life. Suppose I take you on a journey and, just for a moment, trap you into my little world where all of my happiness was taken away.

Usually, stories that begin with 'once upon a time' will automatically make you think of classic fairytale stories with characters that we've all grown to love and some that we love to hate. My name is Anneka Snow, and my story is a tad bit different. It doesn't start with 'once upon a time', and it sure as hell ain't a fairytale.

If you are here for a story that's wrapped in a pretty bow, I suggest you keep moving to the next story because my tale possibly won't end with an enchanted kiss. The way my tale is told, we are on the streets of New York, and things here sometimes end with a bullet…

Into the Hood: Pierre & Anneka

How will my story end?

“So when were you going to tell me this? Why did you all hide it?”

“Anneka, trust me. I wanted to tell you. All types of crazy shit went on in my head the moment I saw him.”

“Why didn’t you try harder? What did he say?”

“It’s not about what he said, sweetheart. I’m simply telling you this because I’m on the fence. He’s begging to see you and acting like shit’s sweet, and truthfully, I can’t call it.”

“Fuck it! I’m going to see him. I’m not running anymore. Today, I promised myself to take back my life, and that’s exactly what I’m going to do.”

“Sweetheart, you don’t want to go alone. If you would wait until morning, I’ll take you.”

“No, I’m going now. He’s going to constantly come after me. He’s taken everything from me, and there’s no way I can keep running from him. I have to go and face him.”

“Well, if you face him, he has to face me.”

“No, this is not your fight. The fact that you have him contained is all I need. I have to see his eyes; I have to talk to him tonight! Please give me your keys and the address. I’ll be fine.”

"Listen to me. I know you want this over and done with, and I do too, but baby, you're not going alone. My conscious won't allow me to let that go down like that. If you feel like you have to go now, I'm going to take you, and I swear to you, if the muthafucka bucks, I'm taking his ass out."

"Please, just allow me to do this alone."

"I can't, Anneka. You have already touched a part of my heart that I never knew existed. If you are determined to face him, you will face him with me. There's nothing else to discuss. Now what's it gonna be?"

We looked into each other's eyes as butterflies began to tickle my stomach. I knew this was the moment that I'd been waiting for. I'd seen it in the movies a million times, and now it was my time to experience this.

The door creaked open, and we turned to see what could only be described as the seed of Satan.

"Well, well, well… I almost missed a beautiful, enchanted kiss. Pardon my tardiness. Had I known it was going to be this congenial, I would have baked a pie; now tell me which one of you muthafuckas are ready to die?" That voice was familiar, and so was that face. My heartbeat began to pick up speed as fear finally snuck in. I wanted this hunt to end, and the only way to end it was to face my fears.

So much was taken from me, and now I must do what my mom told me to do. FIGHT!

Chapter 1- Eva

"Anneka, baby, bring me my medicine, and help me get this dinner party together. Mommy isn't feeling the best, and you know your father will have a fit if this shit isn't done," I spoke in exhaustion, wishing like hell that this party would come and go so that I could allow my body the rest that it required.

I sat in the multifunctional room of our condo and prepared for this party that my husband, Leo, wanted to host for a meet and greet after he took the senate seat.

These parties meant the world to my husband because when it came to him, image was everything, and everyone needed to play their part and make him look good, or there would be hell to pay.

"Here you go, Mommy. Why do we have to do this song and dance for him? I'm sick of this shit," Anneka spoke, and my eyes went up and caught her scowl.

"Anneka, first off, watch your damn mouth. This is your father, and you know he's going to want things perfect. When you step out and get married, you'll understand how to make and keep your husband happy."

Into the Hood: Pierre & Anneka

"Mommy, how? You do everything for Daddy, and that still don't stop him from sticking his dick in other women."

"Anneka! That's enough! Yes, your father has his flaws, but young lady, trust me when I tell you a man is going to be a man."

"Well, a man can be a man without treating me like shit. I'm sorry, Mommy, but that's the way I feel. I hate how he treats you. I love Daddy, but I hate the way he treats both of us. We are supposed to be the apples of his eye. I'm supposed to learn how a man should treat me based on the way Daddy treats us both. I'm sorry, but seeing this, I don't think I'll ever get married."

"What goes on between your father and I is our business, and you shouldn't be concerned. Your father has a lot going on now, and it's up to us to help him get through this. Neka Pooh, I know you see and hear a lot, and now that you're eighteen, I can't pull the wool over your eyes, but trust me. Your father is a good man, and he just needs our support."

"Mommy, stop with the Neka Pooh. Seriously, Mommy, what about you? No disrespect, but he ain't shit for asking you to do this, knowing that you're not feeling well. I mean, damn, Ma. You just got home from chemo;

you need your rest. I'm so sick of him treating you like this. Ma, the only reason I haven't moved out is because I'm afraid of what may happen to you when I'm out of the house."

"Sweetheart, I know your heart is in the right place. I don't want you feeling as if you can't live your life simply because of my battle. This cancer won't win. Mommy will beat this."

"You're beautiful, you're strong, and you're my shero, superwoman, and truly the queen of New York. Mommy, I may not have a lot of life experience, but I thank you for always being a real mother to me. I may act spoiled at times, but it's only because you raised me to want and demand better. Let's get this meet and greet together for this no-good ass bastard."

"Anneka, that is still your father, so hold your tongue, and don't speak like that about him. Listen to me, sweetheart. If I haven't taught you anything else, I know I taught you to trust, love, and respect. Respect is taught at home, and without it, this is a fucked-up world to be in. No matter what, always honor and respect your parents. I won't tell you again to watch your mouth, young lady."

"I'm sorry, Mommy. I love you, beautiful."

"And me you, Neka Pooh. Now help me get this together. We only have a little bit of time."

...

The multifunctional room was decorated to perfection, the food was perfectly placed, and I had an hour to get ready. My body was tired, and every last one of my outfits seemed to swallow me with the weight that I'd lost from my battle with cancer.

I was standing in my full-length mirror when I saw Anneka standing in my doorway.

"Come in, Neka Pooh," I spoke weakly as I sat on the bed, trying to collect myself.

"Mommy, please lay down. I'll host for Daddy. You really need your rest. Did you take your second round of meds yet?" Anneka asked with so much concern.

"Not yet. I needed to get your father's things in order before he got in. He said he would only have time to shower and dress, and he needed everything laid out."

"That selfish son of—"

"Anneka, stop."

"I'm sorry, Ma. Just lay down. I'll take care of everything. If I haven't learned anything else from you, I know how to entertain, cook, and clean. Allow me to step in on your behalf. You need your rest, beautiful."

"Just give me about ten minutes, and I'll be up and refreshed."

"Sleep, Ma. I'll take care of everything."

"Neka Pooh, please don't let me sleep too long. I just need a small power nap."

"Okay, Ma," Anneka spoke as she helped me get tucked underneath the blankets, and I allowed my body to relax.

Looking up at my daughter, I wondered how much time I really had left with her. I knew that with each passing day, this disease was taking me down, and soon I'd be out. Leo and I sheltered her so much that I felt like if I left now, she wouldn't be able to function in this world as she knew it.

Anneka was my heart, and each day that I was here to look into her beautiful eyes, I was thankful to God that she was on my side.

It was like I was afraid to not fight this thing because my heart told me that Leo wouldn't step up to the plate and do right, but I could only pray.

Into the Hood: Pierre & Anneka

Anneka took the brush that was on my nightstand and began brushing my short, stringy hair. This chemo was really taking a toll on me, and Anneka did all she could to make me comfortable.

At times, I felt bad because she really didn't have a life outside of me. Anneka was homeschooled simply because when I was first diagnosed, she was going into her high school year, and this cancer started aggressively, taking over my body. Leo was really into politics, so he didn't spend a lot of time at home, and getting Anneka back and forth to school by trains wasn't feasible to me.

I was finally relaxed as Anneka stroked my hair, and I allowed my body to rest. I was nestled into my covers, dreaming of better days, when I was snapped out of my slumber by Leo's rage.

"Eva! Is this your idea of handling things? Why aren't you dressed? What the fuck are you doing?" Leo ranted as I sat up in the bed, trying to adjust my eyes and focus on what was going on.

"Oh, so you're going to sit there, looking dumbfounded? Why in the hell are you not dressed? Get up and get moving! I think you're trying to fuck up my night!" Leo screamed, and Anneka, of course, came to my rescue.

"Daddy, she had chemo today. Did you not see that everything was set up and ready to go? You don't have to talk to her like that."

"Anneka, please, give your dad and I some privacy. Mommy's alright."

"You're not! I told you that I will do it for you. Please lay down, Ma."

"Anneka, I'd advise you to take your ass in your room and listen to what your mom said. You will do as I say, show up for ten minutes, allow me to show off my family, and then you will bring your ass back in here and sit in your room until we return," Leo spoke in a tone that let me know that he was going to put hands on my child, and I couldn't allow that to happen.

I used every bit of strength that I had and rose from my bed to address a now pissed off Anneka.

"So are we puppets now?" Anneka sassed, and then Leo's nose flared.

"Anneka, please! Do as your father instructed," I commented as I put a little space in between the two.

Anneka was as stubborn as a bull, but she got it honest because Leo was the exact same. Anneka gave

Leo a cold stare as she backed out of the doorway and did as instructed.

"Eva, I'm getting real tired of her smart-ass mouth. If I didn't have this meet and greet tonight, I would have put my fist down her throat. Get your ass dressed, and I hope you bought a wig. I won't tolerate you looking like a weak bitch, trying to represent me," Leo spat as he walked into our bathroom and jumped into the shower.

I sat at my vanity, tried to complete my makeup, and then placed a wig cap over my head. As I stared in the mirror, I didn't recognize the woman that was looking back at me. I was once strong and confident, and now I was weak and insecure. I could only hope that Anneka wasn't taking a page from my current book, because I didn't want her weak.

I struggled to get the wig placed just right, and my hands started to tremble. Leo emerged from the bathroom and began putting on his clothes that I had laid out and pressed perfectly for him.

"Are you almost done? We have ten minutes, and you know I loathe tardiness," he said as if he hadn't noticed my struggle.

Taking in a deep breath, I spoke just above a whisper. "Leo, I don't think I can make it. I'm not feeling the best."

"Well, it's a good thing that I didn't ask you to think, because you are going to make it. Now hurry the hell up."

I swallowed hard and called out for Anneka. "Neka Pooh, come help me please," I managed to get out, and Leo shook his head and walked back into the bathroom, slamming the door.

"Ma, what do you need help with?" Anneka questioned as she walked into my bedroom.

"Help me get dressed, sweetheart," I said, trying to hold back my tears.

Leo used to be the most loving man before I took ill, and ever since this disease had taken over my body, he'd been verbally disrespecting me more, and his cheating was getting sloppy. Leo thought that I didn't smell the perfume that emitted from his body when he first came in, but I smelled it just as I had the past few years. I simply sat back and ignored his cheating and disrespect because I knew the image that he wanted us to uphold.

Into the Hood: Pierre & Anneka

"Mommy, no matter what, you're beautiful with or without this wig. Come on, beautiful. Let's get you into this dress," Anneka spoke as she looked me in my eyes.

I knew my daughter felt my pain, and I begged her with my eyes to remain silent and allow me to fight this battle. I simply wanted to prepare her for the absolute worst just in case I transitioned to my creator sooner than later.

Anneka touched up my makeup and pinned my gown perfectly to fit my tiny frame. "I love you, beautiful."

"And me you, Neka Pooh."

Anneka placed a kiss on my cheek, and she escorted me to the living room as we looked at the view of the city while waiting on Leo to come out of the bathroom.

"Mommy, no matter what happens, know that you are worth so much more than you're getting now."

"Neka Pooh, this all may seem as if your dad is mistreating me, but sweetheart, know that he's under a lot of pressure, and things will get better."

"Well, regardless of what you say, Mommy, I'm here with you, and we will fight together."

"Are you two finally ready to go?" Leo asked as Anneka leaned in and gave me a hug.

"We're ready, Leo," I spoke as Anneka took me by the hand and led me to the multifunctional room down the hall.

As we approached the room, Anneka opened the door, and the flashes from the cameras were blinding. Leo finally took me by the hand and began his performance as a loving husband and doting father.

Anneka wasn't smiling but more so had her eyes and focus on me. I kept up my act and tried to speak with confidence and make sure that I was doing everything just the way Leo wanted it.

The citizens of New York who came by were more than amazed with the setup and enjoyed the food. I took pride in knowing that I was the cause of the chatter that centered on the décor and food.

With the night almost coming to an end, I detached from Leo's arm and took a seat to rest my body.

"Are you trying to fuck things up for me? Get your ass up and smile for these people until the last one leaves," Leo spoke through gritted teeth and a fake smile.

He planted a kiss on my cheek and pretended to dance with me.

The onlookers cooed as the reporters continued to snap pictures.

Thankfully, the night ended, and Leo demanded that I clean the multifunctional room so that we wouldn't get a hundred-dollar fine. I didn't know why he was being so cheap with things when we had the money. I simply smiled until the last person was gone and then went back into our condo to change so that I could come back and clean.

"That went well. It could have been a lot better if you would have worked the room the way I wanted you to," Leo said as he undressed and prepared for bed.

"I'm sorry, honey. I'm not feeling the best."

"How long are you going to use that as an excuse, Eva, dammit! Look around, Eva. This is New York; people are living with cancer daily and have more energy than a toddler. You want sympathy and always want to talk to people about your battle and struggle when you should have been talking about the expansion that I'm over. I don't ask for much, and you can't even give me the little shit I'm asking for. What the fuck are you even here for? Shit!"

Tears began rolling down my cheeks as I quickly changed to go back out to clean the multifunctional room.

As I was leaving from our bedroom, Leo spoke. "Turn those fucking lights out. I'm trying to get some rest."

Turning off the lights, I thought about how much more of this I would be able to take.

After closing our bedroom door, I looked toward the city and spoke quietly. "Lord, how much more can one person take?"

I didn't know my daughter was there waiting to help me, and she replied. "We can leave whenever you want. Just say the word, and this will all be over." I looked toward Anneka's voice and wiped away my tears. She came to embrace me and said, "Mommy, you deserve better." And in that moment, I knew she was right and knew things needed to change.

Chapter 2- Anneka

I helped my mom clean the multifunctional room and get it back in tip-top shape. I started thinking of ways to help her to regain her strength, and then it hit me.

"Ma, do you think going to Dad's doctor is a good idea?"

"What do you mean, Neka Pooh? We've been going to Dr. Osbourne for years. You know I trust him."

"Well, I don't. Ma, before you say anything, listen to me and hear me out," she stated, and I took in a deep breath and sat on the sofa that was in the room and gave her my full attention. "Ma, since you've gotten really sick, it doesn't seem as if you're getting any better. I've been doing a little research, and I think it's the combination of your medicines that's acting as a catalyst with your body. There's this doctor; her name is Vanessa Brown. She's young, black, educated, and she deals with natural cures, and just at thirty years of age, she's making great strides to a modern way to treat and naturally medicate the body for complete healing."

"Anneka, you know all that stuff you see and read about is just a plot to get people to give money for things we know won't work. In my case, they caught the cancer too late, and it has attacked my body so bad that my fate is pretty much written."

"Mom, don't say that. I need you here, and if we are going to fight, we are going to swing with everything we have. Trust me, Mommy, just like you always have me, I always have you."

I looked at my mom with nothing but love in my eyes, knowing that my gut was telling me to try things differently with her. Mom loved Dad, and that was cool I guess because of the years they'd spent with each other. Here lately, my attitude hadn't been the best because of the way I was seeing my dad.

He'd always been a jerk to some degree, but here lately, he'd been a bigger jerk, and I didn't trust his ass, so I needed to do whatever I could to ensure that my mom had the best chance of survival.

"Mommy, I made an appointment for you for tomorrow. Please, let's go and see for ourselves. If you don't like it, we will walk away and continue things just like you want it, but Mommy, please, for me, let's just try," I begged, showing my mom that I was in the fight with her. Cancer wasn't going to beat her; we were going to fight this thing together and kick cancer's ass.

Into the Hood: Pierre & Anneka

Turning off the lights and taking the leftover food back into our condo, I placed the food on the counter and helped my mom get into her bed. She had a long, tiring day, and I set my alarm to get up early so that I could take care of breakfast and get her to Dr. Brown. I had a feeling that this would be just the thing we needed to get my mom in the best of health so that I could do the things my heart desired.

…

It was 4:00 A.M. when my alarm sounded. I sprang out of bed, took care of my hygiene, and immediately put the coffee in the grinder to make my dad a fresh cup. He would be ready to eat by 4:30 and out the house by 5:00 A.M. That was always his Monday-morning ritual, and I wanted to be sure I didn't miss a beat.

With his coffee going just the way he loved it, I had one of the biggest spreads on the table.

He stepped out his room and held a glare that I knew oh so well. Ignoring his stare, I prepared his plate and sat it on the table at the head where he always sat.

"Morning, Father," I spoke with a hint of attitude.

"Anneka, your behavior has been less than perfect lately, and you're acting like you don't appreciate what I do for you around here. You know that I don't take too kindly to disrespect, and we will have to address your behavior."

"Father, I'm eighteen, and I'm not an idiot by any means or stretch of the word. I am my father's child, and my behavior is nothing more than the mere reflection of what I'm seeing," I sassed, making sure that he knew my actions were only a reaction to his own behavior that he displayed here lately.

"Since you pointed out that you're eighteen, I guess that means that you're saying that you're grown."

"I'm not saying that. I know that I'm grown. Father, I won't take a beating from you ever again, and since we are on the subject of behavior, let's address yours."

"I don't know who the hell you think you're talking to, little girl. You won't sit at my table and sass me. Do you understand?"

"I understand perfectly well, Father, and as your daughter, I'm telling you that the things you're doing to mom are unacceptable, and I hope like hell that you are prepared to take everything that you've dished out. Remember when you told me that you reap what you sew? Well, Father, you're sewing a bad seed, and I'll be there smiling when it's time for you to reap your harvest."

"Leave my presence before I forget that you're my daughter and do something that I might or might not regret," my father spoke, and I was laughing on the inside, knowing that I'd gotten to him. Maybe my mom was too weak to stand up to him, but I wasn't, and I was going to try my best to put his attention on me and off my mom.

I got up from the table and walked back into my room to prepare for my day. I heard my father in the kitchen slamming things down, and that only meant that he was pissed. *Good. Now he's feeling the same shit that he places on my mom,* I thought as I glossed my lips and tied a beautiful, red, silk headband on my head.

The door slammed, and I knew he was gone, so it was the perfect time to clean up after him and get my mom's medication, clothes, and food ready so that we could start our day and get to the doctor's office by 7:00 A.M. It was the only appointment Dr. Brown had, and I was going to make sure we didn't miss it.

…

We arrived at Dr. Brown's office with fifteen minutes to spare. The aroma in the waiting area was so calm that I felt as if we were surrounded in perfect peace.

"Anneka, baby, you have to stop arguing with your father."

"Ma, can we not talk about him? I just want us to focus on trying to get you better," I stated, holding her hand.

"Eva Snow, the doctor will see you now," the office assistant announced, and I grabbed my mom by the hand and took her back to see the doctor.

"Here, beautiful. Have a seat," I said as we sat in the office, and Dr. Brown stood with a smile as she watched me take care of my mom.

"What a beautiful sight. Having a strong support system is just what you need to fight this beast that we call cancer. I'm Dr. Brown, and when I saw your case, I couldn't pass up the opportunity to provide you with my services. Make yourself comfortable," Dr. Brown stated with a smile.

"Dr. Brown, here is all of the medications that my mom is taking. I'm Anneka, and I'm the one who demanded to speak with you the other day on the phone."

"Oh yes, you're just as persistent as your father." She laughed.

"You know my father?" I queried.

"Only from television. I thought it was an honor that the great Snow family wanted me to oversee this case, and that's why I told you not to worry about the cost or insurance. It's my pleasure to take on this case and show you all that there's life after a diagnosis of cancer. We will beat this—together."

I loved her confidence, and I took in everything she said as she carefully went over my mom's condition. This woman was black, educated, and a force to be reckoned with. I had a feeling that we were in the right place, and I was going to make it my business to see to it that my mom got everything she needed to get better.

"So remember, Eva. Toss all of this away, and we will start your new plan immediately. With Anneka's help, I'm sure you'll have your strength back in no time."

"Are you sure I need to throw this away?" my mom asked with confusion in her tone.

"Unless you want to continue to wither away, then by all means, continue to take those medications, but if you want to regain your health and take control over your life, I need for you to trust me."

"We trust you. I trust you. She's done with this, and we are ready to do the work to get her back healthy and strong," I interjected, and Dr. Brown smiled as she stood to shake my hand and give me the natural things needed to get my mom back on a healthy track. We said our goodbyes and were able to make a follow-up appointment. I almost danced out of the office.

...

Arriving back at home, my mom was feeling a lot better with a natural energy booster that Dr. Brown made herself. She gave us a week's supply and said that we would start Mom's process with five of these a day with protein and vegetables for one meal per day.

"So tell me, Mom. What did you think about Dr. Brown?" I asked as I smiled and put away the natural juices that the doctor gave us.

"I think that she's confident, beautiful, and smart."

"So are you glad that I found her?"

"We will see, Anneka. One day at a time."

I smiled because I knew that meant she was happy. She didn't want to outright say that I was right, but I knew deep down inside, she was loving Dr. Brown just as much as I was.

I sat on the couch and decided to have a conversation with my mom that was long overdue. "Mom, it's getting a bit crowded in here with you and Dad, and I think it's time for me to find my own place."

"Neka Pooh, you know I need you."

"I know, Mommy, but it's been time for me to find my way and learn the things that I like. I mean seriously, Ma. Dad and I are constantly bumping heads, and it's only a matter of time before he tries to kick me out anyway. I've been doing a little research, and I found a place here in Manhattan, but you know I'll need your help until I get my studio up and running," I spoke, giving my mom my plans.

"Neka Pooh, you know that I believe in your dreams and want you to have your happiness, but this world is evil, and I don't feel like now is the time."

"Mommy, before you give me a hard no, let's just see how your new treatment goes, and we can work from there."

"I know you want to see the world with a new pair of eyes, and Lord knows I don't want you to wither away and not find love on account of me being a burden to you."

"Mommy, stop. You know I'll take care of you forever and a day. I just want to open my own health studio and teach yoga. You're going to be my first customer, so stop with all the crazy talk. When it's meant for me to find that special person, he will come, but right now, I'm focused on my studio, and of course you, my beautiful queen."

"Neka Pooh, Mommy is far from being a beautiful queen."

"Says who? As long as I'm your princess, you will always be my beautiful queen. Mom, you have to stop allowing Dad to live rent free in your mind. You are gorgeous. I would know because I look just like you." I laughed, meaning every word.

I sat in the living room and talked to my mom about my hopes and dreams and started seeing things in a new light. I knew that she needed me, and it would only be a matter of time before she was healed, and I would be on my way to finding my independence.

Mom had a pretty eventful day, so I helped her into bed and put on my running gear, grabbed my beat headphones, and went jogging around our area on Roosevelt Island.

Things were going to work out. It was only a matter of time before they did, and I was ready for this change.

Change meant to become different, and little did I know, life for me was about to become very different.

Chapter 3- Eva

4 Months Later

I couldn't believe that Dr. Brown's methods had completely changed my life. I had so much energy, and I was starting to feel like myself. My tiny frame started to fill out in all of the right areas, and my hair was growing like weeds.

"Whoa, Anneka, slow down. Mommy can't keep up with you." I panted as I ran behind my daughter out on our morning run.

Anneka spoke to Dr. Brown, who encouraged her to get me out and about daily for at least thirty minutes a day, and Anneka pushed me to a full hour, and I had to admit that I felt great.

"No, Mom. Keep up. We're almost there!" Anneka yelled as I pushed myself and gave this run everything I had.

Finally making it to the stairs of our building, I sat on the bottom step and tried to catch my breath.

"Girl, I won't have to worry about cancer killing me. If I keep running like that, you're going to kill me," I joked as I held my hand to my heart, trying to gain control over my breathing.

Into the Hood: Pierre & Anneka

"Stop it, beautiful. You have a long life to live. Let's get your after-workout protein drink going," Anneka said as I got up from the step and made my way into the entrance of the building.

The elevator chimed, and we stepped in, holding the door for one of our neighbors. He spoke his good morning with a smile and then stated, "Mrs. Snow, you're looking stronger than ever. You know that we are all rooting for you to fight this thing."

"Thank you. Every day is another chance for me to fight stronger and harder. Thank you for your positive thoughts," I commented and waited for us to get to the fourth floor.

Stepping off the elevator, I heard Leo having a heated discussion. Anneka rolled her eyes and barged in, having no regards to his conversation.

"I have to go, but trust me, this won't stop anything," he stated as he hung up the phone and diverted his attention toward me.

"What is this, Eva? You're going through a midlife crisis or some shit? Why are you trying to keep up with that girl? You know Dr. Osbourne called me and said that not only haven't you been getting your medication, but you haven't been to any of the standing appointments that he had for you. Eva, I go out of my way to make sure you have the best of care. Don't make me look bad."

"Leo, haven't you noticed that I haven't been as sick lately? Sweetheart, I haven't been going to Dr. Osbourne. In fact, Anneka found me this great doctor who specializes in natural healing, and her methods are really working, and I'm feeling better than ever."

Leo's face turned angry as he wasn't receptive to what I was saying. He marched over to me and put his hand around my neck as he spoke through gritted teeth.

"I don't give a fuck what that bitch of a daughter found. Take your ass back to Dr. Osbourne and get the treatment that he's suggesting. I'm sick of you making me look bad."

Leo released my neck, and I sucked in air and grabbed my phone. Calling Dr. Osbourne, I had tears in my eyes and made the appointment like Leo suggested.

I drank my protein shake and walked back into my room as I tried to figure out why Leo didn't see that I was getting better.

I walked in the room, and he had papers in his hand, and he sat on the bed beside me.

"Look, Eva. You may not understand why I do what I'm doing and need for you to do things just the way I planned. I'm in a position now that governor's mansion is looking rather good, and it's only a matter of time before the presidential seat will be mine. Look. Do what I say, and everything else will fall into place. Sign these papers, and have them on the table ready for me tomorrow morning."

Leo put the papers on the bed, kissed my forehead, and left out for the day.

Leo thought I was dumb and was going to sign his papers without reading them. For the past few years, I've been hiding money in an account under an assumed name that myself and Anneka only had access to. I hadn't told Anneka about this account as of yet, but when the time was right, she would have everything she desired.

I looked through the paperwork and saw that Leo had changed everything and also made himself power of attorney over my life, and that was when it hit me. Leo didn't want me better. I was worth more to him dead, and everything Anneka was saying for the past few months was ringing true. It was time for me to take a stand and do everything in my power to make sure this man didn't see a dime of my money.

I contacted a great attorney and a long time special friend of mine so that I could make sure things were perfect for Anneka.

"Hello, Robert. This is Eva. I know it's been a long time, but I really need you." My heart was pounding fast, not certain of how I was going to explain this situation to Robert, but it was time for me to put my big girl panties on and get this out. I didn't have a clue of how Robert would react, but I knew if anyone could help me, it would be him.

Robert and I chatted and caught up for a bit, and I sent him things that he'd been wanting for years, and when he got them, I heard that smile through his voice, and things were seeming to be on the right path.

After taking a few trips back down memory lane and agreeing that our friendship needed this conversation, I told him in the strictest of privacy my full dilemma with Leo, and he was more than delighted to help.

After I faxed him the documents, we devised the perfect plan where I would come out the victor in all of this if, by chance, I passed on sooner than later. It was time that I, Eva Snow, began acting like the queen my daughter saw through her eyes.

Into the Hood: Pierre & Anneka

…

I was refreshed from my afternoon nap and ready to take the rest of the day by storm. I started brushing my hair and smiled at how thick and full it had gotten, and not to mention, it went from being almost bald and stringy to thick and touching my neck."

"Hello, beautiful. Here's your energy booster," Anneka spoke as she held one of the natural drinks that Dr. Brown had been making me for the past four months.

"Thank you, sweetheart," I stated as I took it out of her hand and began drinking.

"Ma, I know you asked me to stay out of things when it comes to you and Dad, but I swear he's not acting like the man I once knew. It's like the past few years, he's been turning into this monster that I'm not able to tolerate."

"Anneka, I told you, respect—"

"Ma, I get it. I haven't said anything and really have been focusing on getting out of here and moving on with my life and the things I want to do. This place isn't big enough for his ego and my attitude."

"Neka Pooh, I thought we had this discussion already."

"We did, Ma. I'm just saying that I don't wish to be around while he's treating you like you don't matter. We need to figure things out for us. I'm not trying to leave you, Ma. I want us to get away and go together. I know we can be happy. We can do this. Me and you, you and me, forever, together. We got this. Come on, Ma. Girl power," she stated, and we both started to laugh. Anneka was smart, and I loved her drive. I knew she put her life on hold just to care for me, but with my new plan in motion, it would only be a matter of time before everything she ever hoped and wished for would surely come to pass. I simply needed a little bit of time to allow things to come full circle.

"Trust me, Neka Pooh. Everything you want, I want for you, and it's only a matter of time before you get the desires of your heart. Trust me, dear. Mommy will handle things. You just leave dealing with your father to me, and trust my process," I stated as we smiled and wrapped into a mother/daughter embrace.

Chapter 4- Anneka

4 days later…

The chill from the morning spring New York air kissed my face as I jogged down Roosevelt Island for my morning run. I'd started running every morning to clear my head from the woes of life that I faced each day I rose to my feet.

My father began putting a lot of pressure on me when my mom, Eva, began turning her battle into victory.

The more he said he wanted her better, the more I felt as if he were lying and trying to manipulate her to use his crooked ass doctor.

My father was a no-nonsense, by the book type of man, but he had to have known that even though he tried to create these rules that he said I must follow, I still had a mind of my own.

My morning runs were my only sense of normalcy when I would get out of the house. With my dad wanting to have this upscale type of image, it simply left me with little time to explore the things that I loved, which were yoga and health fitness training.

I'd been talking to my mom a lot about my goals and aspirations to be the best health and fitness trainer who ever came out of New York, but with the way my father was and my mom being sick, that shit didn't seem like it would ever become my reality.

As I finished my jog and was standing in front of my building, The Octagon, I took in a deep, cleansing breath and prepared myself before going into the building. I knew that my mom would need me, and it wasn't a problem at all. I just hated seeing her in this condition and wished that I could do something to help her ease all of her pain. Dr. Brown was doing an excellent job with getting her healthy, but it seemed as though my dad was doing all he could to disrupt the process.

I stepped inside the building, headed to the elevator, and pressed the number four. Once the bell chimed, I got off on my floor and approached 445, which was our apartment number. A sick feeling rested at the pit of my stomach the closer I got to my apartment.

I approached the door, which was ajar, and I had a clear view of the living room, which overlooked the beautiful skyline of New York City. Not having to put the key in the door, I pushed the door open, and my eyes rested on a horrific scene.

"Do you think anyone is going to miss you? Huh? When your ass is dead and gone, I'll have the pity of the city and women tossing themselves at me to stand at my side and do the job of a wife that you couldn't do."

With a pillow over her face and her energy drink on the side of the couch, I watched in horror as my dad suffocated my mom. I placed my hand over my mouth in shock. Tears began to well in my eyes as I listened to what my father was saying to my mom. Careful not to alert him of my presence, I continued to listen.

"Every morning, you're begging for fucking attention, taking your ass out on runs with that bitch of a daughter, and thinking you're going to get healthy. That bitch Dr. Brown is scamming you. You're not getting healthy. You're a weak withering bitch, and you're still not able to stand like the proud beautiful woman I married. With the insurance money I'll get from you, I'll send that bitch of a daughter away and live the life that I was supposed to have."

My words were caught in my throat as he continued to push the pillow deeper into her face as her body began to flop like a fish out of water. I couldn't take it anymore.

As the lump in my throat blocked my words, I choked out, "Father, stop! You're gonna kill her!"

His eyes darted to the door, and it felt as though I was looking in the face of the devil himself. My eyes landed back on my mom as her hand went down, and her chest rose and fell, and the life left her body. The horror that was planted on my face caused my father to look at my mom, and I took that as my opportunity to get the fuck out.

I turned on my heels and ran as if I were being chased by a pit bull.

"Anneka, stop! Come back! It's not what you're thinking. You don't want to do this, Anneka!" My father yelled behind me.

I knew that I could outrun him, and I relied on my ability to sprint long distances to help me get as far away from him as possible. I took the stairs, going down at least four at a time, trying not to lose my balance.

As I reached the first floor, I was winded but knew I couldn't stop. I had five dollars to my name, and I heard the dinging of the elevator and knew I needed to get the hell out of this building.

As luck would have it, the Red Bus was out there and pulling away from the curb. I began to bang on the back of the bus as if my life depended on it, and I started yelling.

"Hurry, let me in, please!" I screamed, and the driver stopped and opened the back door. I looked back to see my father on the steps of the Octagon as the driver took off, and I went to the front of the bus, out of breath, with my five-dollar-bill.

"I'm sorry, miss. We only take quarters."

"Sir, please don't stop this bus. At the next stop, I can get off and get change, please," I begged, and a guy who was seated got up and paid my fare. I thanked him and sat down in the seat across from him. My breathing began to turn back to normal as I sat and allowed the events to replay in my head.

I allowed the hot tears to spill from my eyes as reality sank in that my mother was no longer with me and died from the hands of my father and not cancer.

The man who paid my fare got up, approached me, and sat next to me while holding out a piece of tissue in his hand and extending it to me.

"Rough morning, huh?" he queried, and I couldn't do anything but nod my head in agreement to what he'd asked.

"I don't know your story or know anything about you, but know that whatever you're going through, trouble won't last always," he said in the most soothing tone.

With teary eyes and a tear stained face, I finally looked up and noticed his distinct features. Since he was seated, I could only gage that he was about five feet seven, kind, soft, hazel looking eyes, appeared to be a little bit older than me, but not by much, and when I finally looked at him, his eyes went down, and he had this goofy, bashful looking smirk that I thought was cute.

"Thank you for your kind words, but I'm not sure I can ever recover from what just happened to me. This is a fucked-up world, and I swear to God that bastard will pay for this," I said as my voice trailed off into the distance.

I was hurt, and I was taking my anger and frustrations out on this man who was being the perfect Good Samaritan. I allowed my tears to decorate my face as I kept my head down, avoiding any and all eye contact. I couldn't believe that my father was so evil that he took my mother's life.

Into the Hood: Pierre & Anneka

He may have had the keys to this city, but what he needed to understand was that I was his child, and with little to no life experience, I would survive this and make sure that I came back to face him to avenge my mother's death.

Leo Snow, you have hurt me for the last time, I thought as my nose flared as my hurt started to be replaced with anger. I was going to mourn my mom forever, but in the meantime, I needed to find a way to take my father down.

"Well, here's my card. If you need a friend to talk to, I'm a good listener, and to be honest, I just want to make sure you're ok."

The gentleman smiled, and I looked up with a tear-stained face and simply nodded. I knew I couldn't get far with the money I had on me, so I had to channel my survival skills and bring this man to justice.

...

The Red bus reached the tram and came to a stop. I as well as others, began getting off the bus, and headed to the tram to get to the next destination.

With no destination in my mind, I stood and stuffed the gentleman's card in my pocket without even noticing the name on it.

I was sure I looked wild and crazy with tears streaming from my face, and I really didn't have a place to go. I knew that my dad would figure out a way to get to me, so I needed to put some distance in between us until I figured things out.

"Excuse me, Miss. I don't mean to be weird or anything, but I bought you a tram ticket. I, um, heard you say that you only had a few dollars, and it seems like you're having a bit of a time this morning. No funny business about it. I simply want to help."

I looked into his eyes, and he seemed to be kind. A bit bashful and shy, but kind. I extended my hand and took the ticket. "Thank you. I'm sorry. I wasn't trying to be rude. It's just that—"

"No explanation needed. I'm happy to help you," he said as his head went down, and he began to blush.

"I'm not sure where you're headed, but we can go up here at the first stop and grab a coffee. I'm a great listener. I swear I'm not a stalker. I just want to be your friend."

New Yorkers were the strangest people from what I was always told, but now, seeing this shit up close and personal, I felt I was in the middle of a shark tank waiting to be eaten alive.

"I'm not sure that I would be great company. I'm about to be dealing with a lot of shit, and I'm not sure you're prepared or even qualified to listen to the shit that's on my mind, let alone process the shit that I've been through this morning.

He offered a smiled and then said, "Try me. We've all been through or had a bit of shit on our plates every now and again."

I offered a slight smile in return and felt that maybe he would be just the friend I needed or at least the friend I needed right now.

As the tram arrived, the passengers each started to fill it up and hold on to the bar as we flew above the awful NYC traffic and held on until the tram came to a complete stop.

We got off on 2nd Ave., and I instantly started running as rats began jumping at our feet.

"Oh my God, this is so disgusting," I said as I ran through the tram stop until I reached the sidewalk.

Laughing and matching my speed, the gentleman, who I still hadn't asked his name, reached me with laughter.

"Don't worry. You'll get used to it," he said as that smirk of his quickly started to grow on me.

"Pardon me for being rude. I know I gave you my card, but I never formally introduced myself. My name is Bernard Post, and if you'd glance at my business card, you already know that I'm an architect designer."

"Are you related to George Post?" I asked in admiration, knowing that the Post family was responsible for designing the Roosevelt Hotel.

"That's my great-great-grandfather," he shyly remarked, and a smile stretched across his face.

"And since you know who I am, tell me who you are?"

We walked and talked, and at first, I was a bit leery on giving Bernard my real information. I didn't know what was going to happen with my father, and I knew I just needed to get somewhere safe until I figured this out.

It was so easy to talk to Bernard, and with what I just experienced, you would think that I wouldn't want to trust or talk to anyone, but Bernard seemed harmless, and more than anything, I thought he could help me. I went with my gut and stated, "My name is Anneka Snow, and I'm—"

Before I could finish my sentence, Bernard finished it for me.

"You're Senator Leo and wife Eva Snow's daughter." He smiled, and I nodded my head.

"I was at the meet and greet that you all hosted a little bit ago, and I saw you and your beautiful mother. I wanted to talk to you then, but I knew you wouldn't have time for a man like me. Plus, I'm sure you have a special person in your life."

He had no idea how wrong he was, and I didn't care what he was talking about in this moment. I just wanted his help in finding a place to hide. I spaced out a bit on his conversation as my mind continued to go haywire. I was brought back to the conversation when he stated, "I'm so sorry to hear that your mom is going through her battle with cancer. She was truly inspiring when she spoke to a few of us at the meet and greet. I'm sure it's not easy for you and your father, and believe me, I've been on that side of the table, but know that with each passing day that she's here, there's a chance for you to tell her how much you love her."

I couldn't hold back my tears. This man had no idea how often I made sure to tell my mom how beautiful and strong she was each day, and now my father had taken that away from me. My mom was ready to kick cancer's ass, and she was doing a damn good job at it, but her devil of a husband decided to play God and end her life.

I knew that my mom wasn't going to live forever, but I knew she had a lot of life to live, and now that had all ended. If I had a gun, I would literally go back to our condo and blow my father's brains out for taking the only person who truly loved me away from me. If I saw that man again, never would be too soon.

"Oh, I'm so sorry, Anneka. I didn't mean to upset you. I just simply wanted to encourage you," Bernard spoke as I stood in front of him with tears painting my face as I thought about my mom. I wanted to blurt out everything to this complete stranger, but I had to make sure that I could really trust him.

I contemplated for a moment, took in a deep breath and put some of my cards on the table. At this point, I had nothing to lose and everything to gain. Wiping my tears with the back of my hand, I spoke. "It's ok. I know that you are only trying to encourage me. This has truly been one of the hardest days of my life, and right now, I need someone I can trust," I spoke openly and honestly.

We continued our walk until we reached Starbucks. Bernard was right; he was such a good listener, and I appreciated his company.

Bernard paid for my white chocolate mocha as we sat in the back of Starbucks and continued our conversation. Bernard shared with me how he wanted to branch out and away from his family and start making a name for himself. For a moment, I forgot all about my own issues, and I began taking in all of his features.

Bernard had a long Rick Ross beard, he was very attentive when I was talking, and he had the cutest bald head, sun-kissed tan skin, and the longest eyelashes I'd ever seen on a man.

"Are you, Anneka?" he questioned, and I was so embarrassed because I didn't hear his question.

"I'm sorry. Am I what?" I retorted.

"Are you running away from something that can't be fixed, or are you simply afraid of the unknown?"

"If this was a day ago, I would say with conviction that I was possibly running away from the unknown, but after this morning, I can say that I'm running away from something that can't be fixed. There's no coming back from this. My life is pretty much fucked up now," I stated as my eyes went down, and sadness covered me.

Bernard didn't pressure me to talk, and I liked that about him. He was probably trying to figure me out because I knew I kept going from hot to cold. He got extremely quiet, and when I looked up into his eyes, his head went down, and he began playing with a button on his shirt and rubbing his bald head.

"Do I make you nervous?" I questioned with a half-smile as I watched Bernard with his eyes focused on his coffee as if he were studying the cup. He shyly lifted his head and spoke.

"I don't usually go out with girls on a date. I mean, I know this isn't a date, and not that I go out with boys. I'm sorry. I'm not used to this. I mean being out with a girl. When you're from a family like mine, everything is mapped out for you, and you're told to just do what they say and produce the things that they want, so I don't have time to go out with girls because of my schedule, so I guess, yes. I'm a little nervous," he shyly stated, and I smiled.

"Well, Bernard, thank you so much for your generosity. I have your business card, and when I'm able to, I'll pay you back," I said as I stood to my feet and attempted to leave so that I would be left alone with my thoughts.

"No need, Anneka. It has indeed been my pleasure. Um, not that it's any of my business, but do you think your father could help you out of whatever situation you're in?"

"No! For God's sake, please don't try to reach out to him on my behalf," I quickly spoke with anger.

"I'm sorry. I didn't mean to upset you, and I'm just a little concerned. Where would you go? What would you do?"

"I honestly don't know, Bernard. I'm going to trust the universe, but at the end of the day, I know I only have myself. From this moment on, I walk alone."

Chapter 5- Bernard

"I honestly don't know, Bernard. I'm going to trust the universe, but at the end of the day, I know I only have myself. From this moment on, I walk alone." Anneka was talking, but I couldn't take my eyes off her lips. The way that her mouth puckered when she spoke my name and the way her tongue moistened her beautiful, full lips had me wanting to be with her in a way that I couldn't explain.

I'd only been around this girl for mere hours, and I was acting like a love-sick puppy, but who could blame me? Her beauty was captivating, and the sweet sound of her voice was soothing.

My stomach began turning in knots because I felt as though our time was about to soon come to an end, and I just couldn't allow that to happen. I wanted to learn all I could about this beautiful, young woman named Anneka Snow.

"Anneka, can I offer you a suite at the Roosevelt? I mean, I don't know exactly what's going on, but I do know that the streets of New York aren't a place for a beautiful woman like yourself to be wandering around alone." I shocked myself with the offer to assist her. My hands became clammy, and my eyes traveled to my feet to prevent looking at her in those gorgeous eyes.

I felt as if she were about to reject my offer, and I didn't know how I would handle it.

"Bernard, that would be amazing if you could do that, but I only have—"

I held my hand up to prevent her from speaking. I knew she was running away from something and didn't have money to get the necessities that she needed.

"Anneka, no need to explain. You've already shared a bit of information with me, so I understand your circumstances."

"But I'm not sure when I'll be able to pay you back, this is just too much, wait, thanks but no…"

"Anneka, sweetheart please slow down. I'm not doing this for any form of repayment. I'm doing this because as I stated, I too sat at the table that you're sitting at, and I watched my mom slip away at the hands of cancer. Allow me to help you by paying forward a good deed, to my new friend."

Wow, this girl had me saying things that I didn't know could even come out my mouth. She was so easy to talk to, and it seemed as though she was simply pure at heart. I wanted to make sure that she understood I didn't want a damn thing from her. I simply wanted to spend time with her and be in her personal space.

I knew it wasn't love, but I also knew I was crushing on her.

I pulled my head up, and our eyes met. Her eyes were glazed over, and I knew her heart was heavy. The pain that she was feeling, I wished I could take it all away, but only time could heal that wound. Cancer was a beast within itself. Once it had taken a bite out of you, your body slowly began to decay.

"Anneka, how long do you plan on staying? I mean, it's not a problem how long. I just want to have your room taken care of."

"I'm not sure. I have to really figure things out, and I don't have the slightest idea of how to even begin."

"Well, allow me to insert myself into your situation. I'm primarily my own boss, and my family owns the most infamous hotel's here in New York. Let's take advantage of this beautiful city and get you the things you need for however long you decide to stay."

Her cheeks became flushed, and her eyes filled with tears. Before I knew it, she'd wrapped her arms around my neck and planted the most sensual kiss on my cheek.

My heart started to race as I was lost for words while holding her warm body close to mine. Her hair smelled amazing as if it had been dipped in vanilla. I didn't want to let her go.

Slowly, she took a step back, placed her hand on my cheek, and stated, "I just can't thank you enough. Even though you don't want to be paid back, I'll find a way to make sure you know how much you are appreciated." Her words were all the thanks I needed as I escorted her out of Starbucks, and we hit the streets of New York.

Going in and out of stores, she was reluctant to spend my money, but after a little convincing, she loosened up and got all the things that she needed. I enjoyed watching her go in and out of the dressing rooms and coming out and asking me how something looked. She seriously had a thing for blue, yellow, and red, and those colors complemented her fair skin.

Just when I thought I'd taken her mind away from whatever sadness she was running away from, the television in Times Square came on, and Senator Snow was making a statement.

"It is with deep sadness that I stand here and address you good people of New York. You all have hung in there and faced this battle with me as I publicly battled this thing we call cancer. Many people say emotional pain is more agonizing than physical pain. I wish that you all understood how deep my love ran for Eva. Before she took her last breath, she looked me in my eyes and said, 'Leo, you continue to fight. You fight all the way until you get to the White House.'"

"He's a fucking liar! I hate him!" Anneka screamed as she watched the crowd in Times Square form as the citizens of New York stood together and mourned the loss of her mom.

I didn't understand her outburst, but I knew she was probably having a hard time with understanding that her mother was gone. The television displayed a rolling banner which read, *Senator Snow's wife has lost her battle with cancer*.

Anneka took off running with bags in her hands, and I immediately followed.

Trying to keep up with her as the crowd seemed to have been getting bigger and bigger by the moment, I kept my eyes trained on her dark, bouncy hair and took chase.

After four blocks, she stood at the side of a building with her chest going up and down and tears streaming from her eyes. Slowly, she started to slide down the wall as the bags rested at her side.

"Anneka, please talk to me. I've been through this before. Just talk to me. It's hard, I know, but I know that you can pull through this," I comforted as I scooped her up in my arms and held onto her for dear life.

"It's ok. I can take you to your dad."

"No! He's a fucking liar! I can't be around that man. I will *never* be around that man again for as long as I live! Fuck him. He caused all of this!"

She pulled out of my arms, and it seemed as if her breathing started to become labored. I wanted to calm her down, so I approached with caution. With her hands placed on the top of her head and tears flowing freely from her eyes, I simply wanted to take away her pain.

"Anneka, it's ok. I get it. You don't want to be around anyone; you want your time. But I think you need to talk to your dad. I can't imagine how he's feeling knowing that he had to address the city and not being able to tell you personally."

"Fuck him! He doesn't fucking care; he never cared. It's all a lie! He… he… he… he stands there, and he's pretending to be hurt, and it's all an act. That man is a murderer, and if he wasn't so well connected, I'd stop at nothing to make sure that he was brought to justice. I want to blow his fucking brains out. My mom is gone, and as far as I'm concerned, that bastard of a father is dead to me."

I was nervous and shocked by her outburst, but I also understood that in situations like this, it was so easy to blame the first person you saw. I didn't know Anneka personally, but I didn't think it was her character to spew out obscenities. Her words were spoken with so much passion and conviction that I felt what she was saying was true, and I felt obligated to help her seek whatever justice she wanted. I made up in my mind that no matter the cost, I would do whatever it took to ease this pain from her. She lost her mother, and I knew that no matter what I said, my words were just that. Words… But I needed to try and comfort her.

"Anneka, I'm sorry for your loss. No words that I can say will comfort you at this time, but I'm asking you to trust me and allow me to help you with every fiber of my existence."

"Why? Why are you so willing to help me? You bought me clothes, shoes, and all of my basic necessities. Why? What are you after? You need building permits signed by my father? What do you want?" she asked with so much hatred seeping from her tone, and I felt that it wasn't really who she was, but this news of her mom's passing was really getting to her.

"I don't want anything. I just want to help a person, I mean, a new friend in need."

"You don't even know me. I have a bad attitude at times, and I'm stubborn, and you'll get tired of me, and then you'll try to hurt and kill me. Just leave me alone. Fucking leave me alone!" She burst into tears, and my heart ached for her. I knew exactly where she was in her level of pain because I took out all of my anger on any and every one in my path when I lost my mom.

"Anneka, I can't say that I know exactly how you feel, but I know the pain of losing a mother. I get it. I know you don't have a reason to trust me, but please, trust me now, and allow me to help you. I don't know you. I don't know anything about you—no more than what I was able to see on TV and when I come to events that your family hosts. Anneka, you may not believe that you need me but you do. Allow me to help you," I begged, hoping that she wouldn't turn me away.

"What makes you think you can help me, and why should I believe anything that you're saying?"

"Listen to me. When you stepped on the bus this morning, you were afraid, horrified, and desperately in need of help. You were alone, no destination, and now you have to deal with your mom's death… publicly. Whatever happened with your father, I promise you, you can put that burden on me, and I'll be an ear. If you decide that you want me to help you in any way, I would be more than honored."

Her body language began to relax, and I felt as if I'd earned her trust.

"No strings attached, you'll help me?" she queried.

"Of course. I only have my word, and I'm giving you my word."

She attempted to pick up her bags, but I quickly intercepted and grabbed them up. She looked me into my eyes, and my head went down. She lifted my chin with her finger and simply said, "Thank you. No matter what happens, thank you."

I hailed for a cab, put her bags in, and we headed to the Roosevelt hotel. On our ride to the hotel, Anneka placed her head on my shoulder and was fast asleep. I made a few calls to prepare the room, leaving little to no information as to whom my guest would be. I knew that she was slowly breaking down her wall, and I was going to get to the bottom of her pain.

We arrived at the Roosevelt, and Anneka stirred from her sleep. I paid the cab fare and took her by the hand as we walked into the hotel. Her eyes darted around the lobby. They began to dance, and I knew I needed her in my life forever; I just didn't know at what capacity, friend or lover.

"Hello, Helen. I have a key that should be waiting on me," I spoke to the front desk clerk, Helen, as she started punching in my information.

"Mr. Post, everything is already set up for you. Here's your key… Oh my, it's you!" Helen exclaimed, drawing attention toward us.

Anneka buried her head into my chest, and the patrons turned their heads and continued their own business.

"Helen, my guest and I want complete privacy. If you want to keep your job, I suggest that you speak nothing about her staying here. Are we clear?"

"Crystal clear, Mr. Post. However, she's all over the news. Her dad is looking for her and has offered a pretty penny for anyone having information on her," she half sassed.

Anneka became tense, and I knew I had to diffuse the situation.

"Helen, it's very important to *me* that word doesn't get out about her staying here. Can I trust you?"

"Of course, you can, Mr. Post. Take the side elevator. A few cops were here, and they were combing the area, looking for her and asking questions. My lips are sealed. Just let me know if there's anything I can do."

I took the key to the room, took Anneka through the side elevator, and went to the top to her new temporary dwelling place.

She walked around, noticing the room and began taking it all in. She turned to me and spoke. "Bernard, do you think you can trust Helen? Her ass seems to be a busy body, just waiting to tell somebody's damn business."

Into the Hood: Pierre & Anneka

"Of course, I can trust her. Her family and my family have history together. She won't go against my family. Just relax."

"Thank you, Bernard. This really means a lot to me. From the bottom of my heart, thank you."

"Anneka, if I'm going to help you, I really need for you to trust me. Tell me everything, and I promise I'll do whatever it takes to make sure you're not only safe, but if your dad needs to be brought down a notch, we have people who can make that happen."

She took a deep breath and started from the beginning.

Chapter 6- Leo

I'd just finished my last conference of the day and finally gotten home to think. I had to work quickly to get the news out about Eva's death. That bitch of a daughter came home at the wrong time, and I wasn't sure of what she saw and heard. Judging by the way her eyes held shock, she saw too damn much, and I wasn't about to lose everything I worked so damn hard for. With her ass on the fucking run, I didn't need her loose lips sinking any ships over here.

I called my associate Sebastian from the boogie down Bronx to carry out a mission to seek, kill, and destroy any and all evidence of her existence. I'd already begun preparing a speech to give to the city when the deed was done and the search party had come to an end. Once that daughter of mine was out of the way, I would rise as the king of New York, and with the abundance of sympathy I'd gain, the White House was now in plain view. I could skip right over the damn governor's mansion.

Sebastian never conducted business over the phone, so I was waiting on his arrival. As I looked out at the skyline, I poured myself a stiff drink, counted the deposit I had for him, and thought about all the bitches and endless supply of pussy this heartbreaking news was going to get me. I would for sure be the biggest man in New York, and no one would dare argue with that fact. I did have a main side chick named Ivanka, and when the dust settled with this shit that I had going, I'd take her as my wife and might be a better husband to this powerhouse of a woman.

Getting my hands on Anneka was the first line of business; everything else should fall right into place. "That little bitch don't have any life skills. She'll be dead in a week anyway." I spoke aloud to myself as I began to process the things going on in my head.

A light tap on my door grabbed my attention. I shuffled to the door and peeped out to see Sebastian standing with his head down. He never looked up when he was in hallways inside of buildings. I guess this was something he did to shield his identity.

After allowing him access into my apartment, his head went up, and he looked me into my eyes. I could never really gage this guy. He was always so serious and had the worst allergies but was the best man for the job.

"Ah-choo... Ah-choo...Ah-choo... Leo, so you have a problem that you need for me to take care of? Ah-choo!" Sebastian asked as he shook my damn soul with his sneeze. I handed him a tissue, and he smacked it away.

"I don't need that shit. This ain't nothing but allergies… Ah-choo!"

"Sebastian, your deposit is yet the same, correct?" I questioned, getting right to business.

With his red nose and droopy looking eyes, he nodded, sneezed, and extended his hand for payment.

After putting the deposit in his hand, I went to the counter and grabbed a picture of Anneka.

"Ah-choo… Is this her?" he asked as his eyes damn near bulged out of his head.

"Haven't you been watching the news? Yes, this is her. She's my daughter, and I need her to go away, but I need proof that she's dead so that I can have another conference."

"Do I look like I watch the news? Ah-choo… *sniff, sniff*. This is a top priority case, so it's going to cost you double, and I can deliver by the end of the week. Just let me know which direction you saw her go in, and it's done," he countered, and I told him everything I knew.

Into the Hood: Pierre & Anneka

Sebastian left, and I felt as if he were on the right path to getting me what I wanted, but I needed extra security, and I damn sure wasn't going to have any of this shit coming back on me. I needed to have some things sealed before any of this surfaced.

I made a few calls, kicked back on my sectional, and took it all in. Not only was I the damn man, but my pockets were about to be on a major come up after I collected on both of those policies. A smile was nicely placed on my face as I clasped my hands behind my head and admired my crafty work. "Oh, what a day," I said as I closed my eyes, taking it all in.

Chapter 7 - Anneka

It was a long, emotional day, and I, for one, was glad it was coming to an end. I never thought that I'd be in a place where I would be running from my dad because he took my mother's life. Cancer was supposed to be her demise, not him.

I dipped my body into the water and allowed the bath beads to massage my aching body. I was practically on my feet all day, running, shopping, and running from the hell of a mess that I was now in.

Although my face was plastered all over the news stations, I wasn't worried, because I felt as if Bernard had everything under control, or at least he did until I figured out my next move.

I sunk my body deeper under the water as I began humming a song that my mom used to sing to calm and soothe me at night when I was a little girl.

Caterpillar in the tree,
How you wonder who you'll be.
Can't go far, but you can always dream.
Wish you may and wish you might;
Don't you worry, hold on tight.

Into the Hood: Pierre & Anneka

I promise you that there will come a day;

Butterfly, fly away.

As tears clouded my eyes, I spoke softly to myself, thinking only of my mother, "Butterfly, fly away. I love you, Mom. Rest well until we meet again."

I rocked back and forth in the tub and allowed the melody of that song to take me to a place of serenity. It was as if my mother came in for a visit just to tell me that she was alright. I began to smell her sweet-scented perfume, and as I wrapped my arms around my body, it was as if I could feel her wrapping me in her arms. I could have sworn I heard her whisper, *I'm flying with wings, baby girl. I no longer have to fight, but when the time comes, you better fight. I'm watching you.*

My head popped up, and my eyes were bucked as I started frantically looking around the bathroom. I wasn't afraid at all; I just wanted to see my mom. I wanted to touch her one last time and tell her how beautiful and strong she was. I wanted to hug her and tell her thank you for all of the lessons she instilled in me while she was raising me to be strong and treating people with the same respect that I wanted to be treated with.

The chill from me standing out of the water caused my body to shiver. I stepped out the tub, wiping the tears from my eyes, and began to towel dry myself. After quickly moisturizing my body, I slipped on a Victoria Secret night set that Bernard picked out for me earlier.

I stepped out of the bathroom, hoping that Bernard was gone and would allow me to simply be with my thoughts, but when I saw his face, I knew I wanted him right here with me. I guess you could say that I was in need of some company, and Bernard was the breath of fresh air that I needed.

"Are you alright, Anneka? I'm sorry. That's a dumb question. Of course, you're not alright. You just lost your mom. What can I do to comfort you?"

Bernard was so sweet, and whomever he married would have one hell of a romantic husband. His soothing tone and bashful ways seemed to keep my mind at ease.

"I'm as good as I can be, considering the fact that, today, I lost my mom at the hands of my dad, and now the whole world is looking for me while he's in fake mourning."

"Anneka, I still say we take this to the authorities. Who knows what he's capable of doing? And I certainly wouldn't want you hurt."

His cheeks were damn near as rosy as mine. As I figured, he had a really bad crush on me.

"I'll be fine. I may have to fight, but I have a feeling that I'll be fine," I retorted as I climbed on the bed, grabbed the remote, and started flickering through the television.

"Bernard, if I had a thousand tongues, I couldn't express to you how grateful I am that you stepped into my life in the moment that I needed you most. Everything you did for me today, I wish I could snap my fingers and repay you for it all."

"I told you, Anneka. You don't have to worry about it. Like I said, I'm paying it forward. Have a wonderful evening. I'll come by to check on you tomorrow."

"Bernard, please, don't go. If you can, please stay with me. I don't want to be alone. Not tonight," I pleaded.

He nodded his head and sat in the corner of the room in the chair.

"Ha ha ha ha, I promise you, Bernard, I won't bite. I just don't want to be alone, and if you're sitting all the way over there, then you may as well leave because I'll still be alone."

He swiped his hand down his face and rubbed them on his pants. He seemed a bit nervous, but so was I. With everything going on, I needed someone here with me, and as long as Bernard was here, I felt protected.

This was the first night in my eighteen years that I would be alone, in a room, with a man. *What's the worst that can happen?* I thought as I pulled the covers back, patted the bed, and beckoned for Bernard to take the space in bed next to me.

...

We talked for hours about my mom, his mom, and both of our hopes and dreams. I'd just finished eating my burger from room service, and then the conversation got deep.

"So Anneka, if you know what your father did, and you're not willing to say anything, how is this going to avenge your mother?"

"Bernard, you may not understand, but I never felt connected to that man. For years, he treated me like I was the dirt underneath his shoes. My mom made sure I always felt supported when he would downplay any and every last one of my accomplishments. I don't want to run to the authorities, because while I was in the tub, I heard my mother's voice telling me to fight. I want to seek justice my way. He won't get away with this. You can never win when you're dirty."

My mind went back to my high school graduation. By my mom homeschooling me, I still had to turn my paperwork in to the local high school. I graduated at the top of my class. That night was supposed to be amazing. I didn't really have any friends, so I depended on my mom and dad to support me.

"Mommy, I'm so excited! Valedictorian! Can you believe it?"

"Of course, princess. You're the best in your class. You worked so hard, and you achieved the goals you set out to achieve, and for that, I'm so proud of you. The principal asked that we come early so that you can get familiar with where you'll be standing and have an idea of how the layout of the gymnasium is."

"Eva, do we really have to waste our time and go to this shit? Damn, Anneka, you have possibly stepped inside that fucking school five times, and now you want to go give a fucking speech to kids who don't know you or give a damn about you."

"Father, I worked hard, and I deserve to stand there with my classmates."

"Anneka, do you know those kids? They damn sure don't know you. This is a waste of fucking time. I could be getting my speech together for the people who know me. I've been working hard in this community, and I'll be damned if I have an off day because her retarded ass want to take a few hours out of my day."

Looking at my mom with tears in my eyes, I made a decision that haunts me daily. "You know, Mom, it's ok. Dad's right. Why should I go give a speech to a group of kids who don't even know my name? Maybe we could just watch a movie and have a girl's night."

"Anneka, it's ok. We can go. Your father is just stressed out."

"No, I'm not. Listen to her. She said we don't have to go, so leave it at that. Eva, get your ass in there, and make me something to eat. I can't believe we were about to get out here and spend money for a fake ass celebration. You probably just checked off that she did all that shit. Who knows how smart she really is?"

"Anneka, you spaced out on me. Are you ok?"

"I'm fine, Bernard. That man took so much from me and beat me every chance he had. If I helped my mom too much, he would get mad and say that she was grown and could do things for herself. If I took a shower too long, he would take my shower privileges away from me. When I would go running, he blamed me for sneaking out, trying to get pregnant, just so he could beat me. This time, I'll be the one doing the beating. He won't have a chance of ever hurting me again."

"Anneka, I understand that you're upset, but I can't allow you to do something that we both know isn't in you. It's not even in me. Revenge may seem sweet, but in the end, so many lives are affected. I promised you that I'd protect you; allow me to show you what I'm able to do without even going to the dark side. Your father will be brought to justice, and if you decide that you don't like my plan and want to move forward with your own, I'll support you in it. I may not agree with it, but I will support you in it. I won't allow you to do it alone."

"Bernard, this isn't your fight. My fight is not your fight; my struggle is not your struggle. What you are doing for me right now is more than I can ever repay you for. My father took something from me so precious that I won't allow myself to do things by the book."

"Anneka, do you think you can seriously take him down?"

"I'll tell you like I told him. I am my father's child. I know that man, and he will stop at nothing to ensure that I'm nothing more than a memory. I know that even if he's caught, he would spend his days behind bars to reach different ones to try to end me. A wise woman once said, "Ego is the anesthesia that deadens the pain of stupidity. Pride is the burden of a foolish person." When my mom spoke those words to me years ago, I never knew what she meant. Now that she's gone, I understand those words clearly."

"Wow, she sounds as if she was so amazing. I only had a chance to speak to her at the last meet and greet, and I would have loved to have been able to suck in some of her wisdom. Anneka, I know this is tough, but this too shall pass. I'll make some calls in the morning, and I promise to do everything I can to help you. You're my friend now, and your fight is my fight. I don't meet strangers. I meet people, and today, I met my friend, Anneka Snow."

I began to smile as Bernard and I talked well into the night until sleep found us.

Into the Hood: Pierre & Anneka

This seemed like the calm before the storm, and I prayed that the storm wouldn't last long, because karma was coming to take back what was stolen from me—life.

. . .

I woke up missing my mom. The events of yesterday were playing heavily in my mind. I got out of the bed to find that Bernard was nowhere to be found. I walked around the suite and started to clean up from the junk-food binge we had last night. I guess Bernard was tired of me being clingy and needed his space. I still appreciated everything he'd done for me thus far.

After cleaning the suite, I took care of my morning hygiene and put on some running gear. I figured with a fitted cap on, nobody in New York would notice me because they all walked with their heads down while conducting business on their phones.

I laced up my shoes and heard the door. Popping my head up, a smile stretched across my face when I saw Bernard. "Good morning. I assumed you left," I spoke with a smile, noticing that he had a bag of food in his hand that smelled divine.

"No, I didn't leave. Well, I left, but I only went to get you something to eat."

"Nothing for yourself?" I questioned.

"Well, we can share this. I went to Grand Central Station because I didn't have a clue as to what you wanted, so I got a variety of things."

I could tell that I was making him nervous, and that seemed almost empowering to me. I kept hearing my mom's voice telling me to fight, and I knew it was time that I started to change my attitude on things in life.

I may have lacked social and life skills, but now was the perfect time to give myself a crash course.

"Bernard, come sit down," I commanded as I made up in my mind that it was time to turn things around for myself. I wanted to make sure that I could manipulate and deceive. It was all a part of my plan to get back at my dad.

Doing as I instructed, Bernard came in closer and sat on the sofa that was placed in the corner of the room. I sat next to him, taking the bags of food out of his hand and placing them on the table that was off to the side of me.

Rubbing on his bald head, I began to blow in his ear, and he immediately began to change the rhythm of his breathing.

Into the Hood: Pierre & Anneka

"Thank you for going to get me breakfast, but right now, I need for you to relax."

"Um, Anneka, um, what are you doing?" he nervously questioned.

"If you have to ask, maybe I need to stop." I continued my torture as I internally laughed at how uncomfortable I was making him. After watching him sweat and squirm, I smiled, stood up, looked him directly in his eyes, and spoke. "My father might be smart, but I'm damn sure wiser. When my mother spoke to me and said fight, she wasn't just talking about physically. She meant in every facet of the word. You see, Bernard, I'm a woman, and what men don't realize is that even when they feel that they are in control, we still have the power to take it away. I have a plan that is almost foolproof to get to my dad without him seeing it coming, but I'll need your help."

Bernard let out a breath that I was sure he didn't realize he was holding and began wiping his hands on his pants. We discussed my plans over breakfast, and although he was a bit leery about them, he assured me that I had his full support.

"Thank you again for everything. Breakfast was delicious, and now I need to get out of here and get in my five-mile run."

"You can't do that. I'm sure someone will see you."

"Not with this," I replied and put on a fitted cap and pulled it down to shield the top part of my face. I figured with my head down and running away from large crowds, this should be easy.

"Anneka, I'm not sure about this. Let me go with you."

"Bernard, calm down. We have to allow the universe to work how it's going to work. If it's meant for me not to come back, just know that you did everything you could have possibly done as a good person to ensure that I was safe. Thank you, Bernard Post. You are one amazing, romantic gentleman." I kissed his cheek, put the room key card in my pocket, and headed out for my run.

...

My morning runs were always so calming, and it was the only time that I could find peace and clear my mind. With the death of my mom at the front of my thoughts, I closed my eyes, took in a cleansing breath, and prayed that my mom would be my angel and watch over me as I ran.

New York was such an amazing city to live in. Although I was primarily sheltered, there were things that I learned about my city when I would make my morning runs.

New Yorkers never made eye contact and were some of the nicest yet rudest people you'd ever come across. The cool thing about New York was that it was easy to navigate once you really immersed yourself into the culture.

I was running through Manhattan with my fitted cap down and focusing only on my run when I felt as if someone were following me. I looked up, and I was at the midtown tunnel. I ran straight to 37th street and quickly looked back and didn't see anything out of the ordinary. I kept running, making a right onto 3rd avenue, and could have sworn I heard someone sneeze.

Blocking out fear, I used my fear to fuel me. I picked up the pace as I continued my run and made it onto 45th street. My body was warm, and my legs were feeling the burn. I slowed and steadied my pace as I came to a traffic light. Hitting the walk signal, I casually turned around, noticing a few New Yorkers on their phones conducting business.

I heard another sneeze and looked up and said, "Bless you," to the woman who stood next to me, who now had a puzzled expression on her face. *Typical rude New Yorkers—too rude to say thank you,* I thought as the walk signal turned white, and we crossed on the crosswalk. After two more lights, I made my way to Vanderbilt Ave. and Madison and was back at the hotel. I took the same side entrance that Bernard took me through and continued to hold my head down.

Stepping off the elevator, I looked at the signs and followed them to my suite.

"Ah-choo! Ah-choo! Ah-choo!" I heard and turned around and didn't see anyone in the hall behind me.

Realizing that this might not be a coincidence, I began walking with a slight jog to hurry to my room, which was at the end of the hall.

My heart rate picked up speed as I prayed to God to watch over and protect me.

Into the Hood: Pierre & Anneka

Making it into my room safe and sound, I pulled off my hat, took off my shoes, and took in a cleansing breath as I sighed in relief.

I walked around the suite, and again Bernard was nowhere to be found. I walked in the section that was deemed to be a living room and found a note.

"Anneka, I stepped out for a bit to grab you more things. I shouldn't be long. If you return before I get back, I ordered you a protein drink like the ones you said you loved after your run."

I smiled because his letter showed that he really listened to me when we had our talk. I felt better about opening up to him about my father and had a feeling that things were going to be alright.

"Bernard Post, you are one hell of a man," I spoke out loud, chuckled to myself, and found the protein drink in the small refrigerator that was cornered in the room.

I drank my shake and began setting out my outfit for the day. I was sure that I wasn't going out, but I wanted to feel good about myself while I was in.

Many days when I would finish my run, I would shower and then brush my mom's hair, and we'd have our stolen moments. Not wanting to cry about something

I knew I couldn't change, I turned on the television and continued laying out my things.

"I will stop at nothing to find my daughter. Good citizens of New York, I challenge you, this day, to help me bring this search to an end. I have the task of burying my wife, and now, I have to find my dear daughter. Please help me." I saw my father talking to the citizens of New York. If I didn't know he was a lying piece of shit and was just on the outside looking in, his little speech would have urged me to want to help.

I shook my head and turned off the television. I wasn't in the mood to hear or see the spiraling fake gestures he was pulling as media stunts.

I turned on the shower, closing the bathroom door so that the bathroom would be nice and steamy. Gathering my things, I pinned my hair into a nice, neat bun, placing a red band around it to hold it in place. I grabbed my robe and headed into the bathroom where the steam welcomed me. Stepping into the shower, the water began to tickle my skin.

"Ah-choo! Ah-choo! Ah-choo!" I heard the same sneeze, but this time, it was so close that I knew it was in the same room with me.

Into the Hood: Pierre & Anneka

My heart began to pound as I tried to compose myself as best I could. Whatever was going to happen was going to happen. Maybe this was what my mom meant when she said fight. I stepped out the shower, turning off the water, and when the steam vanished, I was face to face with a man who held a death glare, a gun, a red nose, watery eyes, and a bald head.

I gasped due to the fact that I was startled, but for some reason, I wasn't afraid. If it was indeed my time to depart this earth, I was comforted in knowing that I'd soon be reunited with my mother.

"What can I help you with?" I asked in the most calming voice I could pull off. Yes, I was a bit nervous, but until a person showed me differently, I always assumed positive intent even when the odds looked as if they were set against me.

"Ah-choo! Ah-choo! Ah-chooooooo! Help me? Do you really think you're in a position to help me? Ah-choo! How about you help yourself and come with me? For the love of God, don't try anything funny. I'm warning you. Ah-choo!"

Chapter 8- Sebastian

Leo must have been that new type of fucked up to want to take out his own daughter. I'd always been called in to do what most muthafuckas couldn't do, and that was kill with one hell of a turnaround time.

This was the second job I'd done for Leo, and to keep it buck, if cancer didn't take his wife out, it probably would have been my third job for him. He'd been wanting to get rid of her ass for some time now, but when I saw the picture of his daughter, I knew this would be my toughest kill ever.

When Leo gave me that picture of Anneka, I was stuck on her beauty, and then I listened to every word that he spoke as he told me about her routine. From what her father revealed, she didn't have friends, and they never affiliated with other family members. I knew she would be easy to find, but the hardest part of this job was following up on what I was paid to do.

I put in a few calls and had some buddies of mine throughout New York looking for this girl. Within an hour, I had a location on her, and sure enough, she was running. Without wasting time, I was all on top of it. My allergies were getting the best of me today, but I knew I needed to complete the task at hand. The moment she slipped into the side door, I followed just close enough to follow her trail.

Getting into her room wasn't a task at all. If you knew New Yorkers, you knew that we were known for making a way even when it seemed hard.

As the steam from the shower disappeared, I was damn near lost in her beauty. I felt as though I was in one of those old movies. She was indeed a beauty to this beast and had my full attention, but I had a job to do. I shook those bitch ass thoughts from my mind because her beauty was becoming my kryptonite. It weakened me.

I had my desert eagle trained on her, and it could have been a clean kill, but my finger wouldn't move, and she stood looking at me as if she wasn't afraid; shocked… but not afraid.

"Ah-choo! Ah-choo! Ah-chooooooo! Help me? Do you really think you're in a position to help me? Ah-choo! How about you help yourself and come with me? For the love of God, don't try anything funny. I'm warning you. Ah-choo!"

"Would you like for me to grab you a tissue?" she asked, and my knees got weak.

"Ah-choo! I don't need a fucking tissue. I need for you to walk your pretty little ass out here and take that towel off."

She began walking and then dropped her towel.

"Hey, what the fuck are you doing?"

"You asked me to take off my towel," she spoke innocently and still stood without fear. I wasn't sure if this was an act or not, but I wasn't taking any chances with her little cute ass.

Closing my eyes, I commanded for her to get dressed. I heard soft giggles from her, and I immediately opened my eyes and noticed that she put on a pair of those skinny ass jeans… "Ah-choo!" And a top that showed her belly button. I had to address the bulge that was growing inside my pants because this woman had my mind gone. Shaking my head and snapping out of this trance that she had me in, I asked, "What in the hell is so funny?"

"Well, let's see. Big, strong, bald man with a gun can't collect on his reward money because his allergies is messed up, and he's taking his eyes off little old me simply because you saw my naked body."

"What reward money? And I wasn't taking my eyes off you. I was respecting you by not staring."

"Well, thank you for respecting me. A thug with manners. That's cute. Oh, and please, spare me the act about not knowing about the reward money. I'm sure you've seen the news. It's fine. It was only a matter of time before someone spotted me and turned me in. I'll go with you. I know my father will stop at nothing until he kills me too. Typical Leo Snow. He can't get shit done on his own, so he sends others to do the job for him. What a coward."

I didn't have a clue what this girl was talking about. She pointed to the TV and sat on the edge of the bed. She seemed so innocent and didn't look afraid at all. I imagined a timid girl on the run, but something about her seemed to have been well composed. She was definitely mad as all hell, but she seemed relaxed and ready for whatever.

I picked up the remote and turned on the TV, and sure enough, on almost every single station, there was Anneka's beautiful face. Her pictures didn't do her justice, but they put you in a tranquil state of mind. Her dad seemed to have been a broken babbling mess. If this fucker hadn't paid me to kill her, I would've definitely thought they had a wonderful relationship. The thing that pissed me off the most was the amount of money he was offering as a reward versus the amount he gave me to knock her off. This fucker was playing with fire and was definitely about to get burned.

I was pissed, and I knew I needed to change the plans. There was no way I was simply going to kill this little lady, but I knew I was going to play with Leo's pockets. It was time to play 'hide the little princess' and take her dad's coins. "Ah-choo! Let's go! Hurry up! Ah-choo! Fuck! These fucking allergies are going to be the death of me," I said as I marched her out of the room.

As we stood in the hall for a second, I made sure I wasn't about to deal with any running bullshit coming from her.

"Ah-choo!"

"Bless you." She giggled.

"Anneka, don't start any shit, or I'll blow your fucking head off." I seethed.

"No, you won't, and don't worry. I'm not going to try anything. If it's my time to go, then it's my time to go. I trust the universe, but I also trust your kind eyes. You know that the eyes are the windows to our souls," she stated, and I figured this girl was simply naïve and didn't know any better.

"I'm a killer…Ah-choo!" And there was nothing kind about my eyes.

I concealed my weapon, and we headed out the same way we came in. Once I guided her down the back street, we reached my brother, Seth, who was parked in his van.

"Wake your dumb ass up! You know good and got damn well what the fuck we out here doing, and you're sleep on the job!" I fussed as I guided Anneka into the van.

"Mutha-fuck you! My muthafucking ass is tired. Been up fucking bitches and shit all damn night, and now you got me out here on a send-off mission. Why isn't that bitch's eyes covered?" he panicked, and I was beyond irritated.

"Don't call her a bitch."

"Shit, let's do her in, collect the cash, spend this cash, and find some bitches to fuck so we can make it rain on their big asses. Shit… I'm sleepy," he said, yawning.

"Move your narcoleptic ass out of the driver seat. You'll fuck around and fuck everything up. That fucker

Leo has been playing us, and I have a new plan for his ass," I stated as I took the wheel and pulled away from the spot we were parked in.

Anneka watched the exchange, and when Seth jumped in the back to keep an eye on her, he looked into her eyes, and I was sure he felt the same shit as I had. Anneka may have been about eighteen, nineteen, max, but she was truly the most beautiful, composed young woman I'd ever seen.

I drove down to the Bronx and kept stealing glances at Anneka in the rearview mirror. Seth was sleep and slobbing on her small yet perky breasts, and I wanted to pull over and beat him until he was awake.

Anneka had her eyes closed, but it didn't appear as if she were sleeping but more so putting herself in a serene place to escape her current reality. I pulled up to my old buddy Dakota's spot because I knew after I went over this information with him, he would offer the best possible solution. See, I was a killer, but Dakota was a planner. He was wise well beyond his years, and he was detail oriented and had an evil side, and the two of us together had no choice but to make things happen. I just had to convince him to get back on my team. We had a deal gone bad and hadn't worked together since, but I knew he would be down for getting this nigga Leo's bread.

"Seth, wake up! We here," I spoke as I put the car in park.

I walked to the back door and helped Anneka exit the car. "Ah-choo! Come on, and please don't give me a reason to hurt you. You will, Ah-choo! Go in here, and don't open your mouth. Do you understand?"

"Of course, I do, but we might want to go to the pharmacy and get you a prescription. Allergies can be deadly, you know."

"I don't need… Ah-choo! A damn prescription. I need you to walk up to this apartment … Ah-choo! And not say a damn word."

We walked up to the apartment, and I rang the bell. We stood outside all of three minutes, and Seth's ass was sleep standing up.

"Nigga, if I have to… Ah-choo! Tell you to wake yo' ass up again, I'm beating yo' ass." I sneered as Dakota finally answered his bell.

"Who is it?" his voice was heard through the speaker.

"It's Sebastian. I have Seth... Ah-choo! With me and a friend. I need your help, Dakota," I spoke, and a loud buzzing sound could be heard; it was the sound of him granting us access to his apartment.

Dakota came to the door, glasses at the bridge of his nose, and appeared to have been buried in books.

"Well, I see nothing has changed," I stated, noticing the mess of literature that surrounded his place. I had no idea how this man was so smart but couldn't get it together to find a maid or a bitch who could clean.

"Well, a lot has changed, Sebastian. What I'm wondering is what brings you here and with her?" he questioned, and I wondered if he knew who Anneka was.

"What do you mean?" I asked.

"I haven't seen you since we had to put away... well, you know when. But what brings you here?"

"Do you know who my friend is?"

"Of course, I do. Now, judging by *your friend*, who is much lovelier than her picture that's circulating on the news and throughout the city, you are here to try to get the senator to offer up more money?" Dakota asked, and that was why I liked him. He was smart, quick, and always had the right idea about things.

Into the Hood: Pierre & Anneka

"Seth, take her into the den," I stated and looked around, and Seth was knocked out on the couch.

"Let him rest. We will go in the den," Dakota spoke and then looked at Anneka through the top of his glasses. "Lovely, simply lovely," he stated with a smile, and Anneka's cheeks turned red from blushing.

I didn't seem to have anything to worry about when it came to Anneka. She seemed to be at peace and wasn't afraid. In the back of my mind, I didn't think she would try to flee, and if she did, I think she figured I would find her.

Dakota and I walked toward his den, and he stopped and asked, "You're not afraid of her leaving?"

"No, I think she's comfortable," I replied and looked back at Anneka who gave a warm smile and wiped her finger on the back of the chair and showed her immediate disgust.

Chapter 9- Anneka

"No, I think she's comfortable," the guy named Sebastian stated as he walked back to discuss business matters with the man I now knew as Dakota.

Dakota seemed smart, a little confused, but nonetheless, very smart, and judging by the appearance of his apartment, he wasn't very clean. My mom used to say that a scattered, messy house, led to a scattered mind.

I hated living in filth, and with the way Sebastian's allergies were set up, he may mess around and die. I had no idea how long we would be here, but I figured if we were here, I may as well make it comfortable.

I started with the books that were displaced all over the floor. If they were turned to a page, I placed a crease into that page and then placed the books in alphabetical order. I found some antibacterial dusting wipes and began wiping down the dusty furniture and straightening things out as I went. The table was sticky, and when I went into the kitchen, I noticed a pile of dishes, and it didn't look as if he could even cook in here with the mess.

Into the Hood: Pierre & Anneka

I put some water and dish washing liquid into a small bowl. I washed down the table and then swept the floor. I then focused all of my attention on the kitchen while boiling a little bit of Fabuloso cleaner to have the lavender scent fill the air.

I began singing a tune that my mom used to sing to me, and I was in a zone. After washing the dishes, mopping the floor, and starting on some lunch, I was startled by Sebastian and Dakota, who were peering at me as if something were wrong.

"What in the hell are you doing?" Sebastian asked, and I was confused. I thought that it was clear that I simply cleaned up, and now I was preparing what I knew to be the best apple salmon crostini in all of New York.

"I'm cooking. Would you like some apple salmon crostini? I mean, you two were back there so long that I got hungry, and of course, I cleaned up. Dakota, you really need to keep a better house," I stated as the men peered at me as if I were carrying two heads.

"Ah-choo! What is that… Ah-choo! Smell?" Sebastian asked as he rubbed his nose rapidly.

"Oh, it's Fabuloso cleaner—the lavender scented one. There was a god-awful odor in this house, and my mom taught me that if I boil the scent, it will linger. Its smells a lot better than the scent that was here before," I replied, sniffing the steam from the pot as I waved my hands around to make the scent fill the air even more.

"Ah-choo! I'm allergic to... Ah-choo! Lavender," Sebastian said before running out of the kitchen.

"I'm sorry! I didn't know. Are you going to be ok?" I shouted behind him as I quickly turned the pot off.

"Don't worry about him. He's allergic to everything." Dakota chuckled, walking over to the refrigerator and opening it.

"You, ummm, know the ingredient that's, umm, secret to a smoke salmon croissant?"

I gave him a puzzled look, confused by his question.

Dakota adjusted his glasses. "I'm sorry. My words get jumbled sometimes. I meant. Do you know the secret ingredient to the perfect apple salmon crostini?" he quizzed, opening the refrigerator door then rummaging through it.

"No, I thought mine were pretty great already," I answered, confused by his question.

Into the Hood: Pierre & Anneka

As far as I knew, my apple salmon crostini were bomb. If I couldn't do anything else, my mom taught me how to clean and cook, and my apple salmon crostini would always bring warm smiles to the table. I used to make them when my father had dinner parties, and everybody loved them. Dakota closed the refrigerator and walked over to me holding a container.

"Ricotta. I mean Goat cheese. That's the secret ingredient." He beamed, and I swear he started to get flustered.

"Umm, are you ok?" I asked as he started fidgeting with the container.

"This stupid container, open won't it. I mean, it won't open," he said, obviously annoyed.

"Aah... this... this... ohhh, mad as hornets!" he shouted, and I grabbed his hands to calm him down.

As smart and kindhearted as Dakota appeared, he seemed to get agitated quickly, and honestly, he was somewhat of a pompous.

"Dakota, let me help you with this. This container seems to be getting you all flustered," I offered, placing my hand on the container.

"I got it. Just carry on, going... What was I saying?" he asked as if he'd confused himself.

He placed the container on the counter and started stroking his chin, looking as if he were in deep thought. His glasses fell on his round, scrunched-up nose, and he adjusted them then started rubbing his potbelly.

"Something smells good. What you cooking?" he asked, and again, I was confused by his question, but I didn't want to offend him. Maybe he was retarded or something, but I didn't want to assume, so I answered his question.

"Umm, apple salmon crostini. It's one of my favorite dishes. My mom taught me how to make this years ago."

"You, ummm, good crostini … Oh, you know the secret to great apple salmon crostini?" he inquired as if we didn't just have this discussion.

I held up the container of goat cheese.

"Goat cheese?" I answered, hoping that we could put an end to the conversation. He was clearly a scattered mess—just as his apartment was before I cleaned it.

"Ah-choo! Anneka… we got to… go. I… I… I… Ah-choo! Can't take it," Sebastian said, standing in the doorway, pinching his nose, and trying to keep from sneezing.

"Oh, no. I was getting ready to serve the food. Are you sure you can't hang out a little longer? I would really like to eat. My damn stomach is touching my fucking back."

Sebastian shook his head no. "Let's go, and watch your mouth. A young lady like you shouldn't say shit like that," he commanded as he stormed out of the kitchen.

"You force me to go with you, and then you try to tell me how to talk. All I wanted to do was eat, damn! I cleaned this nasty ass apartment and can't get a meal."

I think I offended Dakota, and that certainly wasn't my intent.

"Just take it with you. I got a jar to put it in. I don't get much cleaning done. Just a lot of reading and studying to keep me on my toes," Dakota said, looking through his cabinets.

I felt bad by my choice of words, I didn't mean to come off as a bitch. I felt it best to say no more, so I didn't bother to tell him that I already had a container with a lid sitting on the counter. I placed the apple salmon crostinis in the container, leaving some on a plate for Dakota.

"Thank you, Dakota. I'm sorry if I said anything to hurt your feelings. That wasn't my objective. I just wanted to eat something. I'm hungry as hell," I said as I gave him a hug.

"No problem. It was a mess in here. Take care and be safe," he replied then kissed the tip of my nose. In return, I kissed his cheek. Then we walked out of the kitchen.

"Seth, wake yo' ass up! It's time to go!" Sebastian shouted as he shook Seth hard as hell. Wherever Seth went last night took all of his energy because all he wanted to do was sleep.

"Damn, can a nigga get some fucking sleep around here?" Seth asked, yawning and stretching. He got up from the sofa and stumbled toward the door.

"Sebastian, remember what I said. To make sure you stay unseen, take the freeway, umm the highway, no, no, the express—"

Sebastian cut him off. "Yeah, yeah, yeah… Ah-choo! I got it. Thanks for reminding me about them. I'll let you know when we get there," Sebastian stated as he grabbed my arm and damn near dragged me out of the door.

"Where are we going, Sebastian? I'm tired of all this running around. I would like to relax for a bit. I know that you're going to eventually take me to my dad, but until then, can I at least have something to eat and a place to rest?" I asked as we got into the van, and I looked at Seth who didn't have a problem getting his rest.

"Eat that shit in the van, and rest while I'm driving. I never told you we were staying at Dakota's crib. You were the one going in there being Molly the maid."

"Don't call my food shit. I take pride in what I cook," I replied as I walked out to the van with an attitude. I flopped down in the back and popped the lid on the container.

"Damn, that shit smells good," Seth remarked and laid his head on the window and closed his eyes.

Sebastian was in the van, and we were about to pull away from the curb. I started eating and allowed tears to fall as my meal tasted as if my mom had herself made it. I quickly wiped my tears away and shoved as much food into my mouth as I possibly could as I pretended to be seated at the table with my mom.

Sebastian began speaking as he started driving. "Why are you so calm, Anneka? Do you know how… Ah-choo! Dangerous I am?"

I took in a deep breath and replied by simply saying, “Sebastian, I can only judge you for the person you show yourself to be, and around me, I don’t see you as dangerous. Your eyes are far too kind. Plus, whatever is meant to be will be.”

I finished my food, laid my head on the window, and closed my eyes to rest.

…

For the first time since I ran out of my apartment on Roosevelt Island, I was scared as hell. Sebastian parked on the street, and I frantically scanned the area. There were homeless men and women, hookers, drug dealers, and women with long nails and different colored hair, and they all looked like they would kill a person with ease. I didn’t see kindness in any of their eyes, but I did see survival. I locked the door, and Sebastian looked back at me and smirked. I hoped and prayed that he wasn’t about to drop me off in the middle of nowhere and leave me with these people.

“Oh, so now you’re scared?” Sebastian asked, and I simply nodded my head, and he unlocked the door and proceeded to get out.

Into the Hood: Pierre & Anneka

Opening up the door, he slapped Seth to wake him and said, "Welcome to Monticello." Although I didn't feel as if this were a place that would have a welcome mat, and if it did, I was sure it would be riddled with bullet holes.

Seth sleepily walked behind us as I grabbed ahold to Sebastian's arm. trying to keep up with his pace so that I wouldn't get lost or left in what could only be described as the ghetto. I was a city girl, Manhattan raised, so walking in the hood wasn't my thing. The closest I got to the hood was watching *Straight Outta Compton*, and I couldn't sleep a whole week from just watching that shit.

We walked for about a block with several people yelling out at us. Sebastian wasn't fazed, and Seth was too tired to even care. We made it to what appeared to be an abandoned house, and I thought I was about to have a heart attack and die. I mean. this house looked as if it were standing on its last leg.

The steps creaked as we walked up to the door. After three knocks, a woman came to the door, and she was the epitome of the word ghetto.

She had two gold teeth, long, pointy witch nails, strawberry-blonde and green hair, and she had on skinny jeans, Chuck Taylors, and a belly top. I kept a straight face because I wanted to ask her if she was trying on outfits for Halloween, but I didn't want to offend her. My mom always said to pick and choose my battles, and this wasn't a battle I wanted to fight.

"Dakota sent us for a makeover for her," Sebastian stated as the woman looked me up and down, put her index finger in her mouth, and began playing with her bubble gum.

"No, Dakota didn't say anything about no uppity ass bitch. She cute and errrthang, but umm, uh ah. This bitch, I can't help. I might have to beat her ass."

"You assume that I'm an uppity ass bitch just like I assumed you were dressing up for Halloween as queen of the ghetto. I don't know anything about a makeover, but I know if you are the one giving it, I decline your services," I spoke up for myself, and I guess that wasn't a very wise move.

"Bitch, did you just try to come for me?"

"What do you mean, come for you? Come where? Please speak English. I'm not following."

"Bitch, your face gon' follow my fists if you don't shut the fuck up," she stated with her nose flared, and thankfully, someone came from the back and saved me from this ghetto back and forth exchange.

"Regina, move yo' stupid ass out the way. She ain't even here for you. You taking her to La," a man holding a video controller in his hand said while opening the door and welcoming us in. If La was anything like the person I was about to meet, I may not make it out of this place. I seriously would have preferred getting captured by my dad rather than being here in the ghetto with a bitch that I didn't understand.

I looked at Sebastian, and he nodded for me to go in, and my stomach dropped. I was wishing that I could be back in the comfort of Bernard's embrace.

I scanned my surroundings as we walked through the house and into a room in the back. Two other men were sitting around smoking weed. One was slouched down in the chair with a goofy grin on his face, and the other one was giving me one of those 'if looks could kill' looks.

"Anneka, this is Geovanni," he introduced, I extended my hand for a shake, and he mumbled something but didn't bother to take my hand.

"Don't mind him. He's always grumpy," the man said as he turned me toward the guy that was slouched in the chair. "This is Harper," he introduced, and Harper hopped out of the chair, grabbed my hand, and shook it rapidly.

"Hi, Anneka. It's nice to meet you. You are so beautiful. Want to sit? Have a seat? You can have my seat." He giggled as he excitedly shook my hand.

"Ah-choo! Harper, if you don't sit yo' happy ass down… Ah-choo! Somewhere, I'mma … Ah-choo! Shoot you. Drake, what the hell… Ah-choo! I tell you about them ah… ah… ah-choo! Damn Kush incense?"

"Man, shut the fuck up, and get you some damn Claritin or Zyrtec or something. Nigga, I smoke loud. I can't have that shit smelling up my house," the man I now knew as Drake said as he grabbed a box from under his chair.

He opened the box, and it was full of bags of weed. He took one out along with a white owl and proceeded to roll a blunt.

"Nigga, that's the shit I don't get… Ah-choo! How you gonna sell that shit… Ah-choo! And smoke the shit up? What type of… Ah-choo! Dope man are you?" Sebastian questioned.

Drake licked the blunt to seal it before answering Sebastian's question. "The type that get a nigga fucked up off that fire shit," he replied.

As the men continued going back and forth, I was starting to get a little annoyed. It had been a long day, and all I wanted to do was lie down, relax, and meditate.

"Excuse me, is there somewhere I can lay down? I'm kind of tired?" I asked.

"Shit, looks like that nigga Seth beat you to it." Harper laughed, pointing over to the couch at a stretched-out, sleeping Seth.

"Aye, Regina! Come here!" Drake shouted.

Regina came in the room with her lips poked out and her hand on her hip, "Nigga, what the fuck you want?"

"Man, fuck you got an attitude for? You worse than that nigga," Drake said, pointing at Geovanni.

Geovanni grumbled something, and then Harper burst out laughing. "Ah-choo!" Sebastian sneezed for about the millionth time today. Looking around at the bunch, I shook my head. I had never been in the company of so many strange ass men, and I was starting to miss Bernard even more.

"Take Anneka to the spare bedroom," Drake told Regina.

She let out a sigh and rolled her eyes. "Girl, come on. You bet' not say no slick shit either. I'll bust yo' ass," she said, and I followed her to the room that she was taking me to.

I was never a performer, but I knew I needed to put on the performance of a lifetime. I may not have been well versed with hood slang and terminology, but I damn sure knew how to sass and curse somebody's ass out.

"You can lay yo' ass down over there. Let me tell you something. Drake is my man. Now, I don't let bitches in my shit, and if you here for drama, bitch, you can get these hands."

"What are you talking about, Regina? I don't even know you. I was tossed in a van and brought here. All I know is that I was getting a makeover. I want to rest. That's it. I don't want your man. Thank you for your hospitality," I said with an attitude.

"Bitch, don't get smart. I know when bitches are trying to be nice nasty to me."

Into the Hood: Pierre & Anneka

"You don't know me well enough to call me a bitch. I addressed you as Regina, so please address me as Anneka."

"Bitch, you not in a deluxe apartment in the sky. This is the hood, and if I want to call you a bitch, then I'll call you a bitch."

"Regina, clearly I'm in your house and wouldn't want to disrespect you, but just because you are living in this environment, that doesn't mean you are the toughest and can beat my ass. I'm really tired and do not wish to continue this back and forth. Again, thank you for your hospitality."

I guess that was my way of excusing her from my presence. I had a long day, and I was pissed that just a day ago, my mom was killed at the hands of my father. Now I was stuck here in this world of the unknown. As crazy as it seemed, with each passing minute that I was in this house, the angrier I was getting, and I felt myself changing. I needed this to be over, and the longer it was taking, the more I wanted to plot an evil, painful death for the man that I called my father.

Welcome to the hood, I thought as Regina gave me a look and walked out after rolling her eyes.

If I couldn't do anything else, I was always a good judge of character and knew when to follow my gut. Regina's eyes held hurt, and I knew she was building a barrier to hide something much deeper. I may not have known all the rules to being in the hood, but I knew I never allowed anyone to talk to me any type of way, and today wouldn't be any different.

I closed my eyes, said a quick prayer over my current situation, and stretched out in the bed that they provided.

It may have seemed strange, but I was wishing that I had Bernard to talk to and listen to me rant until I was captured by sleep.

I reminisced on our conversation from last night and closed my eyes with a smile on my face. *Maybe we will meet again. If it's in the cards for me, we will meet again,* I thought until I found sleep.

Chapter 10- Bernard

"I don't know, Mr. Post. I hadn't been here all day."

"Helen, I trusted you. After all my family has done for your family, and you betray me like this. It's been hours since I've been back, and even if she'd gone for a run, it's after 8:00 P.M., and she's not back."

Helen stood behind the desk, frantically typing away at her keyboard to see if Anneka changed rooms. I just couldn't imagine what could have possibly happened.

"Mr. Post, I'm so sorry. I don't see anything," Helen assured as she gave a sympathetic look.

"Helen, get with security, and please look at the tapes. Better yet, don't look at them. Tell security I need a copy of the tapes within the next twenty minutes in my suite. I'll get to the bottom of this." I walked away from the desk with Anneka heavily on my mind. I just couldn't believe that she'd left. I thought I did everything right. I gave her a place to stay. I got her clothes and food, and I made sure to listen to her every word. The only time I spoke was when I was reassuring her that I was indeed listening and interested in what she was saying. None of this made sense to me as to why she was gone.

When I got back to the room, her scent was yet lingering from possibly this morning. The aroma of apple blossom filled my nostrils, and I immediately began to smile. "Anneka Snow, where are you?" I asked aloud as I looked out the window of the suite and watched the many cars pass by.

Sitting on the bed, I noticed a neatly folded towel. I picked it up, and it was damp. I pulled it up to my nose, and it was as if Anneka was standing here.

Taps at the door pulled my attention away from my daydreaming about Anneka.

"Who is it?" I called out, and security responded.

Opening up the door, I was greeted and handed the footage.

"Mr. Post, as you have requested, here is the footage from today, leading up to the last ten minutes."

"Thank you, Roland. I appreciate this."

"Mr. Post, is there anything that we could possibly assist you with? You know that we have the best team here and can possibly be a great pair of eyes."

"No thank you, Roland. This is plenty." I dismissed Roland and walked to the DVD player and put in the disc. Grabbing the remote, I started the disc and began scanning the footage. I saw Anneka blending in as she went out for her morning run. As I fast forwarded the footage, I saw her return.

Things were looking normal. I continued watching, and there it was. Slowing down the footage forty-five minutes after her return, she was walking back down in the lobby and exiting out the door. The only difference in her exit this time was a man walking closely behind.

I needed another pair of eyes on this footage, and I knew exactly who to go to. I had my reserves about reaching out to him simply because even though he was so hood, he was such the charmer, and it seemed like every woman I thought I was interested in, he ended up charming them, and they'd forget about me, but if I wanted to find Anneka, I knew I had to reach out.

I called the number that I dreaded to call, and he picked up on the third ring.

"Pierre speaking, what do you want, and who in the hell is this?"

"Pierre, it's Bernard," I started, and he cut me off.

"Nigga, you finally over that bullshit that happened two years ago with that Sasha chick? Man, you should be. She was a handful. You didn't need those problems, and neither did I. What can I help you with?"

"I have a problem."

"And if you have a problem, you know I'm the nigga to solve them. What you need?"

I knew I could trust Pierre. He was a street dude that played by the rules. He wouldn't snitch no matter what I told him, so I started from the beginning and ended with me telling him about me being in this room watching this video.

"Damn, B, that's heavy. So this Anneka chick, she got an ass on her? She thick with it?"

"Pierre, I need to find her. Did you hear me when I said that she watched her dad, Senator Snow, kill her mom? And now he's looking for her because I'm sure he wants to shut her mouth… permanently."

"Alright, alright, alright, what does she look like?"

"Turn on any news station, but trust me, Pierre. Her pictures don't do her any justice."

"Aw shit, you feeling this girl? It's not even about her dad; you want some of Miss Snow's pussy…"

I took in a deep breath, and Pierre paused.

Into the Hood: Pierre & Anneka

"Hello? Hello? Pierre?" I questioned as I looked down at my phone to make sure we were yet connected.

"Yeah, I'm here. This bitch is a hottie," he said, sounding as if he were mesmerized by her looks, which wasn't hard for any man to be wrapped in her enchanted beauty.

"Pierre, please stay focused. Can you help me find her? And for the love of God, don't call her a bitch. She's not like the girls you're used to."

"I sure can help you. Give me twenty-four hours."

"Ok, I'll call you in twenty-four hours."

"Yeah, you do that…" Pierre retorted, and his voice sounded as though he was preoccupied, and then the line cut off.

I kept replaying the footage until sleep found me, and I began to dream about Anneka and the short time that we spent together.

…

"I love you so much, Mr. Post," my wife said as she sat on top of me, straddling me. She leaned forward and planted a soft kiss on my lips.

"I love you too, Mrs. Post," I replied, grabbing the back of her head and pulling her down to hungrily kiss her.

It was our honeymoon, and I was anxious to consummate our union. My wife was innocent, and pure. She wanted to wait until our wedding day to make love. I loved her wholeheartedly, so I didn't mind waiting for my wife to give herself to me. She removed the clip from her hair, let it fall to her shoulders, and shook it a little bit. I couldn't help but run my fingers through her soft, thick locks.

"Baby, I want to feel you inside of me," she whispered as she nibbled on my earlobe as she started dry humping me.

I grabbed her ass cheeks with both hands, lifting her up a little so that I could slide my fingers into her opening.

"Mmm..." She moaned as she closed her eyes and threw her head back.

Moving my thumb in a circular motion, I applied a little pressure to her clit while my two fingers danced around in her wetness. She exhaled heavily as she licked her lips and ran her fingers through her hair. I sat up, cupped her breast in my hand, and started circling her nipple with my tongue.

"Aaah," she breathed out as her body shuddered from my touch.

I nibbled then sucked on her nipple then switched my hand from her box to her other breast so that I could give it some attention as well.

"You're so beautiful," I said, stroking her hair. I kissed her before flipping her on to her back.

Her body was tensed and trembling as if she were afraid. Her chest was rising and falling at a rapid pace, and her heart was pounding so hard that I could feel it beating against my chest.

"Relax," I coached her, staring deep into her eyes. She nervously smiled, and my heart skipped a beat.

"I love you, my wife," I spoke slightly above a whisper as I thrusted slowly inside her.

"Ow." She groaned with a distorted face and dug her fingers in my flesh.

I held her tightly, kissing her to comfort her as I continued ease my way into her sweet spot. After a while of me slowly grinding her, her body started to relax, and I could feel her pussy starting to open to receive me.

"Mmm, Bernard..." She moaned softly as she raked her nails up my spine.

Speeding up my pace, I wrapped my hands around her shoulders, pulling her downward so that I could go deeper.

"Damn, baby, you feel soooo good," I grunted out.

She was lying there like a dead fish, and honestly, it wasn't really pleasing to me. I didn't want to offend her or make her think that I wasn't enjoying her, but I had to tell her the best way that I knew how.

"Baby, in order for both of us to get pleasure out of this, you have to move your hips to match what I'm doing," I instructed her, guiding her hips forward and backward.

A few seconds later, she was rocking and rolling her hips, matching my rhythm.

"Yeah, that's it, baby. Gimme that pussy," I coached, feeling her pussy walls gripping my rod tightly.

"Oh, oh, oh!" she shouted as I picked up my pace, plowing into her as deep and as far as I could go.

"Bernard, yes, yes, yes, I love you!" she cried out as her body started convulsing, causing my tool to pulsate.

Into the Hood: Pierre & Anneka

My toes were curling, sweat was dripping from my body to hers, and we were both panting as the trembles in our bodies increased.

"Oh, my!" She hissed with a look of fear on her face. "What is happening? I feel weird." She huffed.

My body was jerking so bad that I couldn't form the words to explain an orgasm to her. Wrapping her arms around my neck, she screamed loudly as she squeezed my dick tightly. Tingling sensations shot through my body, then I felt warm liquid spilling onto my legs.

Breathing rapidly and sweating profusely, I shot up in the bed, disoriented. I blinked my eyes several times to regain my focus as my heart rate started to return to normal, and I took several calming breaths to regain my composure as I came to the realization that I was only dreaming about Anneka Snow. She wasn't really there, and we weren't married. However, my boxers were wet from my own nut. I shook my head.

"Damn, Bernard, you haven't had a wet dream since you were twelve. You spend one amazing night with Anneka, and you're nutting all over yourself in your sleep," I mumbled to myself. "Who am I kidding? A woman like her would never go for a guy like me," I added.

Feeling embarrassed and blushing at the same time, I hopped out of bed and ran into the bathroom to take a shower. As the warm water dripped down my spine, thoughts of Anneka flooded my mind. I didn't know what it is about this girl, but I was falling for her hard.

"Don't worry, Anneka. I won't let anything happen to you. I promise. I'll find you soon," I said aloud, hoping that somewhere in the universe, she was hearing my words.

After showering, I went into the bedroom and changed the sheets on the bed, picked up the towel that held Anneka's scent, and began thinking about Anneka. I started praying for her safe return until my eyelids got heavy, and sleep found me.

Chapter 11- Leo

Three days later

"Fuck!" I yelled, slamming my fist on the table, making the glass shake. "I didn't pay Sebastian all that damn money to not get any results," I ranted.

I'd been calling Sebastian for hours now, and he hadn't answered or returned any of my calls. Meanwhile, Anneka was running around the state of New York probably running her mouth to whoever would listen to her little story about me killing her mother. And I couldn't have that. Although I was a very rich and powerful man and could make the situation disappear instantaneously, I didn't want or need any type of scandal tarnishing my good name.

I picked up the phone and called Sebastian one more time. The phone rang a few times then went to voicemail. This time, I decided to leave him a message.

"Sebastian, it's imperative that you get in touch with me, asap."

At first, it wasn't my intent to kill Anneka. I was just gonna ship her away and supply her with enough money to live happily ever after, but then she walked in on me killing her mom, and when she ran, it was clear that she saw and understood what I'd done, so now I had no choice but to take her out.

Anneka was so young and naïve. By the time I was eighteen, I had my own shit and was figuring out this world on my own. Eva had handicapped that child into believing in fairytales when, in actuality, this world was fucked up, and you had to have a dog-eat-dog mentality in order to make it. Yes, she sassed and had a smart-ass mouth, but that was about it. She had no real-life experiences. She only had book sense, and that wouldn't get her ass far.

When I met Eva, I thought she would be my rock, but the bitch failed to disclose to me that the females in her family mysteriously carried some fucked up bone disorder that caused cancer.

I never signed up for that shit. Yeah, we said 'until death do us part,' but I didn't say shit about sickness. I said in health, and in love. I purposely didn't mention sickness in my vows because I just wasn't the type of man that had the time or patience in dealing with that shit.

Anneka would never understand. That bitch of a mother of hers had been a burden on me for years. Eva was nothing to me but a trophy wife, and when she was well, she played the hell out of that role, and that shit kept me happy. She did many of the things I required as a powerful man who only wanted his wife's help in gaining even more power.

Eva wasn't all bad at first when I thought about it. She cooked and kept our home immaculately clean, she took the time to try to be the best mom she could be, and she always hosted the best parties for my friends to enjoy and become envious of us, and that was the shit I enjoyed the most, but even though she did those things, she didn't take care of my every need. As a man, I really needed my wife to be a lady in the streets but a freak in the sheets.

When I first met Eva, she was just as young and as beautiful as Anneka, with a body fit for a model. She was slim yet curvy and had nice, full breasts and a tight, round, plump ass. We used to go at it like two horny jackrabbits, and I was the envy of all men, and all the women were wishing they were in Eva's shoes. I loved the attention she received when we stepped into a room, but when the guest would leave, and I wanted her to roleplay for me, that was when shit got fucked up in our marriage. Eva loved to make love slow and steady, but I was a man who loved to fuck nice and hard.

I would have to beg her ass to do what I thought was simple shit, like talk that shit to me while I was busting up in those guts. Tell me I had a big dick and you wanted more, but Eva was too conservative at times, and when she got sick, shit really changed, and I started fucking these young bitches who were always thirsty for a come up.

The more time I spent fucking around on Eva, the more I hated coming home. To top it all off, Anneka was turning into the woman that I thought I married, so I began to grow hatred for her as well and started treating her like shit.

The day I knew it was time to rid myself of Eva was when I came home from a conference that she couldn't make it to, because she claimed to be so tired and could hardly move. I started to notice her for whom she'd become, and I knew this wasn't the life I signed up for. Her luscious, silky, long hair seemed to have turned thin and stringy, her fair skin became pale and clammy, and all of her curves seemed to have disappeared. I married Eva for her looks, and that bitch had the nerve to lose them.

Into the Hood: Pierre & Anneka

Anneka was into all types of natural shit and found a doctor to help Eva recover, but by then, it was much too late. I was deep into my new relationship, and the plans we had for this insurance money was closer than ever. Had Eva gotten better, it would have fucked it all up. I made sure Dr. Osbourne knew what to give her so that I could continue to demean her and keep her feeling lower than shit, so she would wither and die. The day I killed her, I felt as if I had no choice because I heard her saying on the phone that she wouldn't miss that appointment and needed more natural juice. She was blatantly trying to defy me, so I needed to show her who was really the boss.

Now that she was gone, all I needed to do was kill her clone of a child she left behind so I could live my life.

My phone ringing snatched me away from my thoughts. Looking down, I noticed it was Sebastian, and I answered on the third ring.

"You wanna tell me why the fuck I paid you, and you didn't deliver on what I paid you to do?" I seethed without hesitation.

"Shut yo' bitch ass up. If you wanted it done your way… Ah-choo! Yo' punk ass would have done it. Ah-choo!"

I was annoyed with his ass sneezing and not being able to deliver as promised, so I needed to show him who was the boss and how this shit was going to go.

"Listen, you punk muthafucka. Do what I paid you to do, or you'll be in hiding with her."

"Ah-choo! Muthafucka, is that a threat?"

"It's a promise."

"You just signed your own death… Ah-choo! Ah-choo! Ah-choo! Certificate," he warned, and silence filled the phone.

"Sebastian. Sebastian… Sebastian!" I yelled into the phone before noticing that he hung up. This shit was getting real, and now I need to show this muthafucka just how long my reach was.

Chapter 12- Anneka

I woke up to the sound of fireworks filling the air. I stood up and began to stretch and walked toward the window to see what was going on.

"Bitch, getcho ass down! You trying to die?" Regina yelled, snatching me to the floor.

"What's going on?" I questioned as we lay on the dirty floor, and then I realized as Regina started to shield her head that it wasn't fireworks but gunfire.

As the shooting ceased, we stood, and Regina spoke.

"Bitch, I don't know what the fuck you think this is, but this is not the fucking four seasons, and you not in that uppity ass apartment yo' rich daddy got. Bitch, this is the hood, and at 5:00 A.M., most of these muthafuckas are finding out some shit that they didn't want to know and end up handling the muthafucka responsible for giving them the information."

Regina had a bad attitude. I got that she possibly just saved my life, but a simple explanation without all of the extra dramatic shit would have been great.

"Regina, I won't pretend as if I know the rules of hood living. I thought I heard fireworks. That's it. You don't need to get an attitude because I'm not as fast as you when it comes to shit like this."

"Girl, you don't even know how to cuss. Shut yo' weak ass up."

"I didn't know cursing was an art."

"The fact that you said cursing and not cussing just proved my point. Next time, I'll let them blow yo' damn head off," she stated and shook her head while walking out the room that I was sleeping in.

Usually, at 5:00 A.M., I was preparing for my morning run, but I didn't want to chance it in this neighborhood, so I did what I was good at. I began singing and cleaning, and once I got done, I figured I would wake the house up with some of my apple butter pancakes.

I began singing Hilary Duff's "Come Clean" as I danced and sang around the room, cleaning. No matter how nice I was, it seemed like Regina was determined to be a bitch toward me. At first, the word bitch bothered me, but the longer I was around her, the more I realized that this was just the way she spoke.

"Bitch! It's too early for all of that singing shit! Take yo' dumb ass back to bed!" Regina spat as I hushed from singing and continued to hum the tune as I cleaned the room.

After I cleaned, I walked into the living space and noticed that everyone was sleeping. I pulled the drapes and was sad because the sun hadn't risen, and darkness continued to fill the sky. I turned on a side lamp and heard the slight snores from Seth and began to giggle.

I began cleaning around them and organized everything they had out, including Drake's weed stash. After everything was perfect. I went into the kitchen and wasn't surprised at the fact that it was dirty. I found the kitchen cleaning supplies under the sink and cleaned the kitchen. By the time I was finished in the kitchen, I'd worked up an appetite, and that was great because I needed to eat.

I cracked and whipped my eggs, took out bread for cinnamon apple French toast, made maple apple bacon, apple butter pancakes, and found a juicer to make homemade fresh apple juice. The aroma from the kitchen seemed to have everyone slowly waking up, and that was simply fine by me. It had been awhile since I hosted a dinner party, and I was excited to do what my mom and I used to do but for breakfast.

Drake came into the kitchen first. "Damn, girl. It smells good than a muthafucka up in here. I'm 'bout to eat all this shit," he said while stretching and coming closer to the stove and standing right next to me.

My heart began to beat faster as his eyes held this droopy haze look. He smiled and then reached over and grabbed some bacon.

"Bitch, who told you to come in my fucking house and try to show me the fuck up? I know how to cook and clean! And why the fuck are you smiling in my man's face? You begging to get yo' ass beat."

I didn't have any friends, due to the fact that I was homeschooled and didn't get out much, but seeing Regina being all insecure made me realize how lucky I was to be a loner.

"Regina, let's be honest. You don't cook or clean, and if you did, your place wouldn't have been in shambles. You keep threatening to beat my ass, but not once have you tried to, so please stop with the fake threats. Breakfast will be ready shortly, and you're welcome."

"Fuck you, bitch."

"I don't swing that way, but thanks for the compliment."

Drake started laughing, and Regina was pissed.

"This corny ass bitch ain't funny."

"She might not be, but she pulled yo' damn card. Hey, Anneka, if Regina didn't like you, she would have swung on you, so she's talking shit to try to intimidate you. She will fight, but you're right. She's not gon' swing on you," Drake offered, and I knew I had her ass pegged right.

"Nigga, you don't fucking know me. Don't tell that simple bitch that. Fuck y'all," Regina spat, and Drake went over to Regina, grabbed her by her hips, and pulled her in for a long kiss, and they hungrily sucked each other's faces. I let out a sigh of frustration as I continued cooking breakfast. I didn't know what makeover I was here to get, but I prayed that it had nothing to do with Regina, and I needed for it to be done so I could move around and focus on the real task at hand, and that was putting an end to my father.

Just as Drake and Regina were finishing sucking each other's face, the other guys started coming in the kitchen.

"What the fuck is all this?" Sebastian asked, and everyone stared at him in disbelief.

"Why the fuck y'all staring at me like that? I got slob on my face, eye boogers, or something?" Sebastian started wiping the corners of his eyes and mouth, wondering if he needed to go wash his face.

"Nigga, you ain't sneezing. That's why we looking at yo' ass." Drake chuckled.

"Oh, I made a mixture of eucalyptus, tea tree, peppermint, and lemon oils together and massaged them on his temples, behind his ears, and on his feet while he was sleeping. The sneezing was keeping me up, and with the dust from the house, he would have been dead by morning," I stated as I picked up the container holding the blend.

"Oh, hell naw! Bitch, you did *not* use my essential oils on that nigga. Drake, she got to go. I can't with her ass. She's making herself too damn comfortable in my damn house. There can only be one woman running this house, and if it's not me, then I gotta go!" Regina fussed, rolling her neck and eyes.

"You run this shit, baby. Calm down. We all wanted his ass to stop sneezing. Hell, you could learn a thing or two from Anneka," Drake said, and I gave a sassy look her way.

Regina gave me a threatening look, threw her hands in the air, and then stormed out of the kitchen.

"Look, I'm sorry. I get that I'm the odd duck in the crowd, but I was only trying to help. I didn't mean to upset her about her oils. I do a lot of natural researching. In fact, right before my mom—" I stopped and got choked up and didn't finish that statement.

"Look, I'm sorry." The guys looked at me empathetically, and Drake finally spoke.

"Naw, you straight. Regina just always has an attitude. She need some of this act right; she'll be fine after that."

I wasn't up to speed on all of the urban, or should I say hood lingo, so I didn't know what 'act right' was, but whatever it was, he needed to hurry up and give Regina some of it because she was getting on my damn nerves.

"Shit, I just did a wake and bake, and I'm starving like a muthafucka. Let's sit down and enjoy this good ass meal Anneka made for us," Drake suggested, pulling out a chair for me to sit down.

Nodding my head, I thanked Drake, and the other men gathered around the table.

"This shit looks and smells so good. Thank you, Anneka. This is so nice," Harper excitedly spoke as he sniffed the air, taking in the aroma.

"Apples, I hate apples," Geovanni grumbled, pushing his plate away.

"Man, shut yo' happy ass the fuck up. It's too damn early, aaaah, for that shit Harper, and Geovanni, you don't like shit." Seth yawned as he stretched.

"Both of y'all… Ah-choo!" Sebastian looked surprised that his sneeze returned.

"Oh, damn, Sebastian. Do I need to put some more oil on you?" I inquired but was interrupted by Regina entering the kitchen.

"Don't touch my damn oil. This nigga needs to take care of his own damn allergies. Take yo' ass to the store and buy yo' own shit, Sebastian. It ain't like you can't afford it." Regina sat at the table and proceeded to fix her plate.

Everyone stared at her in shock as she piled her plate with food.

"Fuck y'all looking at? Y'all better dig in, shit, acting like y'all asses not starving. Y'all better eat all this shit 'cause y'all know I'm not feeding y'all asses."

The men all burst into laughter as they began fixing their plates.

After eating, I cleaned the kitchen while the others went about their way. As I was sweeping the crumbs off the floor, I started thinking of Bernard. He would've sat in the kitchen and conversed with me as I cleaned. None of these men really talked to me, let alone had a full conversation. I was starting to get bored, and all I wanted to do was to get the makeover I was here for and move on.

Once I made sure the kitchen was spotless, I started down the hall toward the room where Sebastian was playing a video game.

Boom! A sudden loud sound hitting the wall in Drake's bedroom startled me, causing me to almost jump out of my skin. Boom… boom… boom… boom. The banging sound was going at a rapid pace, and suddenly, I heard Regina cry out, "Aaaah, Drake, shit!" I clutched my invisible pearls, praying that he wasn't hurting her.

"Whose fucking pussy is this?" Drake shouted, and Regina answered in a loud droning voice.

"It's yours!" she cried out.

At the realization that Drake and Regina were having sex, I covered my mouth with my hand as to not make a sound then rushed down the hall and into the room with Sebastian. I may not have had sex before, but I did know what sex was, and after hearing that, I wanted to have an experience of my own.

Truth be told, my mom asked me to save myself for marriage, but the more I hung around these people in this hood, I didn't know what would happen.

I walked in the room and took in the scenery. As usual, Seth was sprawled across the bed sleeping, Geovanni was slouched in the chair looking angry, Harper was on social media laughing at videos, and Sebastian was playing the video game and smoking a blunt.

"Ah-choo! You ok?" he asked when he noticed me standing there.

"Yes, I really want to know when I am getting my makeover. I'm ready to move on. I need to get as far away as I can. It doesn't seem as if you're taking me to my father, so I need to do what I was planning on doing before you came and interrupted my life," I spoke as I sat next to him on the foot of the bed.

Sebastian started smiling and staring at me as if he could eat me or something. I felt a little uncomfortable, but it was just Sebastian. He was harmless.

"Aye, Anneka. Regina's gonna be out in a second. She's taking you to get your makeover or whatever the fuck it is," Drake informed, walking in the room with his hand down the front of his pants and a blunt hanging from his lips.

He adjusted himself then slapped Seth's legs. "Nigga, wake yo' ass up. Always muthafuckin' sleeping. You got one of those hoe bitches you be fucking with pregnant?"

Seth yawned and stretched. "Fuck that. My pull-out game is real strong. I ain't dropping no seeds in no bitch. Y'all niggas never let my ass sleep. I'm always running around with this muthafucka." Seth pointed at Sebastian.

"Nigga, you don't do shit but sleep in the fucking car. Fuck you talking about?" Sebastian slapped Seth in the back of the head, and the two of them started play fighting.

Regina walked in the room with a big smile on her face. I stared at her in shock. It was the first time since I'd been here that I saw a smile on her face. Drake noticed the look on my face.

"That's that act right," he whispered, grabbing the front of his pants.

I laughed, finally catching on that he was saying that she needed some dick in her life to make her happy. If dick was going to keep her smiling, maybe he needed to give her more of it because I was sick of her damn attitude.

Regina playfully slapped Drake's arm then gave Drake a kiss.

"Y'all stop all that bullshit. Y'all not outside," she said to Seth and Sebastian. "Come on, Anneka. Let me get yo' bourgeois ass together so I can get back to my man." Regina grabbed my hand and led me out the room and out of the front door.

"Regina, where in the hell are we going?" I asked, looking around at the neighborhood with a look of disgust on my face.

"Girl, I'm taking you to my girl Laquanda. She gon' hook yo' little bourgeois ass up. Maybe take some of the proper out yo' tone," she replied, walking fast as if she were marching. I had to step up my pace to keep up with her.

"Regina, who is Laquanda, and does she dress like you?" I questioned out of curiosity.

"Bitch, don't get smart. La is one of the most underrated and might be the baddest stylist in all of New York. Shit, she ain't famous or nothing, but she gon' hook yo' lil' bourgeois ass up."

I knew that Regina and I were from two different walks of life, and I was almost certain that my idea of being hooked up by a stylist was clearly not the same as hers. I could only hope that this wasn't a disaster waiting to happen.

...

Being around Laquanda and Regina, I was slowly picking up the hood language. Hell, these two could possibly teach a class in it. I was waiting on my reveal when Regina called out, yelling in the back where Laquanda was transforming me, or snatching me as they say, and she was loud as hell.

"Bitch, please tell me you hooked her ass up. I mean, she cute or whatever, but the chile needed a complete makeover for real!" Regina screamed from the front of the house back to Laquanda.

"Bitch, who the fuck am I? Who's in charge of the girls? Laquanda is in charge of the girls!"

"Well, I hope you worked yo' magic on that bitch!" Regina continued yelling.

"Girl, shut up! She didn't need too much, but here she come. I need to show her first, damn!" Laquanda stated, and I got nervous. I felt as if I had a tight helmet on my head. And although I saw the clothes as I put them on, I didn't know how I looked in them, because Laquanda said I wasn't ready for the mirror.

"Aye, Anneka, bring yo' ass out here! Let me see what you looking like!" Regina hollered.

"Bitch, shut up! She coming! Let me show her first just to see if we need to make a few changes." Laquanda pulled me in front of a full-length mirror, and I saw myself differently for the first time.

I was hesitant about the look because I'd never worn anything like this a day in my life. Plus, it wasn't my taste. Yellow skinny jeans, a blue V-neck form-fitting crop top that was trimmed white around the neck area and red on the short sleeves. It was a tad bit colorful and a little tacky for my liking, but being around these two allowed me to welcome the change and go with the flow.

"Girl, if you don't bring yo' lil' bourgeois ass out here!" Regina shouted.

I glanced at myself one last time in the mirror. It might not have been my taste or style, but in the words of Regina and Laquanda, I was slaying this shit. I walked out with my head held high, and just as I thought, Regina said the exact words that were swimming in my head.

"Biiiiitch, you slayed this shit!" Regina excitedly spoke as she walked around me, giving me a once over.

"Did I do it, or did I do it?" Laquanda questioned, and Regina and Laquanda both burst into laughter.

"Girl, all we need to do now is give her a quick lesson in Ebonics and take that proper shit out her tone, and we may actually start to claim her ass around these parts. Might be able to get her a piece of dick to lighten her up."

"As tempting as that's sounding, I really just wanted to get over here and get this done for whatever reasons Sebastian wanted it done and then move on. You both know what I'm dealing with, and although this is cool and everything, I'm not into this shit. I can't think about anything else but my mom."

"Bitch, we all been through shit. What you going through is public information. I may not know the ins and outs of it, but I know your father is devastated and looking for your ass, and hell, if the hood didn't have snitching rules, I would have turned yo' lil' ass in for the reward money."

"Look, you don't know the half of it. Don't believe the shit you see on television."

"Girl, don't she sound funny as shit cussing? Told you her ass was weird." Regina laughed, and I was trying to be serious.

If I despised anything about this experience in the hood thus far, it was the fact that these bitches were self-centered.

"Anneka, are you cool?" Laquanda asked.

"No, my head hurts, my heart is broken, and I'm with two chicks I hardly understand, getting a makeover I didn't damn want."

"Bitch, you do cuss funny. Say you wit' two bad bitches that snatched yo' damn soul today and got you all the way together," Laquanda teased as she and Regina slapped fives.

"Girl, that good ole sew in gon' last yo' ass for about a good three months," Regina countered, playing in my beach waves that Laquanda curled with a wand.

"She ain't gon' keep that shit up, girl. We should take her to Pierre's party. You know niggas is gon' be on her cute, thick, slim ass."

I was starting to feel annoyed with the both of them standing here talking about me like I wasn't even in the room.

"Look. I may not have ever had a weave, wig, tracks, extensions, or whatever you all call it, but as you can see, Laquanda, I do take care of my natural hair. Don't stand here and talk around me like I'm not standing right the fuck here. That shit is starting to piss me the fuck off."

"Yeeeesssss, Biiiiitch! You better read!" Laquanda stated, snapping her fingers, and she and Regina laughed.

"Look, I'm sorry if I'm not like you guys, but I'm not dumb, not by a long shot, and I'm not gonna continue to stand here and be disrespected."

"Girl, calm down. La is just saying that you reading us, you know. Like doing that shit you thought you were doing earlier, being nice nasty. Petty, if you will. Look, bitch. We like it."

"Well, clearly, I don't know all of the lingo, and if I feel like you're trying to disrespect me, I'll speak out on that shit because that's something I will never tolerate. If I respect you, dammit, you will respect me."

"Well, damn, she does have a backbone. But shit, even when you trying to go in on somebody, you sound too fucking nice. We gonna have to hood yo' ass up," Regina stated, shaking her head and rolling her eyes as we prepared to leave.

"Anneka, what's yo' nickname?" Laquanda queried.

"My mom only called me Neka Pooh, and other than that, I don't have one."

"Well, I like you and all, but fuck that. You're Neka, and you can just call me La. I appreciate the fact that you stand up for what you feel is right. It may be dumb as shit to do that in the hood, but hey, I like yo' style. Glad to be of service to you."

"Neka is fine with me, but um, La, can you loosen this weave up? This shit is snatching me bald as we speak."

"Girl, that shit ain't nothing. It will loosen up in about a week or two."

"No, I can't take this, and if this is what Regina had, I see why she's so damn angry."

The girls laughed because they said I was funny even when I wasn't trying to be. La took me to the back to address the concerns I had with this sew in. About an hour later, Laquanda was putting the finishing touches on my hair and then immediately wanted to try some makeup on me and was anxious to see how I looked.

"Regina, get up, girl. Come look at lil' miss bourgeois over here," La instructed, and Regina hopped off the sofa and rushed over to us.

"Yaaas, girl, now that's what the fuck I'm talking about. That hair is fierce, and that face is beat to the Gods. Anneka, girl, you doing it."

I actually started to feel this style. It was different but edgy, and with the shit I was facing, change was welcomed. I was checking myself out and preparing to leave, and then La stopped us.

"Wait. Put this jacket on first," La said, passing me a black moto-style leather jacket with a red interior.

I put the jacket on then headed over to the full-length mirror to check myself out. I must admit that I looked damned good and nothing like my picture that was circulating on the news.

"I like it!" I beamed, running my fingers through my sew-in.

"Girl, like it? I love it," Regina complimented.

"Laquanda, I love it. I wasn't sure about all of this before, but it's beautiful. Different doesn't always mean bad, and proper doesn't always mean bourgeois. I can pull this off." I couldn't stop smiling.

"You do look good, Ms. Bourgeois. Now, if I could just understand if that was a read or compliment, I would be straight. Girl, you be blowing me, but anyway. Thanks, La. We will get up with you before Pierre's big birthday bash," Regina commented, and she and Laquanda were laughing because I guess they were trying to get used to me.

I looked at the exchange between the friends and knew that was missing in my life. I didn't have siblings or friends to go through any of this with, and I guess that was the hardest part about my unknown journey.

With a new look and learning a new style of speaking, I guess I can pull off this Anneka in the hood vibe, or should I say swag, like Regina and La, I thought as we prepared to make our exit.

"Aight, La. I'll see you Tuesday for my shit to get redone," Regina told Laquanda.

Laquanda walked us to the door, and I thanked her again for the makeover. Then Regina and I stopped to grab a bite to eat, and I was loving the attention.

"See, lil' bourgeois. Yo' ass fit right in. You a classic boujhetto bitch." Regina laughed, and I joined in this time.

I guess you could say that we got off on the wrong foot, but these last few days, we were slowly but surely understanding each other, and to be honest, I would say we were creating a bond.

Chapter 13- Drake

When Regina and Anneka walked in the house, my mouth literally dropped. Anneka was already beautiful before the makeover, but got damn, shorty was banging. I hopped up off the couch and walked over to her so that I could get a closer look. She had a nigga drooling, and I was trying to keep my third leg from bricking the fuck up. Forgetting that Regina had just walked in with Anneka, I spoke in admiration.

"Damn, shorty. Laquanda hooked you up. You look good," I affirmed, trying to keep my cool. Regina was eyeballing the shit out of me, and I didn't want to give her ass a reason to go the fuck off.

"Thank you, Drake. I think I look good too. I mean, different, but good," she spoke in the most pleasant tone. If I hadn't noticed her ass before, shorty definitely had my attention now.

"Yeah, my girl be doing the damn thing. She hooked bad and bourgeois right the fuck up," Regina excitedly spoke as she spun Anneka around, giving me a full view of all of her assets.

I nodded my head in agreement then made my way back over to the couch so that I could finish my blunt.

Regina walked over to the stereo system and turned on some music. I was high like a muthafucka and ready to shoot for the fucking clouds. I lit my shit and then watched Regina and Anneka do that girlie shit.

"Girl, get over here so I can teach you how to dance. If you gonna be hanging with me, you got to know how to work yo' shit on the dance floor," Regina said as she grabbed Anneka's hand and pulled her to the middle of the room.

I was excited to see some ass shaking, so I sat up and started blowing my trees as I watched the two of them gyrating their hips. I slouched back on the couch with my arm behind my head, stretched out my legs, and enjoyed the damn show.

"Yes, bitch, loosen those hips up. Move that body like a fucking snake," Regina coached as she demonstrated what she wanted Anneka to do as she rotated her hips.

Regina started damn near caressing her own body, and Anneka followed suit. I almost nutted on myself when Anneka started twirling around in a circle while slowly moving her hips around. I had to reposition myself on the couch because my dick started jumping around in my pants. A nigga was ready to play and wanted to bend Regina and Anneka over and give them this pole.

Anneka's eyes met my gaze, and I swear her big, brown, doe eyes looked as if she were using them to seduce me. She bit down on her bottom lip as she started feeling the music. Shit, I imagined myself walking over to her and sucking those sexy, full muthafuckas into my mouth.

As the girls continued to dance, I couldn't take my eyes off Anneka. I couldn't help my thoughts as my eyes continued roaming her body; she was slim but had a neat little hourglass figure. Her hips were the perfect size to hold on to while plowing into her pussy. Her waist was tiny, which made her breasts look a lil' bit bigger.

I closed my eyes and imagined her and Regina both walking over toward me ready, willing, and fucking begging to give me the business. Shit, it had been a long time since I'd had a threesome, and I was ready to fuck the shit out of both of them. I could see it now. Anneka, innocent, and shy; then there was Regina, freaky, and aggressive just like I liked her.

Into the Hood: Pierre & Anneka

The shit that was going on in my mind had me ready to pop off in some pussy. In my mind, *I wrapped my hand around Anneka's plump breasts and teased them with my tongue. She giggled and then let out a soft moan that let me know that she was ready for me to devour her breasts. I slid my hand up her thigh until I reached her honey pot then started teasing it a little. She threw her head back as she opened her legs wider and welcomed my thick fingers into her tight little pussy while Regina deepthroated my dick.*

I opened my eyes, and Regina was bent over twerking while Anneka looked on, embarrassed. I licked my lips as I watched Regina reach up and bend Anneka forward. I grabbed my dick as I thought about smacking her ass cheeks, leaving my handprint on her fair skin. Then I spread her cheeks apart and slid up in her. Shivers went through my body as I thought of how warm and tight her pussy had to be. I bet that shit would latch onto my dick and squeeze it while I was pumping in and out.

"Aye, Drake, let me hit that," Regina said as she flopped down on the couch beside me.

Without taking my eyes off of Anneka, I passed Regina the blunt. "Ole girl coming out of her shell, huh?"

Regina asked, pleased with the way Anneka was dancing in the middle of the floor.

"I guess so. I mean, if anyone could help her come out her shell, it would be you," I replied, trying not to show my excitement.

"Let's see if we can loosen her lil' bourgeois ass up a little more. Let her hit this shit. See what these uppity ass bitches look like high as giraffe pussy," Regina said then puffed on the blunt and called Anneka over to join us.

"Here, hit this," she instructed as she passed Anneka the blunt.

You could tell that Anneka had never been around this shit as she took the blunt from Regina's hand and popped it with her hand.

Regina and I started cracking up laughing as Anneka held a puzzled expression on her face.

"Bitch, yo' ass dumb for real. Hold the shit in your hand, suck in, hold that shit in your lungs, and blow out. You ain't never had a cigarette?" Regina asked, and Anneka was looking so beautiful and lost. I was drawn to her innocence.

"No, not at all. I don't think I want to hit… anything. Smoking is bad for your health, and I want to specialize in fitness," Anneka commented.

"Girl, specialize in this blunt. You not going out with me if you can't hold yo' own. We got a party we hitting soon, and I refuse to have yo' square ass out and about with me. Matter of fact, chug this first. Then hit this shit fo' I beat yo' bourgeois ass," Regina teased, handing Anneka a shot of vodka.

Anneka was reluctant to drinking and smoking, but with the pressure that Regina was laying heavy on her, she couldn't resist and took the shot and tossed it to the back of her throat.

Grabbing her chest, which I was sure was burning the fuck outta her, she began to gasp as if she were struggling to breathe. Her hand was beating her chest, and tears rolled from her eyes.

"Oh, shit… Fire… It burns… *Burp!*"

"Fuck that shit up! You'll get used to it. Hit this. Remember what I told you," Regina coached, and Anneka didn't do too bad.

She took a hit of the blunt and choked a bit, but after a few more pulls, she started to mellow out. I, for one, was happy to see that. I was about to ask for one of my fantasies and hoped that Regina would allow us to bring Anneka into our bed.

While Anneka was blowing trees, I took the opportunity to lay some dick in my baby, Regina. Hopefully, this would loosen her up to the idea of bringing Anneka in with us. I had to sample that pussy. I was so fucking horny. I couldn't wait to bust up in my girl.

"Let's go in the back so I can give you a lil' something," I whispered in Regina's ear. Laughing and giggling, she took me by the hand and escorted me to the back.

I looked at Anneka and winked as I walked behind Regina. She smiled and put her head back on the couch, and I was hoping that sooner or later, I'd have a chance to rock and roll in her pussy walls.

Regina and I had just got going. I'd just finished eating her pussy and was putting my dick in at the tip of her opening when Anneka burst in.

"Regina! Come quick! La is out here, and she need you now!" Anneka spoke as if it were an emergency. Jumping out of the bed and heading to the living room, our mouths dropped as we looked at a badly beaten La.

Chapter 14- Leo

"Uh, ahhh, oooh, Leo. Baby, that's my spot. That's my fucking spot, daddy. Hit that shit!" Ivanka moaned as I pumped her juicy pregnant pussy walls full of my nine-inch-thick pulsating rod.

Ivanka and I no longer had to meet up in faraway hotels, sneak in and out of restaurants, or pretend that we didn't know each other when Eva was around. Eva was dead, and I was slowly but surely working on my woman Ivanka to move in with me.

Ivanka was smart, young, beautiful, and most importantly, she had a wicked side that I was drawn to and loved.

"I'm about to cum, baby!" I moaned in her ear as my pumps began to get rapid.

"Right there, daddy! I'm cumming too!" she exclaimed as she wrapped her arms around me and pulled me in deeper. We both erupted and were breathing heavily as our sex juices mixed together.

"Your pussy is going to be the death of me, my love," I spoke, kissing her on the cheek.

"No, your daughter is going to be the death of you if you don't find her ass and kill her," she responded, out of breath, and I simply got agitated.

"Ivanka, we just finished enjoying each other. Must we bring that shit up right now? Damn, baby. My dick not all the way soft, and it's still inside you, and you're ready to get back to business," I spat, rolling to the side.

"Leo, I'm two months pregnant, and eventually, I'll start showing. It's only going to be a short while before people start to piece together that we are an item. Exactly how long do you think I can play the role of your new executive assistant? Hell, if people really wanted to dig around in my life, they would find out that I'm overqualified for that position," she sassed, pulling the cover over her naked body.

"Baby, I get it. You want things done right now, but these things take time. Plus, I have to make the announcement today about Eva's services," I stated, and oddly enough, a wave of sadness took over my tone.

"Oh, so now you want to grieve? That's cute," Ivanka spat as she sat up in the bed and looked me directly in the eyes. "Leo, that bitch of a daughter needs to be found, and this little announcement that you want to make? Cancel it. Tell the people that you want to grieve in silence and want the city to respect your privacy. Hell, after all, the sooner you get her in the ground, the sooner we can collect on that fucking policy."

"Ivanka, if I fuck this up, I would be looked at as the prime suspect. I don't want to give them any reason to perform an autopsy on her body. I told them I needed things done quickly."

"Leo, for you to be so smart, you're a fucking idiot. Think about it. She died at home. They have to automatically perform an autopsy to make sure there wasn't any foul play," she sassed, and I was confused.

"Wait. So what does this mean?"

"It means that you're fucked unless you listen to me and do everything I tell you to do. This won't be easy for anyone else, but for me, this is like taking candy from a baby." Ivanka's eyes seemed to have gone dark, and she began smiling as if she were holding on to a secret that nobody knew but her. I didn't want shit to fall apart and erupt like a pimple coming to a head.

I took in a deep breath, looked her in her eyes, and spoke. "So what do we do?" I questioned, knowing that the ball was definitely in her court. I had no idea about how much trouble I could have already possibly been in, but I knew that Ivanka wasn't going to let this all crumble.

"We kill Anneka and then live happily ever after." She smiled as she rubbed her stomach that housed our baby, and she closed her eyes as if things were simple. I knew that this was going to be a long, drawn-out battle, but I was at her mercy if I wanted to keep my freedom. Now I was stuck wondering, *Why did I kill Eva?*

Chapter 15- Ivanka

The look on Leo's face was priceless as I closed my eyes and pretended to take a nap. Feeling him move around and about the room gave me a sense of peace. "Please turn the lights out, dear," I simply stated as I smiled internally, knowing that I had him right where I wanted.

I felt his presence over me, and then I fluttered my eyes open to a disturbed looking Leo. "May I help you, dear?" I questioned coolly.

"Ivanka, why would you tell me to do her in when we both knew that it was only a matter of time that she would have eventually passed on? I feel like you're playing games with my life, and that's not a smart move for you."

I wasn't shocked that Leo was starting to piece this shit together. I was simply grateful that men loved thinking with the head between their legs rather than the head that God intended them to use. I sat erect in the bed as I turned on the table lamp. As the light illuminated the room, I spoke in almost a whisper.

"Leo, I never told you to kill Eva. I told you to hurry and take care of our problem. Now, however you took that, well… that's not on me. But to answer your question directly, I'm not playing with your life. I'm simply securing our future," I stated as I rubbed my belly to remind him that our baby was growing healthy and strong.

"So what does this mean, Ivanka?"

"Leo, since I have to spell things out for you, listen to me, and hear me when I speak loud and clear; you must do everything I say in order to remain a free man. I'm the only person who can make this all go away. Now, since we're talking, what are your plans to rid us of Anneka? I don't like problems. That's why I never majored in math," I spoke directly.

Leo exhaled a breath that I was sure he didn't realize he was holding in, and with a puzzled look resting upon his face, he spoke. "I've hired the best of the best to track and find her. It seems like the task is damn near impossible because he hasn't been able to locate her."

"Nonsense. An alone, naïve, afraid eighteen-year-old girl with no sense of reality, who clearly will stick out like a sore thumb, hard to find? Leo, that's laughable. Who did you hire? Who is this incompetent fool?"

"Only the best in New York. Sebastian."

"Ha ha ha ha, the sneezing fool from the Bronx? Now that's comical. If the saying 'you want something done, you have to do it yourself' didn't reign true any other time, it's definitely our truth now."

I swung my legs to the side of the bed and allowed the sheet to fall at my feet. I strutted my naked body toward the bathroom and Leo questioned, "Where are you going now?"

"I'm going to do a job that you couldn't do. Your lack of follow through is just as lame as your pull-out game—nonexistent," I spat as I walked into the bathroom, hit the shower, and started to wash away Leo's scent and semen.

…

After cleansing my body, I'd gotten dressed and had to leave from Leo's presence. His incompetent ways had my anger at an all-time high, and not to mention, I couldn't get the look of hurt out of my head as he spoke about Eva.

Leo knew he fucked up, and it was great that I showed him a few of the cards that I was playing. I wanted to make sure that he stayed in line, so I told him just enough to show him how much he really needed me.

Into the Hood: Pierre & Anneka

I picked up the phone and called my friend Dennard. He was the one who was performing the autopsy on Eva. I needed him to make sure he gave me two reports. "Dennard, darling, how are things going for you?" I questioned as I kept my phone on speaker as I made my way to my high rise in Manhattan.

"Things are going well, and I'll have your reports to you first thing in the morning."

"Perfect. You always come through for me, dear. Always come through. So Dennard, should I be expecting you this evening?"

"Of course, you can expect me. I've been craving you all day and can't wait to get to you as soon as I close up here."

"Good. See you soon, and bring that oil that I love, and hey Dennard. Is your friend Larry still in the hunting game?"

"He sure is."

"Good, I have a job for him and can't wait to see you, dear."

"Not if I see you first," he flirted, and we disconnected our call.

The chips were falling perfectly, and the odds were in my favor. Now it was time to tighten up my plan and get Leo's ass in gear.

Chapter 16- Bernard

Days Later

It had been over a week since I'd met Anneka, and I couldn't seem to get her off my mind. I went back and forth to my family's hotel, simply hoping that I'd run into her. Constantly watching the news, and checking the reports, just wanting anyone to say that they spotted her was driving me insane.

I was in one of the biggest meetings of my career, yet I wasn't able to function. Her scent, her eyes, and her features were eternally etched into my mind. I had to find her.

"Mr. Post! Did you hear the question?" one of my investors spoke in an annoyed tone.

"I'm sorry. I didn't hear you. Can you please repeat the question?" I asked, embarrassed.

"Mr. Post, do you think that you and your family would be able to accommodate Senator Snow and his team? Doing this would only put the hotel in a position to expand. With the news of his wife and the constant, tireless search for his daughter, I think it's wonderful that he wants to announce the funeral plans here on Friday."

I heard the investors speaking but became angry when I heard that this monster wanted to use our hotel to capitalize on a lie that he told to cover up a crime he committed.

"Hell no! We can't do it; we won't do it!" I stated, and with the look of shock on the investors face, I politely rose to my feet, turned to exit, and was now facing the demon himself. Leo Snow.

"Ah, Mr. Post. You seem to be a bit troubled by my presence," Senator Snow stated as he walked closer, being in my personal space.

"Troubled? No, not at all. I was simply advising my team that we aren't able to accommodate you and your team."

"Mr. Post, I can guarantee that it would be worth your time, not to mention the money I'm pouring into the development of a new location," he added.

"Why would you want to invest in a new location just to have a conference here? That seems a bit too generous to me," I stated as I stood with my arms crossed and my head tilted to the side to look this demon in his face.

"I see that you weren't informed. Allow me to catch you up to speed," he started, and then a woman stepped in and cut him off.

She was wearing a black, hooded-cape overcoat. She slowly removed the hood then unfastened the gold and ruby circle-shaped closure, revealing a strapless purple dress that hugged every curve on her body. She flipped her hair to one shoulder as she stood erect, glancing around the room at the other gentleman as if she were demanding respect. Mr. Snow was beaming as he gave her a once over. Her eyes fell on me, and she peered at me with a wicked glare before slowly walking closer to me. Her walk was powerful, her voice was commanding, and her eyes seemed to hold the same amount of evil as Senator Snow.

"Pardon me—"

"I don't have any grey poupon," I interrupted because that was exactly how snooty she was speaking to me.

Shaking her head, she spoke. "Funny… I'm Ivanka Vanzant, Mr. Snow's publicist, and it would behoove you to take what we're offering and maybe even fix up this little dump of a hotel that, you, um… think that you're running. Ha ha ha."

"Lady, I'm going to ask you and Senator Snow to leave my establishment. You're not welcome here," I spoke in a tone to let them know that I wasn't playing.

"Bernard! You apologize to our guests this instant!"

I turned, noticing my aunt Veronica had somehow made her way into the conference room.

"I'm sorry, Aunt Veronica. I just can't," I said, walking away and leaving them in the conference room to sort out whatever it was that they were going to decide.

I heard my father calling out to me and knew it was going to be hell to pay when I had to face them again, but right now, I knew I needed to find Anneka because I was almost certain that my aunt and dad would allow those bozos access to the hotel, and I didn't want to chance Anneka coming back and running into her dad.

…

I walked out of the hotel and started walking toward the metro. Taking out my phone, I called Pierre. When he didn't answer and the call went to voicemail, I pulled out my Bose earbuds and was about to play

Pandora when Pierre's name and number flashed on my phone.

"Hello!" I answered on the second ring, making sure that I caught him before he hung up.

"Nigga, what the fuck you want? You know I'm trying to get my party together. I'm about to be the big 2-5," he spoke, and it seemed as if he had a million things going on and wasn't paying me any attention.

"Pierre! Did you do what I asked? It's been a week, and I haven't heard anything. I need to find her like now," I expressed while Pierre was yelling at someone in the background over the details of his party.

"Hey, nigga, I'm trying to get this shit in order, but I haven't forgotten about you. That girl ain't been seen no damn where. I thought I might have had a clue, but shit, it wasn't her, but I fucked that bitch the niggas brought back to me. Ohhh wee! That bitch had an ass on her! Bounced on my shit, had me looking like I was a stroke patient the way my face was all twisted up."

"Pierre, as much as I would like to continue hearing this conversation, I really need for you to find her. It's imperative that you find her like yesterday. I have a feeling that something is going to happen, and I can't allow her to be in the crossfire of that. Can I count on you?" I questioned, getting on the B train.

"Yeah, nigga, I got you, but you need to slide through my party. I bet when you see the bitches on my roster, that Anneka chick will be the furthest from yo' mind. Slide through so you can lose yo' virginity," Pierre teased, and I didn't give him the satisfaction of knowing that his words were getting to me. I ended the conversation, hoping that Pierre would get the ball rolling and find Anneka. I just couldn't have her out here alone and afraid.

The B train let me out at my stop. I walked a few blocks, taking in the city. When I walked past the store, I saw Senator Snow in my family's hotel, making yet another announcement. "My good citizens of New York, we have worked tirelessly and put forth the best effort into finding my daughter, Anneka. I thank you all for the hours and dedication that you have extended to me in my time of need. It's with a heavy heart that I must lay my beloved wife to rest and pray for the safe return of my daughter."

I couldn't watch anything further. He was the biggest liar ever. I was now on a mission to find Anneka even more. I needed to protect her from this monster of a father. "I'll find you, Anneka. I'll always find you," I spoke in a hushed tone to myself as I arrived at my destination.

After knocking three times, the door flung open. "Bernard! It's been a minute. Come in," my friend said as I walked into his high rise.

"Well, after all of this time, if you are here, that means you have an issue."

"Larry, I need your help, but before I say anything, I need to know that no matter what I say, I can trust you. Like really trust you," I spoke, and Larry's eyes went up, and I took in a deep breath after he nodded his head, and then I spoke.

"I need to find Senator Snow's daughter. She's in trouble."

Chapter 17- Anneka

Regina was out in the living room, and when her eyes landed on La, she went completely bonkers.

"What the fuck happened to you? Who the fuck did this shit? Where they at?" Regina was mad, and La was talking fast.

La was standing there in a ripped shirt with a bloody nose, and her wig she had on earlier was missing. She had braids going straight to the back that only touched the top of her hairline.

"Oh my God! Please, La, come in. Damn, who did this? Have a seat. I'll get you something to clean up with," I stated as I started to move back and forth, grabbing things to help. After all, La had given me an amazing makeover. It was the least I could do.

"Lil' Bourgeois, stop all of that shit. Me and Regina 'bout to handle this. This bitch think I'm fucking playing with her. She and her sister got another thing coming. I'm smoking her and her weak ass sister," La spoke, and I was nervous.

I didn't know what La was referring to when she said she wanted to smoke some girl and her sister. I could understand the smoking trees things, but I wasn't sure how to smoke people. I swear, you had to be here to understand what I was hearing, and none of this shit made any sense.

After watching them go back and forth, clapping their hands with every word they spoke, it finally hit me. They wanted to kill the girls who did this. *I gotta learn this damn lingo*, I thought to myself as I turned my attention back to Regina and La.

Regina picked up what seemed to be a box cutter, and she and La ran out of the house without so much as another word.

Drake was standing there, shaking his head, and then our eyes met.

"Too much excitement for you, Neka?" he spoke, and I smiled. I never told any of these men that my mom used to call me her Neka pooh, and I'd always loved the name. The way that it sounded when Drake said it had me feeling all tingly inside.

"How did you know my nickname is Neka?" I questioned as I stumbled a bit, trying to make it back to the sofa.

Assisting me and breaking my fall, Drake spoke. "Anneka is too damn long, and you look like a Neka more so than an Alex, so I just went with it," he stated, and I stared into his droopy, red eyes. I wonder if Regina told him, but that wouldn't make sense for them to be discussing me, so I simply thought of it as him being charming as I smiled and crossed my legs to settle down from the excitement. I was high and drunk. I knew what was going on, but I really didn't. It was kind of hard to explain. Nonetheless, I thought this would be the first and last time I would willingly drink and smoke.

"Why are you sitting all the way over there? You've been around us long enough to where you should trust me," Drake said, and I didn't know what these feelings were that were coming over me.

I scooted over closer to him, and he pulled a blunt from his ear and lit it up, and after inhaling the smoke, he pressed his lips against mine and blew it in my mouth.

Giggling, I pushed back. "Drake, I don't think we should be doing this." I spoke as he licked his full lips seductively, and I immediately felt wetness in my panties and became embarrassed.

I tried to get up from the sofa, but Drake pulled me back down. "Stop running, and let this shit happen. You know you feeling a nigga, so stop all that extra shit," he said, and my heart rate began to pick up speed.

Grabbing my face, he turned my face to his, and we were staring into each other's eyes. "Drake, I don't think this is a good idea. I just got into a good place with Regina, and I'm not that type of a person to try to go after her man," I spoke softly as he started to kiss my neck.

"It's not a good idea; it's a great idea. Just enjoy yourself. Regina wants you to loosen up," he urged, and I could honestly say that although it was feeling good, it seemed like this would end bad.

"Drake, I, I've never…"

"You will, and you will enjoy it," he stated as if he already knew what I was about to say.

Our breathing changed, and Drake laid me back on the sofa. Taking a puff of his blunt, he blew the thick cloud of smoke into my face. He pulled my pants down, and a smile stretched across his face.

"Fucking beautiful, baby. Simply fucking beautiful," he complimented, and I knew my cheeks were rosy from blushing. I knew this was wrong, so I put my arm over my eyes and tried not to enjoy this feeling so much.

Drake pulled down my panties and stuck his thick fingers inside my wet tunnel of love. I knew his fingers were full of my juices, and I was embarrassed because this had never happened before, and I didn't know what to do. I was nervous, scared, and having mixed feelings.

"Oh… Drake…"

"Oh, baby, don't scream my name until I'm in this juicy pussy," he stated, and more juices escaped my body, and I couldn't stop it.

Seeing sex on television was a lot different from having sexual experiences, and I was seriously nowhere near an expert in this subject matter.

"Drake, this isn't right. Please stop. I'm not going to do this. Stop!" I stated, and the next thing he did sent me into overdrive.

Drake started kissing and sucking my love box, sending a feeling of the unknown through my body.

"Ah-choo!" A loud sneeze could be heard, and my eyes popped up to see an angry Sebastian.

"What the fuck… Ah-choo! Is going on here?" Sebastian asked, and I grabbed my things and ran into the bathroom.

Chapter 18- Sebastian

"Nigga, what the faa… Ah-choo! Fuck is wrong with you?" I barked, shoving Drake back onto the couch.

He started laughing as he got up and stepped in my face.

"Fuck it look like, nigga? I was about to fuck the shit out of shorty until you came in and interrupted us."

"She's fucked up, Drake! Is that what you doing now? Ah-choo! Taking advantage of women?"

"Fuck you, Sebastian. She wanted it just as much as I did. We grown, and grown people can fuck if we want to." Drake laughed, and I was pissed.

"Fuck you mean, Drake? You can tell that she's not used to being around shit like this. Look at her! She's fucking drunk! I could smell the shit before I even approached, not to mention she's high. How the fuck you gon'… Ah-choo! Try that ignorant ass shit? Ah-choo! What you gon' do… Ah-choo! When Regina finds out? You need to stop to fucking think. We are supposed to be protecting her, not taking advantage of her."

"First of all, Regina ain't gon' find out, 'cause you ain't gon' say shit. I already started warming Regina up to the idea of a threesome anyway. From what you told me, this started off as a job that you couldn't fucking complete. Then it turned into us protecting her. Never once was it spoken that we couldn't fuck, so are you mad that you didn't get her to spread eagle first?"

"Drake, don't allow your words to get your ass into something that it can't get out of."

"Nigga, it's new pussy in my house. What the fuck you thought was about to happen?"

"Drake, kill that idea… Ah-choo! I would hate to have to lay yo' ass down over a misunderstanding." I mean mugged him to let him know that I wasn't for the shit.

"Tell the truth, Sebastian. You mad? You wouldn't be this mad if you didn't have it bad for her sexy ass. Come on. Tell me the truth. Yo' ass trying to fuck. She don't want yo' post-nasal drip having ass. Shiiid, that pussy just needed a man's touch. Yo' hating ass coming in here talking shit. I tell you one thing. Her mouth was saying no, but her body was saying something different." He stuck his fingers in his mouth and sucked on them. "Yeah, that wet pussy taste good than a muthafucka." He smirked.

Before I could ball my fist to knock his ass out, Anneka came back into the room.

"I… I don't feel—" She threw up all over herself before she could finish her statement. I snatched the towel off the couch and started wiping her up.

"Come on. Let's get you cleaned up and in bed."

Looking over my shoulder at Drake, I mugged him as I shook my head in disgust.

I took her into the bathroom and set her on the side of the tub. I wet the towel and started wiping her up.

"Ah-choo! You gon' be alright, Anneka. I got you. I ain't gon' let nobody fuck with you," I affirmed as I continued cleaning the vomit off of her.

Once I had her clean, I took her into the back room where she'd been sleeping. I didn't want to disrespect her, so I didn't bother to change her clothes. She'd been through enough today, and I simply wanted to make sure that she was as comfortable as possible.

As I laid her onto the bed, she wrapped her arms around me. "Sssseabbbbastaian, why, why, why, are we…" she started and then passed out.

I knew she was tired, so I sat at the side of the bed and began watching her as she slept. I wasn't sure what the fuck was going through Drake's mind, but I was gon' make sure that his ass didn't try shit with Anneka again.

Removing her arms from around my neck, I laid her in a comfortable position on the bed. She began squirming and holding her stomach. "Mmm, Sebastian, please don't leave. Come here please."

She sounded as if she were in so much pain, and I obliged her request. Climbing in the bed next to her, I pulled Anneka close to me. She continued to squirm, and you could tell that she wasn't feeling well, so I wrapped her in my embrace.

"Sleep tight… Ah-choo!" I kissed her on her forehead and rocked her to sleep.

…

Tossing and turning in my sleep, I turned to the right and was immediately awakened by Anneka's stank breath. I covered my nose and mouth as I looked at her in disgust, not believing that someone so beautiful could produce such a foul odor. I knew it was from all of the alcohol and weed she had last night, but mix that with morning breath… Whew, that was a fucked-up smell.

"Ah-choo!" My loud sneeze shook Anneka out of her sleep. She looked kind of crazy. Her hair was all over the place, and she was looking around the room with wide eyes.

"You ok?" I asked, moving her hair from her face, which appeared to be damn near glued to the side of her face. She had a stream of slob that was coming from the corner of her mouth, and I simply shook my head at the sight.

She nodded her head as she started smacking her lips and swallowing, trying to moisten her mouth.

"Let me go… Ah-choo! Get you some water." I got out of bed then made my way to the kitchen.

I got her and myself a glass of water. As I was leaving the kitchen, Drake was coming out of the room with a blunt hanging from his lips.

"About last night, my nigga." He licked then bit down on his bottom lip as he smirked at me. "Don't you ever try to block shit that I got going on again, my nigga," he stated with a cocky grin.

As bad as I wanted to beat the shit out of him, I had to tend to Anneka. I didn't say a word to Drake. I simply took the water to Anneka and made sure that she was alright. I gave her two Excedrin because I knew her head was going to be pounding.

"Thank you, Sebastian," she said then gulped down the glass of water with the two pills.

Into the Hood: Pierre & Anneka

"Anneka, you need to… Ah-choo! Go in the bathroom and brush your teeth. You might want to get out of those clothes too. The aroma isn't a great… Ah-choo! Smell," I honestly spoke.

She looked around, embarrassed, and I felt like shit, but she needed to be told. "Oh my, I could only imagine that I smell like a brewery. My apologies to you. I need to go and freshen myself up," she said as she attempted to get out of the bed.

"Whoa, damn, the room is spinning." She stumbled and fell back on the bed.

"You good?" I inquired as I helped her sit up.

"Yeah, I just feel dizzy, and my head hurts. I don't know what's wrong with me."

"You just have a hangover. That's all. That's why I gave you those pills. The pounding and the pressure will go away. You need to stay hydrated as well," I replied, popping a Claritin pill in my own damn mouth to stop this damn sneezing.

"What's that you're taking? Do you have a hangover too?" she asked with concern.

"I'm taking everybody's advice. I'm tired of always sneezing," I said, holding up a box of Claritin.

She smiled, and my heart melted. I got up from the bed then went over to the side of the bed where she was sitting.

"Come on. Let me help you to the bathroom." I pulled her off of the bed and helped her into the bathroom.

Standing outside the door of the bathroom, waiting for Anneka, I pulled out my phone and started browsing the internet for a place where I could take Anneka. After the shit Drake pulled last night, it was best that I found a safer place for us to go. I didn't want to chance anything happening with Drake. That nigga wasn't afraid to cross the lines.

"Sebastian, let me tell you the fucked-up shit that went on last night," Regina said as she came storming down the hallway.

Just as she was about to start running her mouth, Anneka came out of the bathroom.

"Bitch!" she shouted, causing Anneka to damn near jump out of her skin. I made sure to keep close eyes on Regina. I didn't know if she found out what happened between Anneka and Drake last night, but Regina was known to cut a bitch, and I wasn't about to let shit go down like that.

"Let me tell you 'bout those bitches that jumped La last night. Those bald-head ass bitches was mad and blamed her 'cause they ain't got no edges. Can you believe that shit? It's all good, though, 'cause now those bitches bald for real. I used my box cutter to cut all their fucking hair off while I beat their asses. Made sure I made those bitches look like fucking skinheads. Shit, I don't let a bitch fuck with me and mine." Regina laughed and kept going on and on, and I got tired of standing there trying to figure out the point of her conversation.

"Regina, Anneka got a hangover and needs to go lay down. We'll get at you later." I grabbed Anneka by the hand and escorted her back into the room. We got back in the room, and Anneka took a seat in the chair. She began staring at the wall at nothing in particular, and it seemed as if she had a lot on her mind.

I could only think that maybe she was nervous about Regina finding out about Drake and skinning her head like she'd just talked about doing to those girls. I had to ask her what was on her mind.

"Anneka, you seemed to be a bit troubled. What's on your mind?" I questioned as I sat on the edge of the bed while facing her as she sat in the chair. She took in a deep breath and asked.

"Sebastian, why are we here? I mean, I got my makeover. Can we just go? It's like when I saw you in the hotel. I just knew you were going to kill me, and I was excited," she stated, and I was confused.

"Excited? Like excited to die?"

"Sebastian, I know my dad sent you to kill me. You saw him on TV begging for my return, but I know he wants me dead. He killed my mom. I saw him. I'm sure he's trying to find me because he wants me dead so that he can be assured that he doesn't go to jail."

"Anneka, you got it all wrong."

"Sebastian, you don't have to lie to me. I'm not as naïve as you all may think. It's ok. Just tell me. When we are leaving, and what's the purpose of the makeover if you're only going to kill me and collect the money?"

"Anneka, I don't want to lie to you, but we'll be leaving as soon as I find us a place to go. We need to get as far away as we can."

"Sebastian, stop it! Please stop it. You kidnapped me. Why? I mean, if you're just going to kill me, why even go through all of this hiding? I'm sure someone will figure it out and beat you to it and collect the money anyway. What's the point of it all?"

Her words were heartfelt, and her questions were valid. I was stuck between a rock and a hard place, trying to figure out how I was going to tell this young woman the truth.

"Man… Ah-choo! Whew… Ok, Anneka, I refuse to lie to you. I'm like a huntsman. I mean, that's what I do. People pay me to get rid of folks. Your father wanted me to kill you. I'm not going to lie; I had every intention of doing that, but then I met you, and I couldn't do it. It's something special about you. There was hurt in your eyes, and when you spoke to me, it was as if I was brought back to the day that I saw my mom laying in a casket. I would do anything… Ah-choo! To be with her again. I wanted to give you a fair chance at life, and that's the conversation that I had with Dakota. We made a plan to get you out here because it's the last place that people would find you. Let's be real. This is the hood. They don't keep up with current events. They are just trying to keep their heads above water and make it out alive," I confessed, and it was like a weight was lifted from me. I saw tears rolling down her eyes, and I wanted to protect her so much that I knew we needed to leave because

Drake would be on some other shit, and I couldn't put baby girl in harm's way.

"If I'm being completely honest, I had a plan to extort more money from your dad since he played me with this money, but seriously, all of that shit went out the window, and I called Dakota to get me a plan to get you out of New York. Once I knew you were safe and living a new life, I was going to collect on that ransom and make sure you never wanted for anything."

"I don't understand, Sebastian. You don't even know me. Why would you go through all of this trouble? Just kill me so I can be reunited with my mom. Fuck all of this shit. I wanted to get revenge, but I don't know the first thing about this type of life, and now that I'm hearing this, I just want to be free from it all. Kill me!" she cried out, and my heart broke.

"No, I wouldn't do that. I'm going to get you safe, and you will live a great life and not in fear. Do you hate me now, Anneka? Do you still trust me and my kind eyes, as you say?" I questioned, waiting on her answer.

"Sebastian, I don't hate you. You were doing a job that you were paid to do. I thank you for being honest with me, and yes, I trust you. You do have kind eyes.

Huntsman or not, you're a gentle giant," she stated, and I felt good about my decision of being honest with her.

"That's real good to hear, but let me ask you this. Do you really want revenge on your old man?"

"More than you ever know. What that man took from me is unforgivable, and I don't have a clue as to how to go about getting revenge, but I know I want to watch him take his last breath, and I hope like hell my mom is on the other side waiting to torture his soul."

"I knew it was the quiet ones that I needed to watch."

"Who said I was quiet? You all assumed and have been making assumptions about me since I got here with you all."

"Like you say. We can only judge you for what you show us, and you seem to be uptight and shit at times. A bit stuffy, but I like this looser version of you. You're pretty cool, Anneka. I'm sorry you're in this situation, but I promise I'll do whatever I can to protect you. Most importantly, I'll help you get the revenge you seek, but we have to plan this shit out perfectly."

"So when you say we have to plan this shit out, you mean you need to call Dakota and get a plan."

"So you think you have me figured out?" I questioned with a smile.

"I only know what you show me."

"So what do you think about this little crew. I wanted to talk to you about that shit with Drake, but I didn't want to make you feel uneasy."

"Honestly, I know it was wrong. It was as if I was having an outer-body experience. The mixture of alcohol and weed didn't help either. It's like my dad kept me sheltered and in so many activities that I was basically separated from the outside world. I had very minimal interaction with guys, so I know I handled that wrong, and I need to apologize to Regina for that. It seems like we are bonding now, and I don't want her to not trust me over something I handled wrong."

"No, leave it alone. At least you acknowledge that shit. Just drop it. So curiously, what do you think about us? I won't be offended."

"Meeting you guys? Well, don't take this personal, but y'all are a strange bunch, and it's really overwhelming. I was trying to read your eyes, and with you, you kept sneezing. Seth is always sleeping. Drake is always smoking, and Regina… Let's just say that I'm slowly but surely starting to understand her language, and that's a bit scary."

"I've been around Regina forever, and when I started understanding her, I knew I was fucked up. Anneka, what do you want to do? In life, what do you desire to do despite all the shit that came your way?" I questioned.

"Sebastian, all I ever wanted to do was take care of my mom until God called her home and open up my own fitness studio. I love health and fitness, and it's killing me daily that I can't get out and run. That's my thing. I wanted to be the best in all of New York, but when my father decided to play God, that all changed in a matter of seconds. I may not have you all figured out, but I do know that whatever we are going to do, I suggest we do it fast. I know my dad, and he will have eyes on the entire city until I'm found."

Anneka was smart, and having this little conversation with her allowed me to see her differently. It was like, slowly, she was changing, and I couldn't say that it wasn't for the better. Her eyes were wide open, and with the hurt that she held in her heart from losing her mom, she would more than likely use that as fuel against her dad. I watched her as she continued to look at the wall, and then she spoke again.

"Sebastian, I just want to go somewhere and relax. I want to try being myself for a while. I mean, I like the changes, and I appreciate the help, but I need a sense of normalcy right now. Wherever we are going, can you make sure I feel normal?"

I didn't know how to respond to that question, so I simply said, "Anneka, I don't want to make you a promise that I wouldn't be able to keep. I do feel where you coming from, and I'mma make sure I find somewhere to go to get you away from all this mess. I promise, Anneka. I'll do all I can to keep you safe."

"Sebastian, thank you for kidnapping me." She giggled as she got up from the chair and walked over to the bed and pulled the covers back. She sunk into the bed and laid her head on the pillow. When she closed her eyes, it was as if she found a bit of peace.

I stroked her hair. "Sleep well, Anneka." I kissed her forehead and pulled the covers over her body. I took the chair that she was just in and watched her sleep. This young woman had a hold on me, and it was my duty to keep my promise.

Into the Hood: Pierre & Anneka

Chapter 19- Leo

Today was the day that I laid my beloved Eva to rest, and my thoughts and feelings were all over the place. I'd agreed to give *Channel 5* an exclusive, and although this started out as me acting, the last few days had shown me that Eva was really a kind-hearted person; I had made a really big mistake, and I was regretting that decision every day that I rose to my feet.

What started out as a quick come up in greed had me realizing that I had everything that I'd ever wanted and needed in Eva. "I'm sorry, Eva. You didn't deserve that," I spoke quietly to the mirror on my wall while I continued to dress for the service.

"Leo, darling, are you finally ready to get through this disaster of a memorial? I couldn't possibly tolerate this for a full day, so let's please get this over with," Ivanka stated, and I had to say that I was offended.

I'd created an environment that allowed her to believe that it was alright for her to disrespect Eva, and now it was getting underneath my skin.

I took in a deep breath, fixed my tie, put my feet into my Velvet Ferragamo black loafers, and grabbed my speech off the counter.

Into the Hood: Pierre & Anneka

"I'm ready, Ivanka," I stated dryly simply because I didn't want to deal with Ivanka and her disrespect. I knew that it was because of me that this environment was created, but I wasn't feeling her with the blatant disregard. I mean, I did marry Eva, so there had to have been some form of love there even if we grew apart. Plus, I'd been getting a bad vibe from Ivanka since her last visit here, and then she'd been distant since that day.

"Leo, let's get this day over with, have this paperwork reviewed by the attorneys, and cash in on a big payday," she coached as she straightened my tie to her liking, and we walked out of my place and headed into the awaiting limo.

...

Our limo pulled up to 5th Ave. as we stepped out and walked into St. Patrick's Cathedral. The soft mournful cries filled the church as I was hit with the reality of Eva's death. My body became weak the closer I approached her eighteen-gauge, steel, ebony and silver finish casket.

As I got closer, I noticed the engraved stitching that read, *loving daughter, wife, mother and a friend to all, Eva Snow*. It was beautiful, as it was scripted in her favorite color, candy-apple red.

A lump formed in my throat as I was now standing in front of Eva's resting shell of a body. Of course, her spirit had moved on, and now her shell was all that I would have to remember her by. A lone tear fell from my eyes as Ivanka nudged me, and I quickly swiped it away. Taking my seat in the front row, many mourners came and shook my hand and offered their condolences. Each time I introduced Ivanka as my publicist, it seemed as if she were aggravated. However, I had to play the role of a grieving widower. To be honest, I didn't think that I was playing a role. I was indeed broken by this and needed to address and express my feelings to Ivanka before things really got out of hand.

As the music began to play, the song "Amazing Grace" was playing throughout the church. Soft cries could be heard from mourners, and I felt like shit that Anneka wasn't here. I was so wrapped up in my own shit and didn't want to be caught up, so I put a hit out on my own daughter.

I began to loosen my tie as I became a bit warm. The program called for me to speak, and ordinarily, the bereaved were simply observers, but in my position, I was sure it was almost a demand for me to share words of expression for my wife.

I took to the podium, cleared my throat, and began speaking from my heart and not referencing the speech that I'd prepared.

"Eva was kind, respected, and a friend to all she encountered. As a wife, she was nurturing, supportive, and never complained even in her darkest hours. There were times when I would recall getting frustrated and even angry because she was having a rough time after chemo. However, I stand here today, wishing, hoping, and even praying that I could hear her sweet angelic voice asking me to do something for her. This has indeed been one of the most difficult times in my life, and as I look out into the audience and not seeing my daughter Anneka, I'm reminded that someone has possibly taken my child away from me, and I'm still working tirelessly to have her brought back safely and unharmed. Anneka, if you're out there, and you're able to watch this, know that your daddy is looking for you. I love you, and I'm so sorry about the pain that you are experiencing with the loss of your mom. Please, somebody, anybody, help bring my daughter home. I feel that I've already suffered a great loss, and I'm not equipped with possibly having to deal with another one."

I broke down and started crying. I couldn't take the guilt and the pain that was inflicted upon my heart. All of the hurt that I put on my family wasn't worth any of this, and I was moments away from confessing everything just to ease my own mind until I felt a hand on my back and smelled Ivanka's perfume. As she grabbed the mic and pushed me to the side. she spoke with a commanding voice.

"Senator Snow is obviously not in a position to continue speaking, and as his head publicist, I'm going to close out this service because it's simply too much for him to handle. Thank you all for your well wishes. Please move expeditiously toward the nearest exit. Mr. Snow appreciates your condolences, and we will be thanking each of you at a later date. Please sign the guestbook on your way out if you haven't done so already."

I couldn't believe that Ivanka closed out Eva's service without the eulogy being given or the obituary being read. I had to control my anger and play it cool as the mourners exited the church. I stepped down from the podium and made my way to Eva's casket. Some of my fellow coworkers in politics were right there to greet me. When Ivanka stepped behind me, her presence caused others to scurry away.

"Leo, that display was a bit too convincing. Please tell me that you're not trying to back out of our plan," she stated in a whisper.

"Ivanka, your presence is much appreciated. However, I think the way you handled things was a bit out of order, and you might have raised a few brows in the process."

"Do you honestly think that I care about that, Leo? We are in this together. Get back on board, or suffer the consequences," she urged as she slammed Eva's casket shut in anger, causing others who were in the back of the church to look our way.

I stood there with Eva's body as Ivanka proceeded to head to the car. "Leo, don't make me wait too long," she stated as the click clacking of her heels began to echo in the church.

I opened up Eva's casket, and a wave of guilt took over me.

"Eva, my love, I've done so many things wrong by you, and all you ever wanted was me to be happy. You supported me when you probably should have given up on me; you nurtured me as well as our daughter when I'm clearly not worthy. Eva, I'm sorry, and although sorry won't bring you back, I can only hope that you know that my apology is heartfelt, and I'm willing to do whatever it takes to get things back on track the way you would have them to be."

As tears flowed freely from my eyes, I thought of the horrible day that I took her out of this world. At the time, it was what I thought needed to happen because I was a coward and didn't want to express to her that I was indeed in a full-blown affair.

I stood there and took in every detail of her body and had to admit that the funeral home did an amazing job with her body, including making her a beautiful wig that seemed as if it was her hair, naturally growing out of her scalp. It was as if she'd regained her youth, and I wanted her back so bad.

Realizing this wasn't a fairytale, and I couldn't snap my fingers or click my heels three times, I simply bent down and planted a kiss on the stiff shell of her remains.

"I love you, Eva. I'm sorry," I spoke as I wiped my tears, closed her casket, and proceeded to the exit.

Into the Hood: Pierre & Anneka

Chapter 20- Anneka

"Uagh!" I gasped, holding my chest as sweat soaked my body, and I was up from my slumber. I didn't know what was going on, but I felt as if something had just happened. I sat erect in the bed and wiped the sweat from my head. Opening up a window, I began to frantically look for the remote.

After locating the remote, I immediately turned on the news. To my surprise, there was coverage of my father leaving from the church, and my mother's body was being carried to a hearse. "Oh my, he had mommy's service," I said aloud, still holding my chest.

I began frantically turning the stations, hoping to find the coverage. I wanted to see my mom. I wanted to be there, and this was the last time I would have the chance.

"Just in, the footage from Senator Leo Snow's wife, Eva Snow has just been released. *Channel 5* had the exclusive, and now we are about to do the replay. Join us now as we take a moment to show you all the heartfelt display of Senator Snow. He truly is a man of great dignity." I stopped as I listened to the reporter talk nothing but great things about my father, but I knew they were all a lie. The opening displayed my mom in her beautiful casket, dressed in all white. I love the small detail of her words embroidered into the casket in candy-apple red.

The camera stayed fix on my mom's body for about three minutes, and I was able to take in every last one of her beautiful features. The camera cut to my dad, and he began talking. I kind of tuned him out and had my face buried inside my hand as I wept for my mom. Something in my dad's voice changed and caused me to focus my attention toward the TV.

"This had indeed been one of the most difficult times in my life, and as I look out into the audience and not seeing my daughter, Anneka, I'm reminded that someone has possibly taken my child away from me, and I'm still working tirelessly to have her brought back safely and unharmed. Anneka, if you're out there, and you're able to watch this, know that your daddy is looking for you. I love you, and I'm so sorry about the pain that you are experiencing with the loss of your mom. Please, somebody, anybody, help bring my daughter home. I feel that I've already suffered a great loss, and I'm not equipped with possibly having to deal with another one."

When my dad began to cry, I felt that his words might have been sincere. There was something different about his eyes.

There was a woman who approached the mic. She spoke and dismissed my mom's service. I again felt robbed and began to get angry. The news reporter came back to the screen and said, "There was an intimate moment between Senator Snow and his wife Eva. Although we weren't sure of what he said, it seemed as if he has his closure. Our thoughts and prayers are with the Snow family as Senator Leo now has the task of burying his wife and still in search of his missing daughter."

A picture of me flashed on the screen, and then a shot of my dad kissing my mom's body and closing her casket. As he walked out, I looked at his eyes. That wasn't the same dad that I knew. Something had indeed changed.

I began crying and couldn't stop. Nothing could have prepared me for the amount of emotions that came rushing to the surface. Every emotion that I had this past week came out in that cry. I felt broken and as if my life were completely over.

"Why, why, why? Why did this have to happen? And I couldn't even be there to say goodbye!" I cried as I dropped to my knees.

As the tears poured out of my eyes, I placed the palms of my hands on the floor for balance and dropped my head to speak to my mom through my pain. She might not have been here in the physical, but I was certain that her spirit was here.

"Mommy, although, I've lost you, I cannot grieve. There's an emptiness inside my heart that will never be filled. As I sit here in my pain, searching for the words to express how I feel, I find that there aren't any. Nothing can truly describe what I'm feeling. No one can truly understand how I mourn for you—alone, trapped in my own silence, feeling lost in this world without you. I'll try my hardest to be the woman you taught me to be—strong, and brave—but honestly, Mommy, it's exhausting."

I slowly curled my body to the floor in fetal position. Wrapping my arms around my body, I closed my eyes and continued speaking freely. I felt as if I could almost smell my mom. and I had to take this opportunity to finish what I was feeling.

"Life has gotten tough for me as of late. I don't know if I can stay strong or fight. I feel so weak. Mom, you always said, 'Be kind, Neka Pooh. Stay true to yourself.' Mommy, you haven't even been gone long, and I'm not sure if I can stay true to myself or continue to be kind. I treat everyone with respect until they show me different, but many people mistake my kindness for a weakness. I need you, Mommy; I wish you were still here. I'll love you forever, Mommy, and miss you always. Fly high and protect me."

A light breeze came through the window and kissed my cheek, causing me to chuckle lightly. I nodded my head as I realized that my mother was finally free. A bird landed on the window sill. I smiled as I watched the bird walking around the window sill, looking out at the city. A warm, comforting feeling washed over me, and I couldn't help but smile.

The bird flapped its wings a few times, and as it flew away, I whispered, "I love you, Mommy. Goodbye."

Sitting on the floor with my knees pulled up to my chest, I took a deep, cleansing breath then wiped away the last stream of tears. A light tapping caught my attention.

"Anneka!" Regina called from the other side of the door.

Pulling myself off of the floor, I took a few calming breaths before opening the door.

"Are you alright? I was in the room, and I thought I heard you crying. Is everything ok?" Regina asked as she followed me over to the bed.

I wasn't sure if I wanted to open up to her. She might not understand what I was feeling, but right now, I really needed someone to talk to, maybe help me make sense of what I'm feeling.

Flopping down on the bed, I let out a loud sigh.

"I just saw my mother's funeral on TV. I wasn't even there to lay my mother to rest. I was supposed to be there." Tears started filling my eyes, but my tears weren't tears of sorrow; they were tears of anger. Regina sat on the bed beside me and placed her hand on top of mine.

"Anneka, I'm so sorry. No one should have to go through what you're going through. Is there anything I can do?" she asked.

I shook my head in response. Regina moved my hair off my face, and turned my head to face her. "Anneka, I'm here for you. I know I haven't been the easiest person to get to know, but really, it has nothing to do with you. That's just who I am. I don't warm up to people so easy. I can honestly say it's been nice having another girl here with all these crazy ass boys." She chuckled a little at the mentioning of the guys.

"Look, we may be a hard bunch to deal with, but Dakota had it right when he sent you our way. It would have been easy to turn yo' ass in, but that's not how shit works in the hood. Plus, we all figured you didn't have shit to go back to, and it seemed like it was safer for you to be with us. We not all the way together at times, but this is our fucked up little family. We all had shit in our lives that we had to deal with. Now, what your father did to you and your mother is beyond fucked up, and I wish I could do something to make this right, but I can't. All I can do is be a listening ear and a shoulder to cry on. I just want you to know that you don't have to go through this alone." She placed my head on her shoulder to comfort me.

"Thank you, Regina. I appreciate that." I took in another deep breath then lifted my head to speak. "I can't believe my father has become this monster. I mean, he was always mean and nasty, but to go to such drastic measures… How could he?"

"Girl, we may never have the answers to those questions. Only he knows how and why he did what he did, but don't make yourself crazy trying to figure folks out."

"Regina, I hear you all talking about me being gullible and everything, and that's cool. I just didn't grow up like you all."

"You sure didn't. Yo' ass would have gotten eaten alive," Regina half joked.

"Seriously, Regina. I'm not sure if this is me being naïve or whatever, but as my dad was speaking at the podium with tears in his eyes, I truly felt that he meant those words he was speaking. I mean he spoke of my mother with such admiration and love. I felt a connection that I can't explain. I wanted him to keep speaking, and then, out of nowhere, some woman grabbed the mic and ended my mother's funeral—just like that. No warning, no nothing, just ended it. I felt robbed in the worst way. It was bad enough he did what he did. I mean, he could have at least given her a proper funeral."

"I feel you, but you can't sit in here and beat yourself up over this. I told you. We can't control what others think and do. Just carry your mom in your heart and know that when she was here, you did right by her. That's all you can do," Regina stated.

"That's a textbook answer. I wouldn't expect you to understand. Nobody understands what I'm going through. If I want to say that this shit is fucked up, then dammit, that's how I'm feeling. You couldn't possibly know what I'm feeling!" I shouted, and Regina stared at me in shock.

I was sick of hearing textbook answers when I was hurting, and I didn't care what came out my mouth. I tried to always be respectful, but dammit, my mom died, and I felt like everything was just taken from me without explanation. I had to really let Regina know how I was feeling.

"I know y'all think I'm just some stupid, naïve, spoiled ass bourgeois princess who walks around with her head up in the clouds, but that's far from the truth. Maybe I don't know the Ebonics language in its entirety, or whatever you call it, maybe I dress differently, and maybe I haven't experienced the things that you all have, but what does that mean? I try my hardest to find the positive in every negative situation, and as you said, I'm in a very fucked up situation."

I paused, not believing the way I was going off on Regina, or as she says, coming for her, and judging from the look of shock that was displayed on Regina's face, she wasn't believing it either. However, I'd been holding all my feelings in. It felt good to just vent.

"My father is trying to kill me for witnessing him kill my mother. No one understands how that shit feels. My mother was all I had in this world. She was the only person who genuinely loved me, and my father took her away—just like that. My whole world crumbled instantaneously, and nobody gives a shit. I didn't even have a chance to mourn my mother's death. Everything happened so fast. I ran from the only life I've ever known and entered into a whole different life. A life that's foreign to me. So forgive me for trying to make the best out of a fucked-up situation."

"I get it, Anneka. I do. Honestly, the shit is foul, and listening to you talk just now was the realest I've heard you be since you got here. You have every right to get that shit out however you see fit. Shit… you right. We are from different worlds, but that doesn't mean that we can't co-exist, maybe even be friends. I can teach you some things, and shit, believe it or not, I can learn a few things from you. Even though yo' ass irritates my soul."

Me and Regina both burst into laughter at her last statement. Regina grabbed my hands.

"Come on, girl. Let's go get us some wine to calm all this emotional shit down. I promise not to give you anymore textbook answers. That's just the shit that people say when fucked up shit happens. Sorry for using that expression again, but hey, it is what it is," she stated, pulling me off the bed.

"Oh, no, Regina. I was sick from drinking. I don't want to feel like that again."

"Girl, that's because yo' ass drank way too much. We just gon' have a few glasses to mellow yo' ass out. It'll be fine. I swear, yo' ass needs to loosen up just a little. This is not a penthouse; this is the hood. We do shit differently around here, and it's 'bout time you start learning a few things, lil' Ms. Bourgeois."

Regina laughed as she led me out into the front room.

"Thanks for listening to me vent, Regina. It seriously means a lot to me," I stated as we walked in the front.

"Girl, it's not a problem. Just don't go all hood on me and dropping fuck bombs and shit. That shit don't sound right coming from you, but I can dig it. I like this lil' hood bourgeois thing you got going on," Regina teased, and I found myself enjoying her company as she continued to comfort me in her own way.

For the first time in my life, I had a real friend, and I couldn't wait to see where this friendship would go.

With Regina being so nice and understanding with me. I was having second thoughts about Sebastian's advice in leaving that shit alone with Drake, but I felt that she needed to know. Having a friend was starting to be hard work. I just had to think about what was best for me in this time.

Chapter 21- Regina

Bandz a make her dance, bandz a make her dance, bandz a make her dance...

The music was blaring through the house as I tried to take a page out of lil' bourgeois' book. I was cleaning and popping my pussy while twerking in the house and getting prepared for a special surprise that I planned for Anneka.

Earlier, when we were drinking wine, Anneka opened up a little more to me, and it was really bothering her that she didn't get a chance to mourn her mother, so I had an idea.

While Anneka went to take a nap, I browsed the internet to see if I could find a nice picture of her mother. Since her father is a politician, I figured that the internet would have pictures of his wife.

I found a picture of her mom, printed it out, and then I searched for a dinner recipe using apples. Apples seemed to be her and her mother's favorite, so I wanted to somehow use them in our meal. I found a recipe for skillet chicken with Brussel sprouts and apples and printed out that as well. I went to the dollar store, got a nice gold picture frame to put the picture in, and found a few candles. While at the grocery store, I got some flowers and all the ingredients I needed to make the dish along with an apple pie and vanilla ice cream for dessert. This was going to cheer her up, and I was happy to take part in this.

…

Arriving home, I was happy to see that Seth had rubbed off on Anneka. She was still sleeping, so it was perfect timing for the guys and me to get everything in order.

"This where you want the stand to go, Regina?" Drake asked while positioning the stand by the mirror on the wall.

"Yes, that's perfect. The reflection of the candles and flowers will help create a nice ambience and appear to look as if they are surrounding Mrs. Snow's picture. She's such a beautiful woman," I stated as my vision was coming to life.

Drake walked over toward me and glanced at the picture.

"Yeah, she was a beautiful woman. Probably the prettiest woman I've seen in all of New York."

I looked at him as if he had lost his mind. I mean, Mrs. Snow was bad, but you don't stand in yo' bitch's face and say another woman is prettier than her. I was seconds from smacking the shit out of him when he grabbed me around the waist.

"For an older woman, that is. Ain't no woman prettier than you," he stated before planting a soft kiss on my lips.

"Yeah, you better have switched that shit up. I mean, I respect the dead, but you was about to catch one real quick for saying that shit."

Drake slapped me on the ass. "What else you need me to do?" he asked.

"Nothing. I'm done cleaning. I just have to decorate the stand and add Mrs. Snow's picture to it. Sebastian and Harper gon' help me in the kitchen."

"Naw, Sebastian's ass ain't helping in the kitchen. Nobody wants his ass sneezing all over the damn food."

"Boy, shut up. He been taking his Claritin. He ain't sneezing like that no more." I chuckled.

"Fuck that. I don't trust it. You and Harper got that. Sebastian can do something else."

"Sebastian gon' help in the kitchen, and that's that, and Geovanni, well, he said he hates cooking and cleaning, so I'm having him take out the trash when I'm done, and Seth, well, shit, if he don't fall asleep, I'll get him to set the table."

"Whatever. First time that nigga Sebastian sneezes, his ass getting the fuck out of the kitchen. Since I ain't got shit to do, I'mma go chill and smoke a lil' bit so I can be ready for the food. It ain't like you cook for a nigga on a daily."

"If you don't get yo' ass away from me, I won't cook for yo' ass no more." I laughed as I placed the red silk covering over the stand.

I placed a gold-plated tray on the stand then decorated it with the flowers and the candles. I took some of the flowers and some vines and attached them to the frame of the mirror on the wall then continued decorating the tray with the remaining flowers. Finally, I sat Mrs. Snow's framed picture in the center of the tray and took a few steps back to admire my work.

"Damn, Regina, you got skills," I complimented myself, feeling proud of the display that I created for Mrs. Snow.

"Ah-choo! Damn… Ah-choo! Regina, this is nice… Ah-choo!"

"Sebastian, you was supposed to take yo' Claritin. Why didn't you?" I asked, annoyed at the fact that he was sneezing again.

"I did… Ah-choo! It's… aaaa… Ah-choo! It's all the flowers… ach… ach… Ah-choo! You got around the place."

"Seriously, Sebastian, you need to go see a doctor about this shit. It's fucking ridiculous that you are allergic to everything," I stated as I started making my way to the kitchen.

Just as I was passing by the entrance of the hallway leading to the bedrooms, I heard Anneka opening the bedroom door.

"Oh, shit, it's Anneka. She can't come in here yet," I stressed as I went into a panic.

"I'll go distract her and make sure she don't come out of her room," Drake offered.

"Naw, I got it. I'll go. Ah-choo!" Sebastian cut in before walking away in a haste.

I didn't know what that was all about, but at the moment, I didn't care I needed to hurry and get the food cooked before Lil' Ms. Bourgeois came out and ruined my surprise.

Into the Hood: Pierre & Anneka

When I got in the kitchen, Harper had already shredded the Brussel sprouts, sliced the apples, and had the chicken already seasoned and ready to cook. About twenty minutes later, dinner was cooked and set aside in serving dishes. All I needed to do was take a quick shower so I could put on something nice.

After showering and getting dressed, I went to Anneka's room and convinced her to get up and get dressed. I told her that I wanted to take her out to eat. I picked out the perfect little dress for her to put on. I didn't want her to go with the traditional black dress. I wanted this to be more of a celebration of Mrs. Snow's life than a funeral. I gave her a royal-blue, sleeveless dress and paired it with a red cardigan and yellow shoes to complete the look. I placed a thin, yellow belt around her waist.

"You look beautiful, Anneka," I complimented as I took her hands and led her out of the room and into the front room where the guys were all dressed in slacks and a button up waiting and standing around the stand.

Anneka's eyes grew as big as saucers as they darted around the room.

"What is all this?" she asked with a hint of excitement in her tone.

"It's a celebration of your mother's life. Since you wasn't able to attend her funeral, I thought that we could have a home-going celebration of our own," I replied, and tears started pouring out of Anneka's eyes.

I led her over to the display then lit the candles. Anneka stared at her mom's picture and began to cry. She looked around the room and spoke. "You guys are simply the best. You just don't know how much this really means to me. Thank you all, from the bottom of my heart. Thank you all."

"Don't thank us. Thank Regina. This was all her," Sebastian spoke with a smile.

Looking at me, Anneka walked to me and began speaking from her heart.

"You all don't know me and didn't know a thing about my mom, but you decided to take a bad situation and make it good. Regina, I've never had a friend, but I'm thankful to have you."

I wasn't a sappy bitch, but hearing her say those words tugged at a bitch's heart.

Anneka held her mom's picture and spoke. "Hey, beautiful. You're gone, and I can no longer brush your hair, take you out on morning runs, or even cook and clean with you for events. Each day that I'm forced to live without you, I find myself getting stronger. Mommy, I don't know where this road I'm traveling will lead, but I do know that I will see you again. Until then, I'll hold you in my heart."

We were all heartbroken for Anneka as we all swiped away tears, watching her express her love and admiration to her mom. I wanted to give her all the time she needed to properly say goodbye, and after she quoted a bible verse, she blew out the candle and told her mom to sleep well, beautiful queen.

"Anneka, I know this wasn't what you expected when this time came around, but I hope you know that you have a group of people around here that want to see you win."

"Thank you, Regina. It was perfect. Thank you all. I appreciate this so much."

"Well, I cooked an amazing meal, and taking a page out of your book, lil' Ms. Bourgeois, I used your favorite. Apples."

Walking into the kitchen, I watched Anneka's face. She was pleased, and she enjoyed this time. In the hood, we were taught to take what we got to make what we wanted, and that was something no amount of money could teach you. We sat at the table and ate as a family, and this was something that I personally wanted to remember.

"Neka, I know we said we are going to celebrate your mom's life, and I figured it would be a great idea for you to go to Pierre's party with La and me. These fools will be there too, but we're not going with them," I said as Anneka ate the food on her plate and smiled.

"Of course, I'll go, but I don't have money for a gift."

"Girl, this is the hood. We just showing up to shake our asses and have some fun. Trust me. Your mom would want you to get your twerk on."

"Regina!" Sebastian yelled.

"Too soon?" I questioned, trying to figure out what the hell I said wrong.

"It's ok. I'll go. I want to have a good time," Anneka replied.

I couldn't wait to get to the hottest party of the year. Pierre was the nigga that every bitch wanted but knew he would never settle down. That was why I ended up with Drake, but I still cooked shit up for Pierre when he needed me. When that nigga called me and told me to bring my bitches through, I knew the set was going to be live. I knew once Anneka saw him, Pierre would knock the bourgeois out of her ass, and she would fit right in even more.

"Great. After dinner, we will freshen up our makeup and have La to run the curlers through our hair."

I never had a gang of bitches I hung around, but being around Anneka made me not only want a few friends, but it was showing me what I was missing having a female around.

I heard Sebastian on the phone with Dakota, saying that he needed to get her out, but I was hoping that she stayed longer because it was good having her around.

We had more than a few hours before the party started, so I was going to clean, relax, and have La to hook us up, but for now, I was going to enjoy this time with my twisted and blended, fucked up version of a family.

Chapter 22- Leo

The burial was over, the mourners were gone, and I was in my condo alone with my thoughts. This was not the feeling that I thought I would have when I first hashed out this plan with Ivanka months ago.

Things seemed to be on the up and up with Ivanka and me until recently, and I couldn't put my finger on when things changed, or how they changed for that matter.

Just when I thought I was going to have my happily ever after and cut off all my other women to give Ivanka all of me, it seemed as if I'd made the worst mistake of my life. All of these thoughts about Eva were taking over my mental, and I wasn't sure if I could pull myself out of it.

I was standing here with my drink in my right hand and my left hand in my pants pocket, overlooking the city. My mind was going a mile a minute, and Eva's face kept coming to me clearly. I couldn't help the tears that started to fall. I wanted to wish it all away and ask God to forgive me for what I'd done. The more I tried to justify the deed that was done, the sicker I became.

Into the Hood: Pierre & Anneka

"God, please don't torture me with my own guilt," I cried as I prayed and begged God for his mercy.

A light tap at my door got my attention, so I wiped my tears, took back my drink, and headed to the door to see who it was.

"Leo, I'm so sorry. I wanted to come by sooner, but I didn't know if you had company. Do you need anything? And I do mean anything," Jessica stated.

Jessica was one of many women I'd had an affair with, and just when I was asking God for forgiveness, temptation found a way to meet me at my front door. I was a widower; however, I was finding out that my heart was yet attached to Eva, and I couldn't allow this woman to disrespect her on a day like today. After all, I'd done enough disrespect to last me a lifetime. I simply just wanted to honor her memory, and Jessica would be a huge distraction.

"Jessica, now isn't a good time. Better yet, I'm not sure if anytime in the future would be good. I'm sorry, but this isn't going to work, and I can't do this, any of this anymore," I spoke in a low tone, still standing at the door with her on the other side, making it clear that I wasn't welcoming her in.

"Leo, you don't mean that. Please, let me in. I promise to show you things that you've never seen before. Let me be here for you. Please, Leo," she begged, and I simply slammed the door in her face and locked it and poured another drink.

Moments passed, and the tapping returned. Agitated from the disturbance, I yanked opened the door and yelled, "I told you Jess—"

I stopped as I realized it wasn't Jessica, but it was Ivanka, and the look that she held didn't seem as if she was up for any type of pleasantries.

Pushing past me and allowing herself entrance into my condo, Ivanka spoke. "Leo, enough of the bullshit. Have you made arrangements for the insurance company as well as your lawyers for the reading of the last will and testament?" she asked in more of an order rather than a question.

"Ivanka, Eva isn't lukewarm in the ground, yet you are here to discuss money. Can you allow me time to get through this?"

"Time, Leo? Leopold Snow, time has run out, my dear. Do you remember it wasn't very long ago, sweetheart, but it was the day that you called me and said,

'My dear sweet Ivanka, I killed the bitch, and now we will have our happily ever after, and hell, we can even make it to the white house.' So um, my dear, you knew the arrangement, and now the trumpets have sounded. The bitch is in the ground, and all we need is that sweet little ditz of a daughter of yours, and that's double payment. You see, Leopold, my future, ah hem, I mean, our future is looking very bright."

"Ivanka, there's no way I'm killing my child now. I've made one mistake, and I won't make another one. As far as the will goes, whatever is there, I'll let you have it. I just want things to go back to normal, and now I have to make things right with Anneka. It's the right thing to do."

"Oh, wow… So when was the devil ever afraid to raise a little hell? So you have a conscious now, Leopold? Well, let's just say you need to get Jiminy Cricket off your back because these papers right here could put you away for a very long time."

Ivanka held up a report that appeared to look just the same as the coroner's report that stated that Eva died from complications of having cancer. I snatched the report from her hand and it read. Death by strangulation. My heart dropped as I now began looking at Ivanka with a new set of eyes. She really was the devil, and yes indeed, the devil wore Prada. However, there was no way I was going to allow her to back me into a corner.

"Go ahead, Leopold. You can have that one. I have plenty more. Now you mentioned you were going to *let* me have something? You have forty-eight hours to get your attorney over here, and also find Anneka. Good day, dear, and for heaven's sake, you might want to wash the tear stains from your cheek. That's so not manly."

She patted my face, planted a kiss on my cheek, and left out my condo in the same manner in which she'd come. I knew I was in deep shit, but I needed to find a way to protect Anneka. The only thing that was stopping me was knowing that I might have ruined my trust with my precious daughter. It might be a difficult task, but I would die trying to mend the heart that I'd broken.

"If it's the last thing I do, I will stop at nothing to save my daughter," I spoke as I locked my condo door, poured a drink, and began to ponder on my next move.

Chapter 23- Ivanka

It was once said that if you wanted something done right, then you had to do it yourself. I knew that statement to be true the moment I left Leo standing in the middle of his condo with a tear-stained face.

For months, I played second to his wife and side bitches, knowing that I was the main bitch. When I first started sleeping with Leo, I used to pretend to be a listening ear and a shoulder for him to cry on. He loved Eva, but I needed to show him just how much she was bringing him down.

Leo was eight years my senior, so after popping my tight pussy for his ass, I quickly was upgraded from the slums of New York to penthouse living in Manhattan, and yes, Leopold funded it all.

For months, I studied women of power and duplicated what I saw and put my own twist on things, and my act became reality.

After understanding the power of my pussy, I simply turned Leo's words of complaint about Eva into my vision of power. He gave me all the material I needed, and you better believe that I used it to my advantage. The power of persuasion was a gift that I had that I didn't mind using.

I was a bitch who admired power and was in love with a twisted and wicked mind. Once I started doing the shit his wife wouldn't do, he started cutting off all his bitches and drew a wedge between himself and Eva. I was now playing puppet master, and that was the type of shit I loved. We started with her medications and ended with fucking up her self-esteem, and the shit was brilliant.

Just as things were going according to plan, Leo decided to have a heart and started slowly changing things in the middle of our takeover. I wouldn't lie; I wasn't really into Leo. I was simply into his money. Once I had the things that I was promised, my man Dennard and I would rise to the top

As my car hugged the pavement, I began taking in my city and really started to understand the New York state of mind. Here in New York, you either sank or swam. It was the city where hustlers and liars were born and definitely the place to rise to the top.

Thoughts of Leo's facial expression began to cloud my mind, and waiting on him to make the first move wasn't the best option for me at this time. Leo knew that now. The time had come to make good on those promises, and he thought a guilty conscious would make this all go away. Well, he was about to learn a new lesson in life; don't fuck with Ivanka Vanzant.

"You will not fuck me over, Leopold Snow. I will get everything you promised me even if it'll cost you your life." I spoke to myself as I grabbed my phone out of my purse and made the call that I should have made the moment little Miss Snow ran away.

"It's me. Ivanka. I'm on my way to see you." No words needed to have been exchanged after I made that statement, so I disconnected my call and headed to my destination.

As I navigated through the horrible New York traffic, images of what Leo would look like while sobbing over his darling daughter's dead body flashed in my head, making a devilish grin spread across my face.

"You haven't seen pain as of yet, Leopold," I spoke aloud, knowing that I would walk away the sole victor in all of this.

Leo was going to find out sooner rather than later that with or without him the show would and must go on. I pulled my car to an open park and killed the engine. After navigating that traffic, I was in need of a drink, but I had a task to complete.

Surrounded in the slums of the city, I shook my head in disgust as I made my way to the brownstone that was oh so familiar to me. After knocking three times, the door opened, and a smile stretched across my face.

…

"Hello, Ivanka. It's been awhile. You look as stunning as ever," Idris greeted sarcastically as he allowed me access into the quaint brownstone.

"Idris. Yes, it's been way too long. We ought to be ashamed with the amount of time that has passed without us speaking," I replied as he closed and locked the door and led me into the living room. With my nose upturned, I glanced around the cozy little room in disgust. "Well, Idris, I see things haven't changed much around here. How is, um… business?" I asked with my nose still turned up while placing the throw blanket on the sofa so that I could take a seat.

"Don't come in here turning yo' nose up at my shit. It wasn't so long ago that this was yo' home too, my dear, sweet little sister. You got around all those rich black folks and found yo'self a sugar daddy. Now you want to come in here acting all high and mighty. You know I ain't with that snobby shit. I see you for who you are. A wannabe rich girl who is nothing but a hoe, sucking dick and pulling the same tricks," he countered, and I internally coached myself to remain composed. I needed his assistance, so I wasn't going to allow his words to upset me.

I simply replied, "Yes, yes, my dear brother. My lifestyle might not be ideal to you. However, it's paying all of my bills, and judging by your apartment, you could stand to take a page or two from my book. Now Idris, let's not do the back and forth; I'm here to make you an offer that you can't refuse. Trust me, it will be worth every penny, and by the looks of your current living arrangements, you can use a penny or two."

"Ivanka, stop it with the Cruella voice. What in the hell can I help you with? Because I'm bored with this conversation."

"Bored, dear? Well, I suggest you listen so that I may change your life. Then maybe you'll have a bit of excitement to look forward to," I spoke, grabbing his attention.

"Last time you stepped foot in this apartment, you said over your dead body would you return, so are you dying?" he questioned, trying to ruffle my feathers.

"Your mouth has always been an issue, but your ability to seek and destroy is why I'm here. Now if you would allow me the opportunity, I will… change your life. Now I'm not talking hundreds. I'm talking about millions."

His eyes danced, and I knew I had his attention. "I'm listening," Idris stated as he finally took a seat on the sofa and gave me his full attention.

I dug into my purse and pulled out a picture of Anneka and handed it to him. I loathed the fact that he was gawking at it as if he wanted to toss her down and make passionate, sweet love to her. I mean, she was pretty, but my God, the way the people talked about her beauty was so annoying. I mean, no one was that beautiful.

I snapped my fingers, bringing his attention back to the matter at hand. "Her name is Anneka Snow. She's Senator Snow's daughter," I explained.

"Yeah, I know. I've seen her picture all over the news. She's missing, right?"

"Yes, and I want her found. Pronto," I replied in a serious tone.

Into the Hood: Pierre & Anneka

"So now you're ready to step from behind the curtain and stop playing the Wizard of Oz and promote yourself to the doting stepmother? Or in your case, the evil, wicked stepmother? So let me guess. You're wanting me to find her, I take the reward money, and then you tell me how to spend it?"

"Idris, that would have been an excellent plan. However, dear, I don't need you. I'm simply extending an olive branch to you. I could have very well taken this offer to any crackhead in New York and offered simply a warm meal, but the reward money is mere pennies in comparison to what you would gain."

I had his undivided attention and loved how I was pulling all the strings. If this shit went left, then I wouldn't be the person taking the wrap for it. He would be. After telling him about the money and guaranteeing him of it being so simple, I knew he was all in.

He raised his brow and then spoke. "So what do you want me to do exactly, and how do you know this is a foolproof plan?"

"Trust me. Everyone is already thinking she's dead. All you need to do is find her and kill her. Tear this city up, brick by brick, and when you find her, bring me her heart."

"Ivanka, her heart? Whoa, you on some other shit now. That man just lost his wife. Damn! What the fuck wrong with you? What? The nigga ain't showing you all his attention, and you want his daughter dead? Is that why she ran away? She found out about you, didn't she?"

"Don't ask questions. Just find the bitch and kill her. You think you can handle that? Oh, before you answer that question, think about the money you'll obtain from this." I was getting annoyed with Idris's questions. He sat in silence, thinking, and then he glanced at the picture again.

"She's a beautiful girl. Damn, Ivanka. You're asking a lot," he said, staring at her as if he felt sorry for her. I snatched the picture out of his hand.

"You in or out?" I inquired.

He shook his head. "Ivanka, you are as evil as they come, but yes, you have my word. I'll find and kill her," he agreed, and I couldn't be more pleased knowing that my brother was on board. It wouldn't be long before Anneka was dead, and I'd finally have everything I wanted.

"Then it's settled. Get your ass in the streets, and get this shit done. Idris, I'm counting on you. Actually, all of New York is counting on you. They only need closure, and you mustn't waste any time. Chop, chop. Get moving," I stated, clapping my hands together as I rose to my feet, placed the picture in my purse, and walked to the door to make my exit.

"Ivanka, this is some fucked up shit, but Lord knows I need the bread. You can count on me," Idris spoke, and my heart was so warm that I embraced my brother and planted a kiss on his cheek.

"Very well, dear brother. Make me proud," I stated as I left with this newfound sense of hope. Things were going to be great much sooner than later.

Chapter 24- Anneka

"Biiitch, I can't wait for this party tonight. It's gon' be lit as fuck," Regina excitedly spoke from the dressing room, trying on an outfit for the umpteenth time.

I was sitting in the chair, bored as hell, with a pile of clothes on my lap. She popped in and out of the dressing room so many times, changing clothes, I could have sworn that I was watching a movie montage.

"Oh shit! Bitch, I think I found my fit!" she shouted as she flung open the curtain, revealing the black, see-through dress that was hugging every curve on her body. "What you think? I get me one of those cute ass bras and some boy shorts! Girl, I'mma be poppin'! Drake gon' lose his mind if he sees me in this."

Twirling around, checking herself out in the mirror, Regina smoothed out her dress then adjusted her breast.

"Girl, I might fuck around and go braless and just put some pasties on my nipples, let my perky ass titties give a little peep show," she continued while popping and twerking in the mirror.

A few other shoppers filed in toward the dressing room, and one stopped in front of me and started staring as if she knew me.

"Wait a minute. It's you! Felecia, come here! Look! It's that bitch! Umm, it's umm…" the girl stated, snapping her fingers, talking loud, and popping her gum. I was so nervous that I thought I was about to shit on myself. I was in full disguise and even had on oversized glasses and looked nothing like my circulating pictures, so I was trying to play it cool.

"I don't think you know me," I said in a low tone and kept my head all the way down, making sure not to make eye contact.

"Bitch, please! You ain't fooling no damn body! You that bitch Farrah that got kicked out of Destiny's Child. Is my sister Beyoncé a real bitch or nah?" she questioned, and her friend Felicia started laughing as my heart returned back to its normal pace.

Stepping out the dressing room, Regina approached, and she was pissed until she walked up on the girl. "Octavia, is that you?"

"In the flesh, bitch! I'm trying to get this bitch Farrah's autograph and tell her to call my sis Beyoncé, but her bourgeois ass acting stuck up! That's why my sis kicked her ass out. Bitch can't damn sing anyway," the girl Octavia said, and her friend Felicia continued laughing.

"Bitch, you all the way. This is not Farrah. This is my cousin Kiara. She in town for a week. You lucky she ain't beat yo' ass. She not used to all this shit around here."

Octavia removed her glasses, got a bit closer in my face, and then started laughing.

"Bitch, you sholl ain't damn her. My bad, but umm, Gina, y'all sliding through Pierre's party tonight? Bring fake ass Farrah. She might enjoy herself. Where she from anyway?"

"Octavia, mind yo' damn business, and yes, we are going to the party. You so damn extra," Regina commented, collecting the outfits that she wanted to purchase.

"Bitch, extra is my middle name. I'll see y'all later, lil' Farrah. Get that stick out yo' ass fo' you come 'round us tonight. Loosen up!" she yelled, and I shook my head and walked to the cash register with Regina.

"I told you yo' ass is bourgeois." Regina laughed as she paid for her items, and we walked out of the store.

Into the Hood: Pierre & Anneka

I was nervous as hell about going to a party. At any moment, someone could spot me, and all of this shit will come to a head. I needed to speak up about it.

"Regina, I don't think it's a good idea for me to go tonight," I spoke as we walked to Claire's to get some accessories for tonight.

"Bitch, it's going to be lit tonight. Why you trying to back out? Especially when you don't have shit else to do but sit in the damn house. Look, Neka. You have to live the life you have no matter what comes your way. You can't sit in the house cooking, cleaning, and talking to birds until the next phase in your life come around. Shit, you're young, sexy, and full of life, and bitch, you're going to act like it."

I smiled, seeing how Regina was slowly breaking down her barrier and allowing me to see a different side of her—in her own way at least.

"So you care about me is what I'm hearing," I stated, and Regina looked at me and laughed.

"No, bitch, I don't. I just can't have you around my damn house cooking, cleaning, and doing shit for my man to notice. He already sweet on you," she stated, and I got nervous.

"What do you mean, he's sweet on me?" I questioned nervously.

"Girl, Drake has been asking and begging for a threesome for hella long, and I refuse to do it. Not that I'm against it, but I'm not a damn fool to bring a cute ass virgin into my mix and have my man crazy about you."

"Regina, I wouldn't—"

"Neka, I'm not saying you would, but Drake has been asking about you, and I know how niggas are. Just tell me if he tries anything with you. Like seriously, be a friend," she urged, and it was burning me up that I couldn't utter the words that I wanted to tell her. I mean, I was drunk and high, but I was aware of what was going on. I pondered back to the conversation I had with Sebastian and decided to keep quiet about it. I simply smiled and responded.

"You have my word. I will be a friend if he ever tries anything."

"Thanks, girl. You know? You're alright, lil' bourgeois," Regina replied, and I felt like shit.

We walked out the mall, and I was in a somber feeling. I felt like a fraud and began thinking that I was no better than my father. He was a liar by choice, and by me having the opportunity to come clean with Regina, I felt that I was slowly turning into my dad.

...

We got to the van, and of course, Seth was sleeping.

"Nigga, damn! We were only in there an hour. Fuck you sleeping for?" Regina sassed as we got into the back with our bags.

"Shut yo' ass up. A nigga works. Shit, I need my rest."

"Nigga, please. Work where? I bet the only subject you passed in school was nap time."

"I bet the only one you passed was ratchet 101," he argued.

As we began to head back to Regina's house, Regina asked Seth to drop us off at La's apartment.

"Seth, take us to La's house. We gon' stay over there until the party."

"Shit, cool with me. I'm tired of fucking driving y'all around. Don't call me to come back either."

"Nigga, you gon' be sleep any damn way," Regina continued.

We sat in the back of the van while Seth blazed a few trees and turned up the music. Regina and I were simply chatting until we reached our destination.

"Lil' Bourgeois, I notice that you were a little nervous when Octavia and Felicia approached you, thinking they recognized you, so that's why we gonna go see La and have her to hook you up with a new look. I'm thinking maybe change yo' hair color or something."

"Change my hair color? No, Regina. I love my black hair. I'm not changing my hair color."

"Bitch, that's what the hell wigs are for. With yo' light, bright, and damn near white ass skin tone, I think red would be yo' color. That shit will be poppin' on you, and maybe a short lil' haircut. Trust me, ain't nobody gon' recognize you. Shit, everybody gon' be too fucked up anyway."

"So you keep going on and on about how *lit* this party will be. To be honest, I've never been to no parties with the exception of the dinner parties my father used to have, and those were pretty boring."

"Naw, Pierre throws the best parties in the hood. He's big time around here, and everybody who's anybody will be there. It's like the party of the year. Niggas can't wait for Pierre to throw a party. When I say the shit is gon' be lit, the shit is gon' be lit. You gon' have a blast. It's his 25th bash, so he's going all out, over the top, and I can't wait."

"Oh… Twenty-five? I'm only—"

"Girl, shut yo' ass up. You grown, and that's all that matters. If it came down to you smashing the nigga, shit, seven years ain't shit. Not like the nigga won't be able to take care of yo' lil' bourgeois ass," Regina joked, but I thought she was kind of serious.

We pulled up to La's house, and Seth parked next to the curb. "Anneka, don't let Regina's ass turn you out," Seth spoke through a yawn, and I was confused by his statement.

"Nigga, shut up!" Regina retorted, grabbing our bags as we headed to La's front door.

"Here come my bitches! Here come my bitches!" La chanted as she gave Regina and me a hug and welcomed us in.

"Neka, girl, that Shea Butter shit you made me got my ass right together. Look… You don't even see the mark on my face. You need to be selling that shit you make. Oh, and look at this," she said, pulling her wig off and showing us her hair.

"Bitttttttcccccchhhh! Yo' edges coming back!"

"Damn sure right! Neka, that shit is about to be flying off the shelf. You need to bottle it up and sell it. Hell, let me be your manager and marketing bitch. All these bald-head bitches in the hood need this shit."

"Bitch, word on the streets is that you snatched out their edges," Regina teased.

"Well, bitch, now I'm 'bout to grow them shits back with my Manhattan lil' bourgeois bitch and her concoction."

We all laughed, and I finally spoke. "La, I was telling Regina that I wanted my own health and fitness center. I want to really focus on natural healing and fitness. To be honest, Dr. Vanessa Brown is my idol, and she's the woman who…" I stopped before I got choked up about my mom.

"Look, I'm not Iyanla, and I can't fix yo' life, but girl, you can do whatever the hell you want because, bitch, you in America, and you got talent."

"La, shut yo' dumb ass up! You trying to counsel by quoting shows and shit, but seriously, Neka. We can help you cook this shit up, jar it up, and label it.

Shouldn't be no different from me cooking up Pierre's crack."

I couldn't believe Regina said that. Actually, I could, but the thought of starting a small business was exciting. It would give me something to look forward to doing.

"Well, I don't have any money to start anything right now."

"You didn't have any money to shop either, but you came out with bags on bags," Regina retorted.

"That's another thing. I get how La would be able to shop. She has her hustle here with hair, but Regina, if you work for Pierre, and he got all of this power and money, why do you all live in that house and live like a basic life?"

"Lil' bourgeois trying to read you yo' rights." La laughed.

"No, seriously. I'm just curious," I commented.

"Girl, look. Truth be told, I love living in the trap. I'm the true definition of trap queen, and I'll trap until the day I die. In the hood, you have to live life on the low. The moment a nigga finds out you have three more dollars than they do, they try to rob you and take you for everything they think you got. Trust, I have had plenty of opportunities to get out, but my heart breathes the hood, and if I'm out in the burbs or some shit, my ass wouldn't know how to survive."

That was deep. Regina was living with a real-life hood mentality. I was making a mental note to address that later, but I didn't think now was the time.

"Well, I guess we need to get started if we're going to get me made over," I said, and La was excited and damn near threw me into her chair.

...

We were dressed, and I must say this look was amazing. I felt good about my outfit and was looking forward to this party.

"Bitch, you look good. Now remember what we said. Hold your cup, nurse your drink, and only pop yo' ass on niggas who can pay for the show," Regina coached, and La cosigned as usual.

"Here. Drink this," La said, handing me a drink that she made.

"What's this?" I questioned.

"It's Pink Panties. Just drink it and shut up. You need to loosen up before we get there. Don't go in there talking all proper and shit. You better blend the fuck in."

"That's right, and remember you're Kiara," Regina reminded me.

"Kiara? Bitch, whet?" La questioned.

"Shit, it was the first thing that came to mind when Octavia and Felicia saw us in the mall," Regina acknowledged.

"Ok, so I'm loving the look."

"Staaaaap! Bitch, you *feeling* the look. Get it together," La coached.

"Ok, so I'm feeling the look, but I'm worried that I won't fit in," I said honestly, not really knowing what to expect.

"Look, just be yourself."

"Don't tell her that shit, La."

"Oh yeah. Ok, do what we do, and you'll be fine." We all laughed and headed out to what I was told would be the party of the year.

Chapter 25- Regina

"Fuck it up, best friend! 'Cause my best friend finna, she finna, she finna fuck it up!"

The DJ was live as we ripped the dance floor up in *The Living Room II lounge.* This muthafucka was packed with wall to wall people and bitches wearing nothing but damn dental floss with their pussies hanging out. Pierre didn't spare no expense as he hired naked bottle service bitches to keep the hoes happy and drunk.

We were fucking shit up, going hard, sweating and drinking, and having a good time. Pierre hadn't made his grand entrance, and it was cool because the food and drinks were flowing, and the DJ was earning every penny of his money.

"You enjoying yourself?" I yelled over the music to Neka.

"Yes, it's nice in here," she replied with a smile, moving her hips to the beat.

I noticed that a bunch of niggas were trying to holla at her, but she was curving they asses as she should have been. I wanted to see Pierre's face when I introduced him to my new girl because truth be told, Drake had been getting on my nerves asking for a threesome with her, and I didn't want to start treating her ass bogus on behalf of his ass, so if she had a man to occupy her time, he would move to the next bitch.

We were feeling the crowd, and the set was mad live, but I needed to keep my eyes on La. Her ass was white girl wasted as she moved and twirled her body on the dance floor.

The DJ slowed down the song, and my guess was that he was about to announce the guest of honor.

"Ladies and gentlemen, bros and hoes… the man of the hour is here! Put yo' muthafuckin' glasses in the air, and salute the prince of the boogie down Bronx, the candy man, that nigga if he don't get no muthafucking bigga, Pierre Charming!"

The crowd went wild, and bitches damn near broke their necks trying to run in stilettos to get to Pierre. He was wearing a pair of faded-wash blue jeans, a white button up, and a red Gucci king snake jacket with a snake going down the center of his back, and to complete the outfit, he had on a pair of tan Polo boots, and I couldn't deny it. His ass was looking good. If I weren't with Drake, my thirsty ass would have given him a piece of pussy in the bathroom.

I shook my head of the lustful thoughts that ran throughout my mind and focused my attention back to Neka. Looking at Neka, I was excited to sec that Pierre grabbed her attention.

"That nigga fine as wine, right?" I asked over the music, never taking my eyes off Neka as she watched Pierre work the crowd.

"Bitch, I know you heard me. You gon' answer, or you just gon' drool like the rest of the bitches?" I continued to tease, waiting on Neka to speak.

"He's kind of cute," Neka shyly spoke, and La immediately jumped in.

"Bitch, bye! Kind of? That nigga can spray all his muthafucking seeds in me, leave me broke, homeless, and with no walls, and a bitch would say I fucking lived!"

"La, shut yo' drunk ass up!" I yelled, laughing, knowing her drunk ass was serious.

Neka didn't say a word, but I noticed her breathing starting to change.

"Bitch, you good?" I asked, not understanding what was going on with her. I turned around, and to my surprise, Pierre was standing behind me. I guess that was what they meant when they'd say a nigga took her breath away because Neka didn't say a damn word.

With the way Neka's tongue was halfway dangling from her mouth, I thought it was the perfect opportunity to introduce her to Pierre.

One thing about hood niggas, when fresh meat came around, they paid attention, and everybody wanted a shot at the title. Pierre was no different.

"So you just gon' be rude as fuck in my party, Gina?" Pierre asked, and I smiled and reached out to hug him.

"Happy Birthday, nigga," I greeted as he pulled me into his muscular frame, and I was enjoying every minute of it.

"Thanks, ma. You look good. Drake's ass let you come out like that?" he asked, giving me the once over.

I twirled around so that he could get a good view of what he missed out on.

"Drake's ass already know he ain't my damn daddy unless he hitting this shit from the back," I flirted, knowing Pierre loved that shit.

Pierre and I both laughed, knowing that Drake's ass was more than likely watching me, and I thought that was good. Angry sex was always the best sex. When a nigga felt like you were giving another nigga some attention, that was when he got his own piece of act right.

"Girl, you crazy as shit. I was meaning to call you, but I was running around trying to get this shit together. Thanks for looking out for that last-minute shit."

"No worries. You know I always got you," I stated with a smile.

"I got you too, Pierre. All you got to do is say, 'La, I want it,' and it's yours, baby. It's all yours, Pierre."

"La, I think you had too much, sweetheart. Thank you all for coming, and enjoy your night. Eat and drink as much as you can hold. A nigga already paid for this shit."

"Pierre, hold up. I want to introduce you to my cousin, Kiara. Kiara, this is the birthday boy, Pierre," I introduced.

"Fuck that boy shit. I'm all man, baby. Pleased to meet you," he flirted, scanning Neka's body with his eyes as he licked his lips. "I'm Pierre." He extended his hand for a shake.

"I'm An … Kiara. Pleased to meet you. Happy birthday, sir," she stated as she took his hand, blushing.

Holding his chest with his dimpled smile and white teeth, he replied, "You're hurting my heart, baby girl. I'm not sir. Just Pierre, and believe me, the pleasure is all mine," Pierre continued to flirt, doing that thing with his lips and tongue that instantly got bitches wet.

Pierre tilted his head to the side a little to get a view of Neka's ass. I was glad she decided to wear those high-waist, yellow skinny pants. They fit her body so well; it was as if they were painted on. Not to mention the blue bustier she had on, her cleavage made her titties look as if they were standing at attention.

Pierre's eyes traveled the length of her body, from the red Pixie cut wig, to her red peep-toe stilettos, and from the look of lust in his eyes, I could say that he was definitely pleased with what he saw.

"Where's my manners? Would you ladies like to come party with me in my VIP lounge?" he questioned.

"Oh, so a minute ago, you were ready to bounce on us and work the damn room, but now we go into the VIP lounge? Hell to the yeah, we wanna go," I replied.

"Gina, yo' ass is too crazy. Come on," he said as he led us to the land of milk and honey.

We were partying and acting a fucking fool. Neka was still kind of reserved, only dancing a bit and nursing her damn drink like I told her. Drake, Sebastian, Seth,

Harper, and even Giovanni were having a good time and enjoying the party.

"Hey, you wanna dip off for a quick minute?" Drake asked as he began grinding on me from the back and kissing on my ear.

"No, I need to keep an eye on La and Kiara."

"Who in the fuck is Kiara?" he asked too damn loud for my liking.

Turning around, I looked him in the face and damn near called him an idiot with my eyes.

Finally catching on, he pulled me closer and whispered. "How about me, you, and Kiara go somewhere and have a little fun."

"Drake, stop that shit. Come on, bruh. We went through this shit already. She ain't down for that shit, so why the fuck you keep asking? You acting a little too damn thirsty," I sassed.

"Come on now. You know who the fuck I am."

"Yeah, you a high ass nigga who keeps pussy on the brain," I retorted, muffing his ass in the head.

I walked away, pissed, and La and Seth were damn near sprawled out on the sofa, and surprisingly, Pierre hadn't moved from Neka's face.

Into the Hood: Pierre & Anneka

Walking over to Neka, I spoke. "Kiara, you wanna go to the bathroom and freshen up with me?"

She nodded her head, and I took her by the hand, and we headed to the ladies' room.

The line was long, and just as we got down there, Pierre made his way to us and asked, "Hey, why didn't you all use my VIP bathroom upstairs? This shit down here for the common folk. Y'all family," he said with a smile.

"Kiara, do you really have to use the bathroom? I would love to hear more about your love for fitness," he said, and I was surprised that she held his fucking attention.

Pierre didn't give bitches any type of attention, and for him to remember something about Neka made me realize that he was really feeling her. With a twinge of jealousy seeping in, I turned on my heels and left them standing there talking.

Headed to the VIP bathroom, Pierre and Neka were on my heels.

"Gina, you need to bring yo' cousin by the spot."

"Hell naw. You ain't fucking her over."

"Come on, Gina. You're giving me a bad name. I wouldn't do that to her. Lil' mama too sweet for me to fuck her over. You know how I love my sweets," he continued.

I made my way back up the stairs and was headed to the VIP bathroom. I turned to make sure Neka was cool. "Kiara, you good? I questioned before leaving her and Pierre.

"She cool," Pierre answered for her. He gave her a wink, and I could see her starting that nervous shy shit, and Pierre noticed too. He flashed her his gorgeous smile, took her by the hand, and said, "Don't worry, ma. You in good hands. You safe with me," he said, and I nodded my head in agreement.

"Ok, well, I'll be back in a bit," I affirmed before hurrying away.

As I was pushing my way through the VIP section, I noticed Drake and Sebastian standing in the corner, looking as if they were in some type of heated argument. My curiosity wouldn't allow me to simply bypass them, so I approached, and when I stepped closer, what I heard had me heated.

"Nigga, he got a gang of bitches. Why the fuck he in her face? I told you I already sampled that pussy, and I'm not stopping until I'm knee deep in that shit."

"Drake, you need to calm the fuck down! You not fucking that girl. Regina will kill you and her."

"Fuck Regina!" he said, and I had to make my presence known.

"Fuck me, Drake? Is that how the fuck you feel? Fuck me? Nigga, I may be a lot of things, but stupid ain't one of them. So you been begging me to have a threesome with a bitch you been bagging underneath my roof?" I questioned with my head cocked to the right.

"Regina, now isn't the time for… Ah-choo! This," Sebastian replied, and I went clean, smooth the fuck off.

"Fuck you, Sebastian. How long have you been knowing about this? So this is 'make an ass out of Regina' day? You make me look after her ass, hold her fucking secret, and then you fuck that bitch right under my nose and then beg me to bed her ass down with you? That's what we doing now, Drake? Nigga, fuck you!"

I hacked up a wad of spit and spat in his fucking face. I turned around and scanned the crowd until my eyes landed on Neka.

Walking with a purpose and stomping hard as shit as if I were stomping roaches, I made a beeline to her lying, deceitful ass.

"You lying piece of shit! Neka, you fucking my man?" I yelled in her face, and the look of shock was expressed through her eyes.

"Regina, I wouldn't do that."

I didn't realize I'd called her by her name until Pierre asked, "Neka? Who is Neka?"

Ignoring his ass, I addressed her. "After all I did for you, this is how you repay me. You fucked my man. Don't fucking lie; I heard him. I asked you to be real, be a fucking friend! That's why I don't fuck with bitches!"

Slap...

I slapped the fuck outta her bourgeois ass, and her wig came flying off. I didn't give a shit. I was hotter than a pussy and wanted to slice her face the fuck up.

Sebastian was fresh on my heels, and before I knew it, gunfire began to ring out.

Brat tat tat tat, brat tat tat tat, brat tat tat tat.

Chapter 26- Pierre

Shots rang out at my party as I pulled Regina and Kiara to the floor. Something was oddly familiar about her when her wig came off, but I didn't have time to try to figure it out. Screaming and yelling could be heard, but as always, I had a way out, and I was determined to make it to safety.

Pulling Kiara to me and shielding her sexy ass body from being riddled with bullets, I made my way to the side door and made a clean exit.

Sebastian, Seth, Giovanni, Harper, and Drake, followed closely, grabbing La, Regina, and a few other girls. Out back, standing next to my Range Rover, I wanted to get to the bottom of this shit.

"Regina, you want to tell me why the fuck you pop off like that in my party? Why the fuck would you slap your cousin, and who the fuck was shooting?"

"That lying bitch ain't my fucking cousin, and Drake, you bet not bring yo' muthafucking ass home tonight. Fuck if I know who was shooting. Nigga, this the hood. Muthafuckas shoot for the fun of it," Regina responded with an attitude.

Looking at Drake, we spoke only with our eyes. He walked to Regina and spoke through gritted teeth.

"Regina, take yo' ass home, and watch your mouth. Don't talk that shit to me."

"Fuck you, Drake! You claiming bitches, wanna make me look dumb as fuck. Why the fuck are y'all out here? This family business. Unless you wanna get yo' shit peeled, I suggest you move the fuck around!" Regina spat, causing the other girls who snuck out the side door with us to scatter.

Kiara had this look on her face, and with Regina being loud as fuck, it didn't seem like she wanted any trouble.

Kiara started walking as if she were leaving in the direction of the crowd. Sebastian and I ran after her and pulled her back toward the direction of my car.

"Hey, lil' mama, that's not a cool decision to go that way."

"Let that bitch roll. She not coming back to my house. Innocent, fake ass hoe. All you had to do was be honest. That's why… I swear to God, I don't fuck with bitches! Oooooh, I wanna fuck you up so bad!" she screamed.

"Regina, I didn't do shit! You coming at me sideways, and I didn't do shit! I wouldn't do that shit to you," Kiara spoke, and her voice was trembling.

"Kiara, are you alright?" I questioned with concern. Before she could answer, we heard a voice call out.

"Anneka Snow…" someone stated, and when we turned toward the voice, he was pointing a gun in Kiara's direction and had a fucked-up expression on his face.

Knowing that I was quick with the draw, and my trigga game was on point, I quickly pulled Kiara to the ground and shot dude in the hand, making him drop his gun.

Sebastian and Seth tackled his ass to the ground and went to work on that muthafucka. I knew they were going to handle his ass, so I grabbed Kiara and pushed her in my truck. This scene was getting hot, and I didn't want to be anywhere around when the laws touched down.

"Don't bring yo' hoe ass back to my house, bitch!" Regina screamed as I helped Kiara into the car and then pulled off, heading to a spot that only my parents and Bernard knew about. I was headed to Jersey.

The car ride was silent as tears began falling from Kiara's eyes.

"Are you alright, Kiara?"

"You know that my name isn't Kiara, and no, I'm not alright. I guess you're taking me to get your reward money, right?" she cried, and my heart was going out to her.

For the life of me, I didn't know why it didn't dawn on me that she was the girl that Bernard was looking for until I glanced over, and we were looking into each other's eyes.

"I only know what you want me to know, so if you're Kiara, then I'll call you Kiara," I replied, trying to get her to trust me.

"Just take me to him. I know that's what you're going to do anyway. This is all so fucked up. Regina thinks that I fucked Drake, and I didn't. I mean, that shit happened so fucking fast. It was feeling good, and I'd never experienced anything like that before, so I didn't stop it. Fuck! I'm sorry! I didn't do shit. I was drunk, and then we were smoking." She started crying and talking in circles. I didn't know if she fucked Drake or not, but I knew something happened, and I wasn't trying to judge. I just wanted to help.

From the moment I saw her, even with the red hair, she simply had my mind gone. As tears continued to stream down her face, I did all I could to hurry to my destination just to keep her safe.

My phone rang, and it was Sebastian. Picking up on the third ring, I spoke. "Speak to me."

After he gave me the info on dude, I told him to take his ass to the spot and wait for my instructions. I killed the line and focused back on Kiara.

"Kiara, I just want to help. I'm not taking you to anyone for any reward money."

"Look. First, that son of a bitch killed my mom. Then Sebastian kidnapped me. He was supposed to kill me. Then some crazy man almost blew my brains out, and now you're kidnapping me. Fuck this shit! Let me out! I'm ready to die! I'm ready to be with my mom so all of this shit can be over! Fuck all of this shit!"

"Sweetheart, I need for you to calm down. I know very little about your situation, but I promise you that you're in good hands with me. Fuck all that other shit. I got you."

I grabbed her hand and interlocked it with mine. We rode in silence until I pulled up to my house in Jersey. Pulling up to my private estate, I drove into my circle driveway, killed the engine, and leaned over the console of the car to face Kiara.

"Kiara, before you walk in this house with me, I have to ask one thing. Do you trust me?"

Kiara dropped her head and started playing with her hair, I lifted her head so that I could look into her eyes when she answered that question.

"Kiara, answer me. Do you trust me?"

"I guess I have no choice but to trust you." She shrugged.

"You have a choice, Kiara. You always have a choice," I affirmed, hoping that I could make her feel comfortable enough to talk to me.

Bernard already filled me in on a little bit of the situation, and based on what he was saying, I just put myself in the middle of some heavy shit, and I needed to know exactly what I was facing.

"Pierre, my life right now is complicated. I think it's best if you just take me back to him. I'm tired of all this. He's never gonna stop until I'm…" She paused and looked down again. Her voice trembled as she spoke. I could feel the same pain in my heart as she held in her eyes. As much as I wanted her to finish what she was saying, I thought that it would be best if I took her inside so that she could get a little more comfortable with me.

"Come on. Let's go inside," I said as I took her by her hand, but she pulled away.

"Wait. Before we go inside, can I ask you something?"

"Yeah, you can ask me anything."

She ran her fingers through her hair. "Can you please stop calling me Kiara? My name is Anneka Snow."

"I know who you are, and I'm more than willing to help you, Anneka, but I need to know everything. Can you trust me enough to tell me?"

She nodded her head in agreement, and I led her inside of the house and into the front room where we could relax and have a conversation.

"Can I get you anything? A drink or something to eat?" I offered.

"No, I'm fine. I just really need to use the bathroom. Can you show me where it is?"

After showing her where the bathroom was, I went over to the mini bar and fixed myself a drink. Even though Anneka said that she was fine, I poured her a glass a wine, hoping that it would relax her and help her open up to me. I went back into the living room just as Anneka was coming out of the bathroom.

"I poured you a glass of wine. Do you need anything else?" I asked as she sat on the sofa and started unbuckling the straps on her shoes.

"All I need right now is to get out of these damn shoes if you don't mind. My feet are killing me." She chuckled slightly.

I chuckled a little myself. She was insanely beautiful, and I couldn't wait to peel back the layers and get to know her. I was truly infatuated by her beauty, and I knew it was something special about her. I just needed to find out what it was.

"Here. Let me," I offered, taking her feet and placing them on my lap. I took off her shoes and started massaging her well-pedicured feet.

"Mmmm, that feels good." She moaned as she laid her head back against the sofa.

Into the Hood: Pierre & Anneka

Even though she appeared to be a bit more at ease and was getting more comfortable with me, she still looked completely stressed out.

"Anneka, it's been one hell of a night for you, I bet… You wanna talk?" I offered.

Removing her feet from my lap, she sat with perfect posture then reached for her glass of wine and took a sip.

"I really don't want to talk, Pierre. Honestly, I just want you to take me to my dad. I'm ready for whatever he has coming my way. I'm just tired, you know? I mean, have you ever just been so fucking tired that you just simply don't give a fuck anymore? That's how I feel right now. I'm done with all this bullshit. All I want is one moment to be me. Just one moment to rid myself of this disguise. These clothes, all this makeup—this shit ain't me. I just want to put on my athletic clothes and running shoes and go for the longest run ever. Just being me, Anneka Snow."

"Fuck, then do it. Take all that shit off. Be you. As long as you with me, you're free to be yo'self. You ain't got to worry about shit. I got you, ma."

She chuckled out of frustration as she threw her hand in the air. "Yeah, Pierre, you got me just like everybody else. It was first Bernard. What a great listener he was, Bernard Post… Anneka, don't worry. I got you." She snickered. "Sebastian kidnapped me then decided that he got me, and finally, the rest of the men over there got me, and still, my father found me. I came face to face with the man my father sent to kill me and almost succeeded, yet everybody got me. Well, get this, Pierre. Senator Snow is a very persistent man. He won't stop until I'm dead. Do you still… got me?" Tears started running down her face, and I pulled her into an embrace, running my fingers through her hair as she cried on my shoulder.

"Look, I have to be honest with you about something. Bernard and I grew up together. We've been buddies for a minute. He was looking for you ever since the day you walked out of his hotel."

"Wait, you know Bernard? Wow, it's such a small world." She beamed, and I was a bit jealous.

Her face lit up, and she sounded as if she had so much hope, but I wasn't counting myself out. I would do what it took to make Anneka mine.

"Yeah, I'm going to call him and tell him to meet us here in the morning, but for now, you can shower, find you something in my room to toss on, and try to relax, I know it's late, and you're probably sleepy," I said, standing up, preparing to get a few things of my own to get comfortable and prepare to get to the bottom of this nigga trying to blow Anneka's head off tonight.

"Pierre, thank you. For all of this, thank you. Um, before I prepare for bed, do you think we can just sit and talk? I mean, if you don't want to, I totally understand, but I love to talk. It helps me to process things," she stated, making me smile.

"Of course, beautiful, we can talk. I would love that. Let's get showered, and we can just… talk."

The look on her face let me know that my words didn't come out right.

"Oh God, no, I didn't mean together. Well, not that it would be anything wrong with that. Shit, what am I saying? Ok, Anneka, please use the bathroom in my master bedroom at the top of the stairs to the left. I'll use the guest room down here. When you're done, just meet me down here, and we can talk."

I had to clear that statement up because I didn't want her thinking that I was trying to simply fuck. I could tell that Anneka was different from the other girls that I usually messed with, and I was determined to pull back those layers and really get to know her. In my mind, she could really become Mrs. Charming.

…

The soft music was playing in the background as I pulled out a bottled water and prepared for Anneka to make her entrance. The sun was damn near ready to rise again, but I didn't give a shit. She wanted to talk, and dammit, I was going to be here to listen.

I began to rest my eyes and take in the smell of her sweet perfume that lingered in the distance. With my eyes closed and a smile on my face, I felt a presence standing over me, so naturally, my eyes opened to what could only be described as a princess.

Anneka stood with her naturally black tresses in a messy ball bun like the girls be having, my tank top that displayed the perfect amount of side boobs, and my Nike shorts with matching slides. It was so simple, but she looked fucking amazing.

"I'm sorry. Are you tired?"

"Not at all, sweetheart. Come sit down. I was simply trying to sort the shit that was playing in my head, but that could be done later. How was your shower?" I queried.

"Amazing. You have the best showerhead ever. I didn't want to get out."

"Then you should have stayed in."

She laughed and then sat down.

"So tell me, Ms. Anneka Snow, what's on your mind."

"Food," she boldly stated, and we both burst out into laughter.

"My chef is gone for the day, but I think I know my way around the kitchen just a bit."

"I can cook if that's alright with you."

"A woman who knows her way around the kitchen? You can't be real. Are you trying to tease me?"

"Tease you?"

"The way to a man's heart is through his stomach," I stated while looking at her into her gorgeous eyes. I took her by the hand and assisted her to her feet. We walked into the kitchen, and then the magic started to happen.

45 minutes later

"Taste it. Come on. Try it," Anneka urged as she dipped her finger in this apple cinnamon sauce that she made to drizzle over the pan-seared prawns.

"I don't know where your fingers been," I teased.

"Pierre, do you trust me?" she asked, posing the same question that I asked her before she stepped foot in my home.

Looking deep into her eyes, I opened my mouth, stuck out my tongue, and when she put the sauce on my tongue, my mouth began to water. Not for the sauce, which was delicious, but more so for her. I began to wrap my mouth around her finger and hungrily sucked the remaining juice from the sauce, and when her mouth parted, and her lips puckered ever so perfectly, my third leg began to stand at full attention.

Out of breath, she spoke, "Is it good to you?"

"Sweetheart, please don't ask me that question. Not right now."

"The sauce, Pierre. Is it good to you?"

"I knew you were talking about the sauce, but sweetheart, let's be honest. The sun is now out, and neither of us are worried about sleep. You're feeling this connection with me as I am feeling it with you."

"I am, Pierre, but I have to be honest. I never had a boyfriend and never had… sex."

"Well, I'm not a boy, but I would love to be your friend, and if we can become great friends, maybe we can visit you being my woman and me your man."

"Oh, I've heard a few things about you, Mr. Pierre Charming. To be quite honest, I thought your last name was fake until tonight."

"Tonight?"

"Yes, I saw your mail on your display."

"Oh, so you were snooping?"

"No, not really. Just curious as to knowing who you really are."

"Well, I think our names fit perfectly well together. Anneka Charming has a nice ring to it. You have to admit Snow and Charming, kind of Disney like, huh?"

We laughed, and her cheeks got a bit rosy.

"Well, my life certainly isn't a fairytale, but I would like to get to know you, Pierre."

Chapter 27- Anneka

I began to stretch as I woke up with the sun resting bright upon my face. I was shocked that I was on the sofa wrapped in Pierre's arms. "It wasn't a dream," I spoke what I thought was quietly when Pierre spoke with his eyes still closed.

"No, sweetheart, it wasn't a dream. Now lay back down on my chest, and let's live in this moment," he urged, pulling me back into him. He was such a gentleman, and I felt as though everything we shared last night only put us in a better position for opening up our hearts to trust.

Laying back onto his chest, I smiled as I listened to his heartbeat.

"What are you thinking about?" he asked, and I wanted to open up to him even more.

"Honestly?"

"Yes, always be honest with me, and I'll always be honest with you. Remember what we said last night?"

"Yes, I remember. We ate our first meal together as trusting and honest friends," I replied.

Pierre sat up on the sofa and looked me into my eyes. I didn't know where these butterflies came from, but I wanted him to be a part of my chaotic life.

"Talk to me, Anneka."

"I don't want to live a lie anymore. I want to be free. I want to follow my heart and pursue my dreams."

"I know, and you will. As far as you living a lie, you can be yourself. I told you. Fuck it, and do what makes you happy. I like your idea about trusting the universe. Just watch. Things will work out just as they are meant to be."

"What about my father?"

"Don't worry about him. He gotta get through me to get to you, and the nigga gotta bring the whole fucking military to get through me." I felt that what Pierre was saying was nothing but the truth. I trusted his words and allowed my heart to simply melt.

"I trust you, Pierre, with my life and with my friendship. I trust you."

Pierre stood up, grabbed his phone, and started replying to some messages. He seemed a bit disturbed and then made a call and left to take the call in the other room.

I sat on the couch, wondering what my life would be like had things gone differently. I had to play the 'what if' game in my mind to chase down what my reality could have been. I needed to run to gain clarity, but I didn't know anything about the neighborhood and didn't have anything but the clothes that were on my back.

I wanted to break down and cry because lately, it was seeming as if I was a nomad, just wandering around in search of food and shelter. I needed to change my circumstances, and today was going to be the day.

...

I'd just finished cleaning the mess that I made after making some lunch for Pierre and myself.

The doorbell rang, and Pierre went to answer it, and I began to hear a familiar voice and shuffling.

I walked out the back from the kitchen, and a handsome Bernard stood in the doorway, holding all of the bags of clothes and shoes that he bought me the day we first bumped into each other.

"Bernard!" I yelled and ran into his arms, wrapping my arms around his neck.

Letting him go so that I could get a good look at him, I smiled, and he started to speak. "I was worried about you, Anneka, and I'm so glad that Pierre was able to find you. I rushed right over when he called, and after he filled me in on things, I figured you might want these," he said, holding up the bags with that amazing smile that I'd missed.

"Bernard, thank you so much. It wasn't a single day that passed since I met you that I didn't think about you," I confessed, and he welcomed me back into his arms into a deeper embrace.

"Are you alright? Do you need anything? Anything at all?" Bernard questioned with so much worry.

"Pierre has been the perfect host. I don't need anything," I stated with a smile.

"Excuse me. I would like to freshen up and use some of my girlie body wash and get myself together. I feel like I need a run. After all, it's the only time that I can really talk to my mom," I stated and smiled as Bernard walked the bags up to Pierre's master bedroom.

"I'll wait for you downstairs, Anneka," Bernard spoke, and I simply offered a smile.

30 minutes later…

I was in running gear, fresh out of a shower, and ready to take in this neighborhood. When I read Pierre's mail, I realized we weren't in New York anymore, but we'd actually came to Jersey.

Excited for my run, I ran down the stairs and called out to Bernard.

"Bernard, Bernard, Bernard!" I called out three times, and still no answer.

"Pierre, have you seen…" I spoke as I rounded the corner to the kitchen and was met by a beautiful woman who was cooking.

"Smells delightful. Are you Pierre's maid?" I questioned as I inhaled the aroma.

"Not at all, dear. You must be the beautiful Anneka Snow. I hope you don't mind me saying this, but your pictures don't do you any justice. I can see why that son of mine is willing to risk life and limb over you. Have a seat," the beautiful woman instructed.

Taking a seat at the kitchen table, I swallowed hard because this woman was very intimidating.

"Anneka, you may very well be wondering, 'what does this woman want, and who is this lady?' I'm Mrs. Charming, and I'm charmed to meet you. I see that you were preparing for a run, and luckily for you, I'm all dressed for the occasion." She pointed to her Nike running gear she was wearing, and I was still trying to figure her out.

"I love running," I offered, trying to rid myself of my nerves.

"As do I. As do I. Now, dear, I know what it's like to lose a mom. I lost both of my parents, and so my heart truly pours out to you. I admire your strength and simply wanted you to know that you aren't alone in this. Both of those men are out there damn near having a pissing match over you," she stated, and I looked out the window, and Bernard and Pierre were wrestling, and I chuckled.

"Be it as it may, I know that being with you would come with a price. I simply wanted to let you know that although I know what it feels like to lose a parent, I don't ever want to know the feeling of losing a child. Be honest with him, and as long as you are honest with him, it's up to him how he would like to proceed. Are you ready for that run? Let me put this pot roast on low," she said, walking over to the stove. I loved how direct she was, but I needed for her to understand that Pierre and I were simply friends who wanted to get to know each other.

After she placed the things on the stove and in the oven on low, Mrs. Charming stuck her head out the back and called out to Bernard and Pierre.

"We're going running. Be back shortly," she stated.

Bernard ran to the door and said, "Anneka, did you want me to go with you? I can go with you."

"Boy, she's fine, both of you. Enough with the nonsense. You two are like a dog trying to fight over a bone. She's not a piece of meat. As you were, gentlemen," she addressed them, and I chuckled, and we went on our run.

Running with Mrs. Charming was almost freeing. As the wind kissed my fair skin, I began to internally have a talk with my mom. I explained to her everything that I was going through and how much I really missed her. This was a tough situation to be in, but this was just the type of cleanse I needed in order to get through my day.

After internally talking to my mom, I thought about our last run together.

"No, Mom, keep up. We're almost there!"

Yes, mom, you're a survivor, you will beat cancer's ass. I was so proud that she made it to the steps and actually beat her last time. She was stronger, and I was feeding off her strength. She sat at the bottom of the stairs, trying to gain control over her breathing.

"Girl, I won't have to worry about cancer killing me. If I keep running like that, you're going to kill me."

I had no idea that I'd made it back to Pierre's house until I looked up. Sweat was dripping from my head, and tears were streaming from my eyes. I looked up toward the sky and screamed.

"Why! Why, God! Why did you let this happen? She was getting better, she was strong, she was beautiful, and she was all I had." I let out a cry that I didn't even know I was holding in. Mrs. Charming rushed to my side and embraced me.

"Let it out, dear. It's alright. Go ahead and let it out."

We walked into the house, and I was crying my eyes out. Pierre and Bernard both sprang to their feet.

"What happened? Ma, is she alright?" Pierre questioned.

"She's fine. She's grieving and surrounded by idiots. Move out the way, and let her get some air." Mrs. Charming took me to Pierre's room and sat me down for a talk. I poured my heart out to her and never felt better. I knew that it was time to really stop running and live my life and walk in my truth.

"Thank you so much, Mrs. Charming. I really enjoyed this talk. You are the first person that truly understands where I was coming from," I stated sincerely.

"Sweetheart, I know what my son does, and no, I'm not proud, so if you were getting advice from the likes of the people that take orders from him, I could only imagine the type of advice they were giving."

"They aren't that bad." I chuckled.

"I didn't say that they were, but during a time like that, and with your dad looking for you, you needed more sound advice. Now, with what you shared with me, you know your father won't stop looking for you. I know my son wouldn't dare go to the authorities, but maybe you could call and talk to them and anonymously give a statement."

"That won't help. He has officers on his payroll, and he will track me down here and kill me."

"Well, take this phone. Let me delete it and set it back to factory. I will have to tell my clients that I changed my number. Call me anytime you want to talk or if you just want a running buddy. I don't live far from here at all, but you need to reclaim your life and stop living in fear. We are women, and if we don't know how to do anything else, we know how to survive. We were born fighters. Always remember that."

Her words hit close to home as I thought about my mom's words to me, telling me to fight. I was rejuvenated and ready to take control over my life. Mrs. Charming said that she was going to freshen up and finish the dinner that she'd started, and I'd figured I'd do the same thing. I ran a hot bath and placed the clothes out on the bed and thought about things the way Mrs. Charming put them. I was going to reach out to my mom's lawyer and Dr. Vanessa Brown too. Today was indeed going to be a good day.

After my bath, I rubbed on my body lotion and allowed the lotion to coat and soak into my skin. I enjoyed this sense of reality as I smiled and looked up my mom's attorney on the smart phone that Mrs. Charming gave me.

I was so nervous about reaching out to my mom's attorney but decided that I would no longer live in fear. I dialed the number and spoke.

"Hello, Attorney Martin. This is Anneka Snow. Do you have a moment to talk?"

Chapter 28- Bernard

Words could not describe how grateful I was when Pierre called me and told me that he'd found Anneka. After hearing everything that happened to her at Pierre's party, I knew better than to call Larry because it seemed that Anneka might have been going to the highest bidder, and I needed to do as I promised and keep her safe.

I'd gotten into a bit of a screaming match with Pierre earlier when it came to Anneka, and that was when I realized that I would be losing yet another woman to Pierre.

Ever since we were kids, this had always been his thing. I talked to a girl and could relate and understand her needs, and once she was ready to give in, Pierre would come in and charm her panties off, leaving me without a girl and lack of many experiences.

Anneka came downstairs, looking just as refreshed as she did the night we had our first real connection.

"Anneka, are you alright?"

"Yes, I am, Bernard. Things couldn't be better. Do you know where I could find Pierre?" she asked, and my head went down.

I thought she was excited to see me, but now she was looking for Pierre. Just like I thought, he had squirmed his way into her heart.

"He's in the kitchen with his mom."

"Thanks, Bernard," she excitedly said as she happily kissed my cheek.

I blew out a frustrated sigh because I simply didn't know how to come at a girl like Anneka. She was indeed the total package, and I wanted her forever in my life and needed to figure out a way of making that possible.

I followed her to the kitchen, and she was holding a phone in her hand and cozying up to Mrs. Charming, tasting her food, and laughing. The entire scene looked as if it were a scene from the Cosby Show. I watched the interaction, understanding that I didn't really have a reason to be jealous, but I couldn't deny my feelings for this woman.

"Oh, Pierre, you know how we were talking about trust, honesty, and loyalty last night?" Anneka questioned, and it was as though she was taking daggers to my heart. Hearing that she sat up talking to Pierre did something to me, and I needed to address these feelings, but I knew that now wasn't the time.

"Of course, I remember, sweetheart. Why? What's up?"

"Well, your beautiful, darling of a mother gave me this phone, and I was able to contact my mother's attorney."

"Yeah, ok… So what does that have to do with our conversation, sweetie?"

I hated that he was really laying on the damn charm, talking to Anneka, and I wanted to fight this man that was more like a brother to me than a friend. I wanted him to stop pushing up on Anneka.

"Well, I wanted to be open and honest with you simply because that's all you have been with me. I spoke to my mom's attorney, and he informed me that my mom left me something, and I needed to come down and sign the paperwork in order to get it. He said that he couldn't discuss in detail over the phone, but it was imperative that I come to his office."

"Anneka, that's great, but do you think it's a setup? I mean like a setup to get you back to your father?"

"I don't think so. Attorney Martin was a dear friend to my mom, and he was the attorney that only handled her business. My dad controlled the things that they had jointly."

"Well, son, it sounds as if you need to check this Attorney Martin out," Mrs. Charming stated, and a bright smile rushed to Anneka's face.

"I'll be happy to check into him for you, sweetheart. Thanks for bringing this to me and not simply rattling off my information to anyone."

"Of course," she said with a smile.

Pierre began walking up to Anneka and pulling her close to him.

"You're beautiful. I don't know what conversation you had with my mom, but there's a new glow about you that I'm loving," he said, and my blood began to boil.

"I'm going to take care of that attorney situation right after I handle that business from last night. Do you trust me?" he asked, and she was putty in his hands.

"I'm going with you. I'm going to check things out for you too, Anneka. Whatever you need, you know that I will do it. Here. Take my card and order some things that you need to make your special meals and creams. See, I remembered all of that."

Everyone was eyeballing me suspiciously, and I didn't give a damn. Pierre was too close to damn near kissing Anneka, and I needed him to stop.

"Bernard, you cool, bruh?" Pierre asked with his hands still resting on Anneka's hips, and he looked over his shoulder until his eyes landed on me, and he had that fucked up scowl on his face.

"I, um, I just need to talk to you. Excuse me, ladies. Pierre and I need to talk."

We walked out of the kitchen and into Pierre's office. I knew how this shit was going to go, but I needed to get this out.

"Pierre, I told you from jump that Anneka is special. Why are you brushing up on her like that?"

Stroking his face, he cockily remarked, "Because I'm a charming muthafucka."

I let out a sigh and dreaded this conversation because I knew I wasn't going to be able to reach him. "Pierre, I really like this girl, and I'm asking, no, I'm telling you to back off."

"Oh, so you're a big man? You're telling me to back off? Look, B. I get it. Shit, I can't even front. She got my head too, but neither one of us can stake a claim to her. Let the chips fall where they may. You need to stop cock blocking."

"Pierre, I'm taking her with me."

"Like hell you are. She's staying right the fuck here where we know she's safe. A nigga almost popped her ass in my fucking face last night. Now if you want me to back up, then you come handle the nigga that tried to blow her brains out… Just like I thought, you're quiet. Continue building shit. You're good with that. Leave the street life and the women to me. I'm a wiz at that." He winked, and then I finally found my voice.

"I'll go. I'll take care of him and find out who sent him, and then I'll take them out too," I boldly stated.

"Wow, big man. You'll take them out? Do you even know how to take someone out?"

"You know, even though I'm not in the streets, I'm the best damn shooter that ever walked New York. It may not have been the lifestyle I chose, but trust and believe, it's in me."

"Ohhhhhh, ok, have it your way, Bernard. Suit up. We meeting in six hours. Until then, we both agree to have random conversation with Anneka, and if it ends with a kiss, then so be it. May the best man win."

"I'm not fighting over her like she's a prize. This is stupid. Just back off, Pierre."

"No, you wanted to get your hands dirty, and now you're going to make good on your word, or we both can simply go out there and tell Anneka what a big pussy you are. Maybe you both can exchange wash regiments, and she can tell you how to clean yours."

"Fuck you, Pierre."

"I don't swing that way, Bernard, but I plan on fucking Anneka. It's something about her that has me like… whoa."

"So you want another notch in your belt?"

"No, I want a wife on my arm."

When Pierre said that he wanted a wife on his arm, that statement shocked me more than anything else he said. For the years that I'd known Pierre, he'd always been cocky and full of shit when it came to women, but never have I ever heard him say that he was wanting a wife on his arms. That meant that he was just as serious about Anneka, and I knew that meant I needed to step aside.

Moments from throwing in the towel, I decided that I needed to prove to myself that I wasn't what Pierre thought, and I was so much better. I was going to get Anneka the closure that she needed, and Pierre was going to help me.

"So you're looking for a wife?" I asked Pierre with a straight face.

"I sure am. I'm sick of my mom begging me for grandkids," he retorted.

"Well, she may have to beg a little while longer. I'm going tonight, and after this shit is over, Anneka is coming with me."

"You sure 'bout that, B? You know this isn't a league you're used to playing in."

"Pierre, this isn't a fucking game. I'm not moving to the side this time."

"B, riddle me this. How in the fuck are you pussy whipped, and you didn't even sample the pussy? Nigga, you damn near sat in the corner shaking like you were auditioning for *Naked and Afraid* the first night y'all were in the room together."

"Who told you that?"

"Nigga, you just did. See, I know you, B. You get all nervous and shit when a beautiful woman is around, but as for me, nigga, I'm cooler than a muthafucking fan. Look, I get it. I may not have always had the best rep when it comes to these bitches and hoes, but I get it, B. Anneka got that shit that make a nigga wanna change his ways."

Pierre walked out the room as cockily as he walked in. I knew that he was serious about pursuing Anneka, and there was nothing I could do to stop him other than to show him that I was just as serious. I may not be a street dude, but I grew up in the streets, and I knew I had one thing going for myself, and that was my aim. I was going to show him better than I could tell him.

Chapter 29- Ivanka

"What do you mean you're not taking the job? Do you know who I am?"

I slammed the phone down and marched into the bedroom where Dennard was sleeping peacefully. I couldn't believe that idiot of a friend of his Larry wouldn't take the job of ending Anneka.

I thought Idris would get the job done, but he wouldn't call me back, and I hadn't heard from him in two days. He said that he was certain he saw her at a party and was going to take her out. Now this brother of mine, who had shit for brains, couldn't be found. I hoped like hell that he wasn't trying to cross me and take her body to Leo for the reward money. That wouldn't be good for him, not at all. That wouldn't be good for him.

I was ranting while charging into the room to wake Dennard.

"Dennard! Dennard! Get up now! We have a problem!"

"What problem now, Ivanka? I'm trying to sleep." He yawned as he rolled over and made himself comfortable.

I walked over to him and snatched the pillow from under his head, causing him to sit up and give me his full attention.

"Sleep when you're dead. Now, get the hell up. Larry refuses to take the job. I need you to get on the phone and convince him to take the job."

"I can't do that, Ivanka. If the man don't want to take the job, I can't convince him otherwise. Shit, we cool, but not that cool to where I'm telling that man to do shit he don't wanna do." He snatched the pillow out of my hand and laid back down.

I couldn't believe the nerve of these people. I was practically changing their lives, and these incompetent assholes couldn't get the job done.

"Imbeciles! I'm working with a bunch of imbeciles!" I yelled out of frustration. "One job! I gave you all one fucking job. I'm literally changing your miserable lives, and you useless bastards can't even complete a simple task. I can't believe this. I'm surrounded by a bunch of idiots," I continued my rant as I stormed out of Dennard's room and into the front of the house.

"Idris, where the hell are you?" I screamed out loud as I paced back and forth.

I knew that I couldn't sit around waiting to see what's going on. Putting on my Gucci shades, I snatched my purse and keys off the table, then headed out of the door on my way to pay Leo a little visit.

I didn't understand how something so small was taking this much time to complete. I called my friend to see if the death certificates were ready, and luckily for me, they were. I had him to place them on hold for me as I headed to Leo's to get to the root of my problem.

…

I circled around Roosevelt Island and used my key pad for the garage. As I parked, I checked my appearance in the rearview, grabbed my purse, and proceeded into the Octagon.

Walking toward the elevator, of course, I was greeted by the staff. After the pleasantries, I stepped onto the elevator, pressed the number four, and waited for the elevator to chime.

I approached Leo's condo and knocked on the door. I waited mere moments, but it felt like minutes—minutes I didn't have to spend outside in this hall.

After a few more moments, Leo finally opened the door, looking god awful, and of course, I was repulsed by his appearance.

"Leo."

"Ivanka." Leo moved to the side and allowed me access into his condo. I walked in, looked around at the mess, and wanted to slap the shit out of Leo for living in filth. "Ivanka, what do I owe this visit? I told you that what we had is over."

"And I told you that I would be back, and you need to get yourself together. Leo, you made me a promise, and you will make good on it. You see, these papers here say that you will do whatever I tell you to do. Not to mention this growing bump causes me to do whatever the hell I want to do."

"Is that right? Now what papers are those, Ivanka?"

"Oh, just your dear departed wife's actual autopsy. You see, my dear. I never play a game that I'm not set up to win. You owe me, Leo, and you will pay me, or you can kiss your freedom goodbye."

"Ivanka, I've already lost everything that ever meant something to me, so your threats don't move me. Do as you will. Just think about this… What type of cell have you picked out for yourself? I'm sure you wouldn't want to give birth in a prison cell."

"What the hell are you talking about, Leo? I won't have my child in prison, but you, my dear, will live your life behind bars if you don't do what I say."

"Just as you have things on me, I have things on you. So when you think about turning me in, think about the cell that you'll be in too. Oh, and babe, it won't be anything like the Ritz. Are you ready for that life?"

"Fuck you, Leo. This shit isn't over. I will get everything you promised me. You just better cash in on those policies, and please don't force my hand in this. My child and I deserve what you promised."

"Ivanka, do as you may. None of that shit means anything to me. When our child is born, we will take the necessary steps to co-parent."

Leo tossed back a drink, walked over to the door, and opened it as if he were telling me to leave.

I looked at him with hatred in my eyes and murder on my brain. Leo thought he was so smart, but what he failed to realize was that he actually signed all the shit over to me in case something happened to him. So I guess he was going to have an accident sooner than later, and if

I could kill Anneka, that was a double payout because I got it all. I rubbed my growing belly and proceeded to the door.

"Good day, Leopold."

"Good day, Ivanka. And Ivanka… before you think about doing anything, think about what I said. You'll be sharing a cell right next to me."

I was furious and walked back toward him and got in his face. I was damn near kissing him and spoke. "Leopold, you've fucked with the wrong woman, and trust me, it would have been so much better to have me as a friend than to have me as your worst enemy."

I left from Leo's with murder at the front of my mind. Why did this girl and his dead wife have so much power over him? I needed to address the situation.

I couldn't wait to give that Anneka the kiss of death. I wanted to watch her in a paralyzed state to where she was trapped in a tomb within her mind while no words would ever escape her lips. I wanted her dead to the world and for all of New York to forget her existence.

There would be no need for a proper burial, as Leopold would be long gone himself. I could see it now—Anneka in a cocoon-like casket, pale skin, ebony hair, and lips the color of crimson blood. Oh, what a sweet day to be the only person to carry on the Snow name and be able to inherit all that was meant for me. I smiled as I rubbed my protruding belly, trying to calm down from the amount of stress I was under. As I turned off Roosevelt Island, I was quickly stricken with pain. "Ohhh."

I yelled in agony as I looked down and noticed that my cream jumpsuit was now painted in blood. "Damn you, Anneka! You will die! You will die!"

Chapter 30- Leo

For days after Eva's burial, I sat there drinking my life away. The guilt was eating me alive, and I hadn't been able to sleep. Every time I closed my eyes, images of me taking the life from Eva, and the horrid look on my daughter's face haunted me daily. Ivanka saying that she would send me to prison really didn't bother me. because my mind was already incarcerated.

I'd been calling Sebastian for days only to have no response. The last time I spoke with him, I threatened his life, and since then, I knew it wasn't smart for me to be out and about. With Ivanka just leaving, making threats, now was the time to be the king that I was and step down from my throne and make shit move and shake.

"Leo, you created this mess. Now it's time to clean it up," I said to myself as I tossed back another shot.

I picked up my phone and made another attempt to call Sebastian. I needed him to know that this thing had to be called off. After allowing the phone to ring three times, I was about to hang up when I heard. "Ah-choo! Nigga, what the fuck you keep calling me for?"

A wave of relief took over my body as I placed the call on speaker to get dressed and collect some money that I had in the house. I didn't care what I needed to do, but if I needed to pay this man, I would pay him to go away.

"Sebastian, I know you don't talk over the phone, but I need that situation called off like yesterday."

"Nigga, you threaten my life and then call me asking for a favor? So… Ah-choo! You got another muthafucka on your payroll to handle yo' business or some shit?"

"Not at all. I just had a change of heart. If you know where—"

He cut me off before I could finish my statement. "Nigga, say less. If you're serious about this, you need to meet me in the boogie down Bronx. I don't trust yo' slick talking ass."

"Yeah, yes, what time? Name the place, and I'll be there. You can actually come here. I'm home now."

"Nigga, you too damn eager. I don't… Ah-choo! Like that shit. I'll give you the time and the designated place, and if you come at me with some bullshit, that will be the end of yo' … Ah-choo! Ass." Sebastian hung up on me, and I couldn't really gage him. It seemed as if he was interested in what I had to say, so I would simply play it by ear and come as protected as I knew how.

I needed to right a few wrongs while I waited on Sebastian to call me back with the time and location.

I picked up the phone and called my attorney. After Ivanka threatened to turn me into the police and threatened me with our unborn child, I wanted to make sure that everything would be in order just in case I ever had to face her in court with this. I wouldn't put it past her. She would do anything for a dime, and I wanted to make sure my ducks were in a row.

My phone rang, and I was excited to see that it was Sebastian.

After picking up the call on the second ring, he gave me strict instructions to follow, and I thought to myself, *This will all be over soon*, as I prepared to go to the boogie down Bronx.

I wasn't a fool by any stretch of the word, so I made sure to suit up for war. After securing my guns, I looked into the mirror and said, "Leo, no matter what, this ends tonight. It's time to bring Anneka home to start healing."

I was now ready for this battle. I was simply praying I came out victorious.

Ms. T. Nicole

Chapter 31- Sebastian

I wasn't surprised at all that Leo continued to reach out to me. I knew I was going to body his ass the moment he threatened my life, and tonight, I'd have the honor of freeing Anneka from the world of hiding.

After getting off the phone with Leo, I went back into the basement of the trap we were in to address this muthafucka who thought he was tough. We'd been torturing his ass for the past thirty-two hours, and still, we had no information, but today, that shit stops here.

I had a good three hours left before the real show began, but I wanted to get some frustrations out. Geovanni was mad as hell, as always, when I walked into the basement.

"Sebastian, this muthafucka shitted on himself, and you expect me to get answers from this stanking muthafucka?" Geovanni growled with his face twisted up.

Harper came down just as bubbly as ever. "Do you think he want water? I have water. I think we should give him some water. Don't want him to pass out. Here, sir, have some water."

I'd seen enough. This was worse than *Killer Klowns from Outerspace.* It was a disaster of a circus act.

"Harper, get the fuck outta… Ah-choo! Here, talking 'bout giving this fucker water. Mutha… Ah-choo! Fuck him." I took the bottle of water and poured it over this fool's face, slapping his ass awake.

He peered through his swollen eyes and tried to address me. "Kill me now. I refuse to talk. It's best that you kill me," he said in a defeated tone.

I didn't know what it was with niggas these days. They claimed to always be ready to die, but when the hammer came knocking at their domes, they started shitting bricks, and in this case, this nigga shitted bricks on top of bricks.

I popped a Claritin to get my sneezing under control because I didn't want to spend any time focusing on my allergies when it was time to put in this work.

Stepping in his face, I spoke. "So you're really ready to… Ah-choo! Die?"

"Are you serious, son? You just sneezed in my fucking face," he said weakly, and I was pissed off.

I began dousing his wounds in rubbing alcohol and enjoyed watching his ass trying to jump out of the chair he was tied down too.

His screams fueled me as I began to beat his ass back to sleep.

"I bet… Ah-choo! That muthafucka don't have shit to say when he wakes back up," I stated out of breath after getting a good workout on that slow fucker. I walked back upstairs to the trap that we were in and noticed Regina had come over to drop off work for Pierre.

I nodded my head in her direction, and she gave me a nod back. I looked at Drake, who was rolling a blunt and acting as if he didn't care that Regina was less than ten feet away from him. With his head focused on his blunt, Regina sighed and proceeded to walk out the door.

"Regina… Ah-choo! Ah-choo! Ah-choo! Wait, come back in here," I called out to her back, and she stopped in her tracks. I started wishing I had that oil mixture that Anneka made me to calm down my sneezing because the Claritin seemed not to be working as fast as I would like it.

"What, Sebastian?" she questioned dryly.

"Come in. We need to work… Ah-choo! This shit out as a family," I stated, looking from Regina to Drake.

"Man, fuck all that. Let her ass go. I can get pussy from anywhere," Drake said with an attitude as he blazed up his blunt.

"Really, Drake? That's how the fuck you feel? Nigga, you know I don't trust bitches, never have, and the moment you convince me to let my guards down and allow a bitch to breathe in my space, you fuck her in my house—our house."

"You wanted to fuck her too, Regina, stop lying to yourself. Don't act like you haven't dipped into the ladies' pond a time or two. Trust me, I was there."

"Drake, what we do in our personal bedroom, is our business, and please, let's not forget that we consented to whatever went on in our bedroom. I never did no sneak shit behind your back, nigga, so don't come at me like that."

"Look, I just wanted to sample the pussy."

When Drake was determined to fuck up his relationship with Regina over something that never happened, I knew he had plans to go after Anneka, and I wasn't going to let that happen. This nigga was high as a kite, and I didn't see any reason for the lies to continue.

"Drake, tell her the… Ah-choo! Truth," I said, looking in his eyes, daring his ass to challenge me.

"Fuck you, Sebastian. Where the fuck is yo' bitch at? Worry about getting yo' dick wet and not about my dick action and my bitch."

"Nigga, I'm not yo' bitch. Drake, you have fucked me over for the last time. Sebastian, we cool or whatever, but I can't stand that nigga. I'm outta here."

"Ah-choo! Regina, wait!" I called out to her again because I was determined to lay this rumor to rest.

"What, Sebastian! I'm gone. This nigga don't give a shit, and neither do I."

Regina left out the door, and I went rushing over to Drake.

"Why do you constantly treat her like that, knowing damn well nothing… Ah-choo! Happened between you and Anneka? For fuck's sake, you were trying to take advantage of her… Ah-choo! But you never fucked her. Why would you have Regina feeling that way when you know her past? That's fucked up," I growled, wanting him to stop with the fuckery.

"What's it to you? You mad 'cause you can't get a bitch, because she's scared of your fucking germs. Nigga, Anneka was just my way out. Regina will always be a good piece of pussy, but other than that, she don't mean shit. Had yo' dumb ass not got involved, I would've busted that sweet pussy of Anneka wide the fuck open. Had that bitch opening up like a beautiful blossoming flower."

I was so pissed off, and just when I was about to beat Drake's ass, I heard, "Is that right, Drake? That's all I am to you is simply pussy? You made me fuck up the only friendship I had over a lie. It was you this entire time and not her."

"Regina, wait. You heard that shit wrong, baby. Stop."

"I heard perfectly clear, and I need you to hear me clear. Unless you want to get cut the fuck up, I suggest you find another place to squat at. Fuck you, Drake." Regina slammed the door, and the look on Drake's face told me that we were in for a long ass night.

...

Drake and I were cleaning ourselves up from our fight. When Regina left, we started brawling as if we were two niggas in the streets and not boys. The fight would have still been going on had Geovanni, Seth, and Harper not broken it up.

Into the Hood: Pierre & Anneka

The sound of the door broke the silence in the room. Pierre came in, and to my surprise, his boy Bernard was with him, and they were dressed in all black and looked like they were in need of answers.

"What the fuck going on here?" Pierre barked, looking around the room.

"Nothing, we were waiting on you to start the show," I answered.

"Well, it doesn't look like nothing to me. Is this a family issue or an outside issue?" he asked.

"Family business. It's handled, though. Ah-choo! You ready to rock this nigga… Ah-choo! To sleep?"

"Sebastian, on some real shit, you need to get that shit handled. You gon' fuck around and blow a nigga's block off with that fucking sneeze," Pierre stated, and the guys started laughing, and the mood was instantly lightened.

"Why is he with you?" I asked.

"Y'all remember Bernard? He's coming to take care of this business."

"This isn't cops and robbers, princess. This is a man's sport," Giovanni grumbled, taking the words right out of my mouth.

"I'm a grown ass man, and there isn't an ounce of bitch in me. Now where is the muthafucka who tried to kill Anneka?" Bernard spat, and we all looked surprised.

The last time I saw this fool, he was upset over a girl that Pierre snatched from him. I figured he was trying to prove a point to Pierre, but before I handled this business, I needed to address the other issue that should be showing up sooner than later.

"Pierre, I know… Ah-choo! How you don't like surprises, and I… Ah-choo! Invited Leo Snow over to join in the festivities."

"Nigga, are you crazy? Why would you tell that nigga where my trap is? You trying to get me put away?" Pierre took out his heat before I could blink, and this nigga was seeing red. I needed to explain myself because he was quick with the draw, and his trigger finger stayed itching—just like my damn nose.

"Pierre, stop. You know I wouldn't put you in heat. Hell, I'm here too. I know I can trust… Ah-choo! Him."

"You can trust the man that put a hit out on his own daughter? I think the fuck not."

Chapter 32- Pierre

It was taking everything in me not to smoke Sebastian's ass. How in the fuck did he think it was cool to tell the fucking senator where the fuck my trap house was?

I was standing in front of this nigga, ready to send his ass to his fucking maker when he said, "My plan is to never allow the nigga to… Ah-choo! Leave. He's coming in, but he's not leaving this bitch alive."

"Suppose he told someone that he was coming. Then what?"

"This bitch will be… Ah-choo! Torched by sunrise, and the only name he knows is mine. There are a million Sebastian's in America, so I'm not worried."

"You better be worried. You're the only one with a fucking allergy issue; I'm sure of that shit." I laughed, and the fellas joined in.

"I have a suggestion," Bernard stated, and everyone's eyes went toward him.

"Anneka lost a lot, and I think before we kill her dad, we allow her to have the closure she deserves."

"Nigga, stop thinking with yo' damn dick!"

"I'm not Pierre. She lost everything. That's the least we can do."

"You really saying 'we' like you about to put in that work."

The bell rang, and everyone got quiet and stared at the door. Walking over to the door, Bernard stood behind the door as if he were about to attack on some sneak shit. This nigga seen one too many movies for me, and I wanted to laugh at his ass, but I had to give it to him. The nigga bossed up quick when it came to Anneka.

Looking out the peephole, I noticed it was indeed Leo Snow. I opened the door and snatched him up and closed and locked the door.

"Wait, what is this, Sebastian? I thought I was coming to make arrangements to get my daughter. I don't want any trouble," Leo said.

"Nigga, when you threatened me, you called the… Ah-choo! Trouble hotline."

"Wait, wait, wait… I brought money."

"Nigga, what else you got? Awww, you think you slick and thought you were going to come in here and smoke somebody?" I asked, finding three pistols on this muthafucka.

"I just wanted to protect myself. I didn't know what to expect."

Into the Hood: Pierre & Anneka

"Nigga, who in the fuck did you tell you were coming over here?" I snarled.

"Nobody. I just came to make arrangements to get my daughter." The fucker was scared, not as confident as I'd thought he would be since he was putting out hits on muthafuckas.

"Let me show you what arrived at my front door. Get yo' ass down those stairs." I pushed his ass down the stairs, and he landed at the feet of the muthafucka who tried to take out Anneka.

That fucker opened his eyes and weakly spoke. "She sent yo' ass off too, huh?"

I was all ears because I wanted to know who the fuck this slow nigga was referring to.

"Who? What are you talking about? Who are you?" Leo questioned, holding his head that hit the concrete floor on his way down.

"My sister. She sent me to kill your daughter, and now you ended up just like me," he said, shaking his head.

"Who the fuck is yo' sister, muthafucka?"

"Fuck you. He knows exactly who she is. He's fucking her, and supposedly, he got her pregnant."

I got up in that fucker's face and asked him again, "I hate repeating myself. Who the fuck is your sister?"

My silencer was on, and I knew this nigga wasn't going to make it out alive, but before I could say anything else, Leo jumped up and started reigning blows on this nigga.

"I told her to call it off! You fucking killed my daughter! Fuck you! Fuck you! You piece of shit!" Leo bellowed out, beating the shit outta this nigga, and we stepped back and allowed him to get his workout on.

"Fuck you, Leo Snow. You put out a hit on your daughter to collect money, and now I'm a piece of shit. You're lower than the shit I flush down my toilet."

"You muthafucka! Ahhhhh!" Leo let out a scream, and we didn't see this shit coming. He picked up a weight and bashed this nigga's skull in. I thought this fucker blacked out because buddy was clearly dead, and Leo kept going in on his ass.

Tears were streaming out his eyes, and Sebastian finally stepped in and stopped him.

"Leo, you need to call your crew to sweep this spot, your blood, your scene."

"Leo, that's one hell of a show you put on. But I know the truth. The truth that you don't want to get out," Bernard spoke, stepping up to a Leo, who still held a bloody weight.

With my gun aimed at him, I ordered him to put the weight down so we could address the issues.

…

Wow, an hour and a half later, the cleanup crew had come and gone. Leo didn't have a problem telling us the truth and disclosing that the bitch who was pulling the strings was his mistress, Ivanka. We left special instructions with the cleanup crew on how to deliver his decaying body.

We were walking back up the stairs with a distraught Leo when Bernard hauled off and hit him in the back of the head. "Bitch!"

"Nigga what the fuck you do that for?" I asked.

"That was for Anneka. He put her through unnecessary hurt. I lost my mom to cancer, and not once did my father try to take her out. He supported her and loved her until she took her last breath." Bernard was in his feelings, and that shit was funny as hell, but now was the time where I had to make a decision.

Trust this nigga and take him to Anneka, or kill this nigga and know that I saved Anneka from any future headaches coming from his slithering snake ass.

I was on the fence when it came to this muthafucka. At times, during his confession, it seemed as though he was speaking nothing but the truth, but he did order the hit out on his own child, which made me believe that he didn't change.

Leo was holding the back of his head and walking up the stairs. I had no idea about how this all was going to end although I'd played it out in my mind numerous times before we arrived.

The bell rang, and we all looked around, puzzled. Then there was knocking and banging as if the door was going to fly off the hinge.

"Open up! It's the police!"

I looked at Sebastian and then looked at Leo. "Both of you niggas are dead."

"Give me your guns," Bernard insisted, holding his hand out as the knocking increased.

The look in his eyes was a look I'd never seen before. It was like the nigga was ready to stand by my side if we had to go to war with the police, and I was glad to have him on my side at this point.

"It seems as if I may have underestimated you, my nigga," I said as I passed him my gun and walked up to the door, not knowing how this would all end.

With both guns behind his back, Bernard nodded his head, telling me to open the door.

"Good evening, officers, how may I help you?" I questioned in the most pleasant tone, being as cool and calm as I could be.

One of the officers eyed me suspiciously while the other officer was glancing behind me. I knew he was trying to see if anything looked suspicious so that they could have a reason to run up in my shit, but of course, nothing was out of place, and everyone was looking calm and relaxed as if nothing was happening.

"We got a few calls tonight, saying that it was a domestic disturbance coming from this house. The callers said that they heard arguing and what sounded like a fight. Is everything ok?" the officer probed.

Just as I was about to answer, Leo stepped up, and it was as if the officers just noticed his ass.

In my head, I just knew this muthafucka was about to say some shit to try to have our asses locked away for good. I glanced at Bernard, who swallowed and then nodded. Sebastian went into a sneezing fit, and finally, Leo spoke.

"Is everything ok, officers? Did my nephew do something?" he asked as he stood beside me with an authoritative look.

"Senator Snow, I'm sorry to bother you and your family, especially after what you have just gone through, but we had some complaints."

"Officers, when family gets together, there is always a bit of excitement. Thank you for your concerns. I can assure you that everything here is fine. These guys have been arguing and fighting for years, but it's simply fun amongst brothers and cousins. Do have yourself a good day." Leo looked at the officers and basically dismissed their asses. I didn't know what it was about this nigga, but I was thinking that maybe Anneka needed to holla at him because he didn't seem to be on that bullshit.

"Good day, Senator," the officer stated and left.

Looking at Leo, I had one question. "Why?"

Chapter 33- Ivanka

"Please! Please! Do anything you can to save my baby!" I cried as the nurses wheeled me back into the room and placed me on the table.

Things were moving so fast that I could hardly keep up with what they were saying.

"Oh… Owww! The cramping is unbearable! What's going on?" I questioned while rocking on the table from side to side, trying to keep my legs pressed closely together.

The nurses struggled to get my jumpsuit off because I was swinging, crying, and fighting to keep my child.

This baby was going to have me with more money than I'd ever seen if I could just make it full term.

"Ms. Vanzant, we're going to need you to calm down so that we might help you," the nurse said as she finally was able to take off my jumpsuit and attempt her examination.

"Calm? I am calm! You idiots get to work and save my baby!" I yelled as tears began to pour from my eyes.

I felt something warm touch against my leg, and when I looked down, I'd passed a large blood clot, which seemed to have tissues within it, and I suddenly lost it. "Stop it! Please stop it! Put it back in! Is that my baby?"

There were three nurses in the room, and they all held the same expression. I knew what they were saying even though they never uttered a word. I knew there was no way to stop a miscarriage once the process started. I was just simply hoping that my body wouldn't continue to rebel against me.

The cramping in my body continued as I knew it was my body's way of expelling my child. I simply laid back, allowed the tears to coat my cheeks, and closed my eyes.

As I lay with my eyes closed, I heard the nurse say something about getting a doctor and wanting to know if I needed to contact someone.

Sadly, I didn't want Dennard here. Of course, it was his child, but I didn't want to face him. Not right now. Dennard knew me and only saw me as a powerful woman, and I refused to allow him to see me as weak.

I never opened my mouth to bless them with a response. I simply remained still with my eyes closed, thinking about nothing else but revenge.

…

Into the Hood: Pierre & Anneka

Mount Sinai was said to be the best hospital in all of Manhattan, but I begged to differ.

Two days later, an empty, baby-less stomach and one hell of a dilation and curettage procedure later, the doctors here decided to release me. I was in pain from the scraping of my uterine lining, yet all I could think about was revenge.

"Ms. Vanzant, will you be having someone to pick you up?" the discharge nurse questioned.

"I didn't have anyone drop me off," I sassed as she handed me a bag, which held my bloody jumpsuit.

Looking down at the scrubs that I was wearing, my spirit was angered. I stood to my feet and walked to the wheelchair and sat down. The discharge nurse placed my papers in my lap and began to wheel me to the exit door. I guess she wanted to give me a textbook speech that I didn't want or ask for. "Know that there's life after a miscarriage," she spoke, and I looked at her with so much disgust

I stated, "Know that there's mints after brushing and flossing."

The look on her face was priceless, and I stood with the last ounce of dignity left within and got up from the wheelchair and put on my best strut to my car. Getting into my car was an immediate reminder of my loss. The blood stains were yet fresh on my leather seats, and I made a mental note to have it all cleaned.

I arrived home in twenty minutes, only to find Dennard getting dressed to go out.

"And just where do you think you're going?"

"Ivanka, don't start that shit. You play disappearing acts all the fucking time, and I'm not allowed to ask you questions while you're working, or should I say working Senator Snow."

"What does that mean, Dennard?"

"It means that I'm tired of your shit—the obsession over his daughter, him, his money. It's all too much. Why the fuck are you wearing scrubs, and is that blood on the side?"

I looked at my side and closed my eyes. I tried to find the right words to say to get Dennard on the right track because he was certainly going to help me get my revenge.

"Honey, I was in the hospital. I lost our baby."

"Ivanka, here we go with this shit! Cut the shit! What's going on?"

"Here, have a look for yourself." I tossed the papers his way, and he began to scan the paperwork, and then his eyes found mine.

Dennard rushed to my side and began planting kisses on my face and lips, offering up his apologies.

"Why didn't you call me, baby? I'd been calling and texting you for the last two days. I figured you were with Leo and decided not to pursue this thing with us. I'm so sorry that you had to go through that alone. I would have been there."

"Well, you're here now, and I need your help."

"What do you need? I'm here, baby. Anything you need, just ask."

"I'm glad you said that because I need you, all of you, and need for you to understand that this isn't a joke. Now that there's no baby, all of the plans that we'd made are null and void. The only thing I have left to attack that man's money is the policy that I have on him and his darling daughter. I have no idea where Idris is, and I need this taken care of today. I'm going to rest now."

I left Dennard with my words. With any luck, payday would be here soon.

Chapter 34- Anneka

3 days later

It had been a few days now since I'd been here at Pierre's house. Things had been strangely normal, and I was finally understanding that there was so much more to life than hiding in fear.

I'd just finished my morning run and internal talk with my mom, and I was ready to jumpstart my day. I was on the porch, stretching out my limbs and thinking about how funny life had been.

I'd gone from having no friends, to one friend who wanted to beat me up, to a host of men who simply adored me enough to not bring harm to me. I took in the fresh air, enjoyed the beauty of the neighborhood, and let myself back in to freshen up.

I was nervous and excited about today because I finally got to feel what it was like to be my normal self. I was going back to the city. I guess you would think I'd be afraid, but I was ready to take on anything that came my way, and my confirmation came from me hearing my mom's voice telling me that things would be alright.

I'd talked it over with Pierre a few nights ago, and he said that he would have his mom take me into the city to see Mr. Martin. I didn't know much about Mr. Martin, but he made sure to tell me that my mom was special, and he offered his deepest condolences. When I spoke to him the other day, he made it clear that he must see me to sign some important papers and had something that my mom instructed him to give me. Knowing this, it brought me peace to simply know that I was going to receive some form of closure when it came to my mom.

I heard the door as I proceeded to walk up the stairs and stopped in my tracks to see Mrs. Charming struggling with groceries bags. I ran down to help her, and she spoke.

"Thank you, dear. Let me hurry to put away these groceries. I don't want to be late taking you down to that attorney. That son of mine said that he has something important to talk to you about, so he needed us to come right back."

"Not a problem. I just want to meet with Mr. Martin and pretend that everything in my life is completely normal."

"It will be, dear. Don't you worry. It will be."

"Thanks so much for everything, Mrs. Charming. You have truly made these last few days tolerable for me. I was sitting on this phone and found myself playing games more so than talking to people. I only talk to you, Pierre, and Bernard. I was thinking about asking Pierre for Regina's number. I think we should talk."

"You're better than me. I wouldn't be bothered with that girl, but I understand you kids need friends and whatnot."

"It's not that I need them. I just wanted to mend that one because of what she did for me with helping me to properly say goodbye to my mom. I never had friends, so I wanted to cherish that one."

"Well, I can surely understand that, but um, dear, have you thought about calling your father?" When Mrs. Charming asked me that question, I had to suppress my anger. The things that my own father did to me and the constant pain of his doing was far too much for me to consider dialing his number.

I looked at Mrs. Charming and boldly replied, "I have, but I left that as a thought. I refuse to call that man."

"No matter what, Anneka, he's your father, and in order for you to completely heal, you must start with forgiving. I'm not saying it's going to happen immediately, but I think you need to start with some counseling, and then when you're up to it, give it a try. You said it yourself that he might have had a change of heart because something was different when you watched your mother's service on television. Anneka, dear, I'm not your mother, and I'm certainly not trying to replace her—"

I interrupted her because I felt that I knew where she was going with this conversation.

"Mrs. Charming, you are the only person that I've come in contact with that has offered me anything close to stability. You may not be my mom, but right now, I'm telling you that I'm enjoying your company and your wisdom. Thank you for bringing peace during the midst of my storm."

"You don't have to thank me, dear."

"Well, I'll consider calling him, but right now, I know I'm not ready, especially with him constantly sending people to kill me," I stated and was tearing up.

"Sweetheart, come here," she stated as she embraced me.

We stood in the kitchen as I laid my head on her shoulder and accepted the comfort that she offered.

"A beautiful sight for tired eyes," Pierre's voice interrupted our moment.

"Hi, son. How was your night?"

"Long. I had a lot of business I needed to handle, and I need to talk to you, Anneka. This is important." The tone in Pierre's voice let me know that something wasn't right.

"Sure. What's wrong?" I questioned.

Just as he was about to say something, Bernard rushed in.

"Pierre, come quick. You need to handle a situation," Bernard said as they both rushed out of the door in a haste.

Mrs. Charming and I stood dumbfounded as we stared at each other in disbelief.

"I wonder what that is about," I said, and Mrs. Charming placed one arm around my neck and held my hand with the other hand.

"My dear Anneka, if I never teach you anything else, don't get involved in business between men," she informed.

"Now, go get dressed so that we can head on out to see your attorney."

…

Into the Hood: Pierre & Anneka

Walking through the corridor of Mr. Martin's building, so many emotions were running through my body, and I began to feel a little uncomfortable. I didn't know what he had to tell me that was so urgent, but whatever it was it sounded serious.

"Are you alright, my dear?" Mrs. Charming asked as she wrapped her arm around mine.

"Yes, I'm fine. It's just that I'm a little nervous. Perhaps frightened," I answered.

"No need to worry, Anneka. I'm right here with you," she affirmed as we made it to the set of glass double doors that led to his office.

As we approached the receptionist desk, I put my head down and spoke, saying, "I'm here to see Mr. Martin."

I never lifted my head or eyes, and the receptionist replied, "Anneka Snow, he's been waiting on you. Don't worry. He already informed me that you would be here. Head straight back through the glass doors. You're going to be safe."

I guess if I weren't technically hiding from my father, her comment would have seemed a bit off, but knowing that my face was all over the news, I guess she wanted to assure me that she wasn't for any funny business.

I began walking, and a handsome gentleman who I knew to be Mr. Martin approached the door. He looked just like his picture on Yelp when I looked up his information.

I slowly began walking, and the closer I got to him, the wider his smile became. He seemed pleasant and very eager to have me here, so I guess you could say that I was eager to know why it was so imperative to have me meet him today.

"Anneka, you didn't tell me that your attorney was so handsome," Mrs. Charming stated, surprising me.

"Mrs. Charming, you're a married woman." I giggled.

She looked at me with raised brows. "Honey, I'm married. Not dead. It's nothing wrong with a little eye candy from time to time." She chuckled as she shrugged her shoulders.

As we entered Mr. Martin's office, I stared at him, trying to take in his features. It was something very familiar about his eyes, but I couldn't put my finger on it. He wasn't a tall man, but he wasn't exactly short either.

He had to stand about 5'10, and even though he was a little thick, he seemed to be fit.

"Come on in, Anneka. Have a seat." He motioned for me to sit in the chair adjacent to his desk.

"Mr. Martin this is—" I started, but Mrs. Charming cut me off.

"Charming, Pamela Charming," she introduced herself as she extended her hand for a shake.

"Mrs. Charming… indeed." He shook her hand then returned to his seat.

Mr. Martin ran his fingers through his jet-black hair, making his strong facial features stand out. His narrow nose widened at the bottom and had a cute little ball. His eyes were big and bright and slanted slightly at the corners. He had full lips that sat quite nicely in his well-trimmed goatee. This man was handsome, and I could see why my mother chose him as an attorney.

"Anneka, sweetheart. I asked you here today to show you a video that your mother made and sent to me in the event of her death. I'm sure that this will be tough for you—"

"She what? I'm, um, sorry, what did she send you?"

"Sweetheart, allow him to explain. I'm right here with you. It may be a last will or something, dear," Mrs. Charming spoke.

I turned my attention to Mr. Martin and stated, "I'm sorry. Please, continue."

"Well, Anneka, before we can continue our conversation, I must play this," he explained as he grabbed the remote.

"Would you like to view this alone?" he asked.

I shook my head as I grabbed Mrs. Charming's hand for support.

Mr. Martin hit a button on the remote, and doors on the wall unit slid open, revealing a TV. He hit play, and my mother appeared on the screen, looking beautiful, as usual, wearing the dress that she had on the night of my father's last dinner party. As happy tears began to roll down my face, my mother began to speak.

"My dear, sweet Neka Pooh. I'm sorry that I had to leave you so soon, but you know we had this conversation for a while, so I would like to think that I'd prepared you for this. Dry your eyes, my sweet Neka Pooh. Mommy is no longer in pain. The pain that you're feeling in my absence will get better with each passing day. Look. Mommy even got all dressed up while you are on your run just so I can show you that I'm trying to be the queen you always saw in me."

She stood up and turned around for the camera and then took her seat and continued.

"You see how I'm filling out? Well, that's because of you. You followed your heart when it came to finding Dr. Brown, and I'm in the best health that I've ever been in. Well, I won't hold you long, because I'm sure you're crying your eyes out since I'm gone, but I want to say, Anneka Snow, I love you; you are and always were my heart and forever my true love. I left you something, and it's all yours. All you have to do is sign on the dotted line. Robert will walk you through the details. There's something else that you will find out, but Robert knows when to give you that recording. I love you, my sweet Anneka Pooh. Mommy is flying high."

The recording went off, and I couldn't help the tears. Mrs. Charming was consoling me as my shoulders shook rapidly as I unleashed all my hurt and pain into her lap.

Finally gaining my composure, I looked at Mr. Martin in his eyes and said, "May I please watch the other recording?"

He looked at me and replied, "In due time, my dear. In due time." He got me more tissue as I looked to him for answers. "Anneka, that envelope there, please open when you are alone. These papers here are the things that your mom left for you. I need your signature on the tabs that are marked, and it's showing that you have a house, car, money, and studio for your fitness training."

"What? How did she? When did she? This is all mine? All of that?" I was at a loss for words, as I couldn't process what was being said to me. I started reading and saw that my mom had a million-dollar insurance policy on herself and appointed me as the sole beneficiary.

I was pleased with what she left me, but I'd give it all back in a heartbeat just to have her here.

…

Two hours had passed, and we were finally finished with Mr. Martin and filling out papers and him explaining my next steps. I was emotionally drained and couldn't wait to get back to Pierre's and rest. Mr. Martin said that all I needed to do was reach out to him when I was ready to go get my new house and studio keys.

Into the Hood: Pierre & Anneka

This was all too much for me. It seemed as if my mom knew she was going to die. These documents for the house and studio were purchased within the last two weeks, and I still didn't have a clue as to the other video that she left.

Mr. Martin assured me that he needed to follow proper procedures so that nothing was compromised.

Mrs. Charming and I were walking back to the car. It had been one emotional ass afternoon.

"Thank you for bringing me here. I don't know if I could have made it through that alone."

"It's quite alright, dear. I'm glad that I could be that shoulder to lean on." We stepped outside, and I was walking with my head down while looking at a text from Pierre.

Pierre: U good?

Me: Yes, heading back now

With my head in my phone I bumped a lady, and her papers fell out of her hand.

"Oh, I'm so sorry," I spoke as I bent down to pick them up.

Placing them back into her hand, I looked up to a familiar face but couldn't place her right now. She never spoke, only stared, and then I apologized again.

"I'm sorry," I said as I hurried to the car where Mrs. Charming was standing with her hand on her purse.

I got into the car, and I could have sworn that lady was going into the attorney's building, but she turned on her heels and walked swiftly in the opposite direction.

"Rude bitches make me sick. I'm sorry, dear. I thought I was about to shoot that bitch."

"Mrs. Charming, you're so silly. I bumped her, so she was probably upset."

"Yeah, and you apologized, but she wanted to swell up her chest and turn up her nose. I know she didn't want these problems," Mrs. Charming said while touching her purse.

"You don't have a… gun, do you?

"Damn right. Just like my credit card, I never leave home without it."

I laughed, and oddly enough, I felt a little safer.

We headed back to Pierre's, and I closed my eyes, thinking of thoughts of my mom.

"Anneka, are you excited about what your mom left you? It seems like you can really get on your feet."

"Honestly, I'm not sure how to feel. I mean, it's definitely everything we talked about, but I just wish she was here to share it with me."

"You're going to always want that. She's not here physically, but she lives within you. Just make sure you do her proud."

…

Later on that night…

Mrs. Charming had just left, and we had a very deep discussion about my life, my goals, and my next moves. She was so involved with my well-being that I was getting so attached to her and close to calling her mom. I knew that Pierre and I weren't an item, but I also knew that he made my heart skip several beats. Then there was Bernard. He was so cute, and it seemed as if he was always trying to impress me when he should know by now that I only ever wanted him to be himself.

I'd turned off the lights in the living room and was heading up the stairs. The door popped open, and it was Pierre.

"Hey, you're home," I spoke with a smile.

"It's good to be home, and now I need to talk to you about a few things. Come here. Sit down."

Doing as he requested, I sat on the sofa next to him, giving him my undivided attention.

"How was your day? How are you feeling?" he asked with concern.

"To be honest, it was a bit emotional. I went to the attorney, saw a video of my mom, which I get to keep and torture myself with later. I received information about the money and things she left for me, which I wanted to talk to you about because I think it's time for me to get up and out on my own."

"Anneka, sweetheart, it sounds like you had a pretty full day, and believe me, I don't want to lay anything else on you. I'm sorry that you had to see your mom on video, but I'm also glad that you have your independence. That's something that you said you wanted and used to talk to your mom about. I'm not sure about how I feel with you wanting to leave me. Can we save that part of the conversation for later? Sweetie, I know you're going to be fine, but I kind of want you here with me just for a bit," he avowed, actually impressing me that he paid attention to our conversations about my independence but making me nervous at the same time with talks about me staying here.

"I know I'll be fine. Today was rough. It really had me thinking, but I'm glad your mom was there the entire way. Her support was appreciated and needed. She's such a sweet lady."

"Yeah, she's pretty damn cool, but hey, be honest with me, are you feeling me?"

"Pierre, I wasn't expecting you to ask me that," I nervously spoke, not really sure how to tell him my answer.

"Just be honest. I do notice the smiles and the stares, but you also get all happy and giddy when Bernard is around, and to keep it buck, I know he has eyes for you. You feeling him or me? I just need to know."

"Well, to be quite honest, Pierre, you're every bit of your name—charming… When I needed you most, it was you who went out your way to make sure I was not only safe, but I was able to regain a fraction of my life and sanity back. Then there's Bernard. The day I lost my mom, I ran into him, and without hesitation, he extended himself in a way that I could never repay him."

"So you want us both?"

"I'm not saying that. I'm saying that I never had a boyfriend, a man, hell, not even friends. Whatever this is that I'm feeling when I see you, I would like to explore, but I'd be lying if I said that I didn't want to explore feelings that I have for Bernard."

"Well, I'm telling you I want you. I mean, really want you in my life. All of this, this life that you've been enjoying, you can continue to enjoy, but I want you to enjoy it with me. I don't care what you have or inherited. I got my own, but what I don't have is you."

I put my head down and began playing with my fingers. Everything he was saying, he was making me want to give in to him.

Lifting my chin with his finger, he stared into my eyes. I felt my treasure box seeping as I knew I was ready to take the next step.

"Anneka, tell me you want me," he urged, and I lost my breath.

I was saved by the ringing of his phone. He stood to answer it and walked into his office.

I rubbed my sweaty palms on my legs and began to coach myself. *Anneka, you got this. He's one sexy ass man, but you got this. Calm down. You're strong, you're beautiful, and you deserve to have real love.*

I stood to my feet to shake my nerves, Pierre came out of his office with a look of worry on his face. He excused himself and walked out the door, and I heard the chirp of his alarm.

Walking back into the house, I saw that he was holding two phones.

"Anneka, I need to talk to you, beautiful."

"We were talking."

"I know, but there's something that I've been trying to tell you and just couldn't seem to get it out." Pierre stood in my face and told me everything that happened with my father. He also said that my father wanted to see me, but Pierre didn't think it was a good idea and might be a trap.

"How could you? You were doing all of this, and you encourage me to be honest with you, but you couldn't be honest with me."

"Anneka, it's not like that, sweetheart. Everything I did, I did it with you in mind. Even Bernard—"

"So Bernard's in on this too? So am I a big joke to you all? Let's see who bags the young, dumb one first?"

"Not at all, baby girl. Listen to me. When I saw your dad the other night, I had no idea he was going to be there. Like I said, that was all Sebastian's doing."

"So when were you going to tell me this? Why did you all hide it?"

"Anneka, trust me. I wanted to tell you. All types of crazy shit went on in my head the moment I saw him."

"Why didn't you try harder? What did he say?"

"It's not about what he said, sweetheart. I'm simply telling you this because I'm on the fence. He's begging to see you and acting like shit's sweet, and truthfully, I can't call it."

"Fuck it! I'm going to see him. I'm not running anymore. Today, I promised myself to take back my life, and that's exactly what I'm going to do."

"Sweetheart, you don't want to go alone. If you would wait until morning, I'll take you."

"No, I'm going now. He's going to constantly come after me. He's taken everything from me. There's no way I can keep running from him. I have to go and face him."

"Well, if you face him, he has to face me."

"No, this is not your fight. The fact that you have him contained is all I need. I have to see his eyes; I have to talk to him tonight! Please give me your keys and the address. I'll be fine."

"Listen to me. I know you want this over and done with, and I do too, but baby, you're not going alone.

My conscious won't allow me to let that go down like that. If you feel like you have to go now, I'm going to take you, and I swear to you, if the muthafucka buck, I'm taking his ass out."

"Please, just allow me to do this alone."

"I can't, Anneka. You have already touched a part of my heart that I never knew existed. If you are determined to face him, you will face him with me. There's nothing else to discuss. Now what's it gonna be?"

We looked into each other's eyes as butterflies began to tickle my stomach. I knew this was the moment that I'd been waiting for. I'd seen it in the movies a million times, and now it was my time to experience this.

The door creaked open, and we turned to see what could only be described as the seed of Satan.

"Well, well, well… I almost missed a beautiful, enchanted kiss. Pardon my tardiness. Had I known it was going to be this congenial, I would have baked a pie. Now tell me which one of you muthafuckas are ready to die?"

That voice was familiar, and so was that face. My heartbeat began to pick up speed as fear finally snuck in. I wanted this hunt to end, and the only way to end it was to face my fears.

So much was taken from me, and now I must do what my mom told me to do. FIGHT!

"Bitch! It's you! You're the bitch that stopped my mom's service! You're the bitch that I bumped earlier this afternoon. Who the fuck are you, and why are you here?" I yelled, walking up in her face.

"Were you really going to kiss her with that filthy mouth?" the bitch asked. I didn't know her name, and seeing her in Pierre's house angered me, and all I could call her was a bitch.

"Are you that Ivanka bitch? I been looking for yo' ass! You get my gift?" Pierre interrogated.

"So my brother. That was from you? This is indeed my lucky day. Vengeance is mine!" the bitch who I now know as Ivanka stated.

"Ahhh!" I screamed, charging at this evil looking bitch. Everything was going so fast that I didn't see her pull out a gun.

Pow! was all I heard as a stinging sensation penetrated my body as my body fell to the floor.

"Bitch!"

Pow! Pow! Pow!

Into the Hood: Pierre & Anneka

I heard Pierre scream, and then everything went black

Chapter 35- Leo

1 year later

What have I done? was the question I'd asked myself a million times standing at the bedside of my beloved daughter, Anneka.

It had been a year since Anneka was shot and slipped into a coma. The doctors seemed to think that there was nothing else to be done, and the best option now was for me to pull the plug.

A year ago, when all of this started, I would have pulled the plug instantly, but now, seeing her laying here, lifeless and looking just like her mother has me doubtful and torn between what I should do and what I wanted to do.

No one should have to suffer and allow machines to breathe for them, but in the same breath, no one deserved the pain that I deliberately caused. The nurse walked in to check her vitals, and I had to ask this question.

"Excuse me, nurse. What would you do?"

"I'm sorry, Mr. Snow. I don't understand your question."

"What would you do if you were in my shoes?"

"Mr. Snow, there's my professional thoughts and my personal thoughts, but ultimately, the choice is yours."

"Tell me. What would you do? Please?"

"Honestly, even though surgery went well, and the bullet has been removed from her neck, Anneka is still unresponsive and showing no signs of improvement. In my professional opinion, nothing more could be done; however, personally, my faith has shown me that God is a miracle worker. If you are a praying man, I would advise seeking an answer from God because it is He who orders and guides our steps throughout this maze that we call life."

She tapped my shoulder and left out the room. Cameras immediately started flashing when Anneka's door opened, and I was beyond frustrated.

Things had become a shit show for the media, and this was definitely not the attention I wanted or needed.

As I stood here with my heart wrapped with sorrow, I tried to stop the mental torture of knowing that I was the cause of this and all because of power and the love of money. No amount of power or money could ever replace what Anneka meant to me as a daughter. I was now the Governor, and it didn't mean shit without being able to right my wrongs with Anneka. I stepped closer to her bed and began to speak as if I knew she could hear me.

"Anneka, I'm sorry for all the pain that I've caused you. It was just a little over a year ago today that I committed the most heinous act that a husband could ever do to his wife. I've been a terrible father to you, Anneka, but I've been an even worst husband to your mother. Honestly, I loved you and Eva, but I let my thirst for greed and power lead me to make decisions against my family, and that guilt I have to live with for the rest of my days."

As I held my daughter's hand, wishing that I had more time with her, I drifted back to the day I held the pillow over the love of my life's face and spoke the most terrible words to her. Tears formed in my eyes. The man that I'd become wasn't the man that I was, and now I would never get to be the father to Anneka that she deserves.

The opening of the door caught my attention, and my eyes fell upon the most beautiful woman I'd seen other that Eva. She had the face of an angel and a body that looked as if she spent hours in the gym to perfect her hourglass figure. With big, beautiful, oval-shaped eyes that slanted in the corners, she held a seductive gaze as she strutted across the room with so much confidence that it seems as if she demanded respect with each step.

"Hello, I'm Leopold Snow, and you are?" I greeted with my hand extended for a shake.

The lovely lady took my hand. "No need for the introduction, Governor Snow. I know who you are. I'm Pamela, Pamela Charming," she introduced with the sweetest sounding voice.

"Pleased to me you, Ms. Charming. Is there a Mr. Charming?" I asked, turning on my own charm. I had always had a way with the ladies, and judging from the gorgeous smile that was plastered on her face, Pamela Charming was no exception. Before she could part her lips to answer my question, Pierre entered the room with Sebastian and the other four gentlemen that had been in Anneka's life.

"Yeah, there's a Mr. Charming. Now back the fuck up out of my mother's face," Pierre commanded, and I was still stunned by her beauty. I stepped back and allowed her to get closer to Anneka.

"Pierre, there's no need to be rude. Besides, I can handle myself." Pamela turned her attention back to me as she stood at Anneka's side. I'd never met this woman before, but I heard that a woman would come up often and read to Anneka. I had no idea it was this gorgeous woman.

"Governor Snow, you ought to be ashamed of yourself. We are here to say goodbye to your daughter, and you're making a pass at a happily married woman. What type of man are you?"

"Obviously, not a man at his best. My apologies to you, Mrs. Charming. Old habits are hard to break," I stated as I offered her my sincerest apology.

"Yeah, well you better find a way to break yo' habits before I break them for you," Pierre warned as he and the other gentlemen made their way over to Anneka's bedside.

"I hate hospitals," the one I'd come to know as Geovanni grumbled as he sat down in the chair with a mug on his face.

"Shut the hell up, Geovanni. I'm tired of yo' grumpy ass always talking about what the fuck you hate. We are here to say goodbye to a girl that we've grown to love, and before you say anything, we all know that you love Anneka as much as we do," Harper said, and everyone peered at him in surprise.

Geovanni held his head down in shame. "You're right, Harper. I do love her as much as the rest of you. It's just hard for me to say it. This is hard for me, Harper," Geovanni confessed.

"Gentleman, thank you all for coming. I know that you all met her because of me and my actions. I want to thank you all for being a protector over her. I want you all to know that this is indeed truly hard for me—" I spoke and was interrupted by the door opening.

"Did they do it? Did they pull the plug?" Bernard stormed in a bit upset with a bouquet of roses.

"Come on in. She's still with us now. I haven't asked them to pull it yet," I commented, and Bernard immediately started crying.

"This is tough on us all, and I truly want to thank you all for the things that you all did to get me to the place that I am today."

The door opened again, and it was a young lady with pink hair, long nails, a basket full of apples, and oversized glasses.

"Excuse me. I know y'all being all sentimental and errrthang, but damn, can a bitch state her peace?"

"Young lady, that mouth of yours!" Mrs. Charming stated.

"Hey, big bourgeois. I just needed to holla at lil' bourgeois," the young lady stated, and we all simply looked at this display that she was putting on.

Things got quiet, and she began speaking. 'Lil' Bourgeois, first off, I'm sorry for accusing you of that shit that I know wasn't yo' fault. That no good nigga Drake been doing the dummy for a minute, so I shouldn't have come at you like that. It's been a minute because I was embarrassed as shit how I acted toward you, but you were becoming my best bitch, and a bitch need some oils, so try to wake up real quick for a real bitch 'cause they trying to pull the plug on yo' ass."

I guess that was her way of getting out her apology. I cleared my throat, and the young lady stood with tears rolling down her face.

I tried to continue speaking my heart, but then, one by one, everyone wanted to say something about Anneka. It truly spoke volumes to her character that she touched so many lives in a short amount of time.

Into the Hood: Pierre & Anneka

Just as Pierre finished what he wanted to say, I called for the doctor to come in so that we could watch Anneka take her last breath.

"I love you, Anneka, and I'm sorry I wasn't the best that I could be." I kissed her cheek, and then, one by one, the men and Mrs. Charming began placing kisses on her body.

The door opened, and I thought it was the doctor until I locked eyes with a man I hadn't seen in more than a month of Sundays.

"What are you doing here?" I asked as Robert walked in with a jewelry box.

"Leo, you know I have every right to be here, and I've been keeping up with Mrs. Charming on the condition of Anneka."

"You know what I discussed with you, and now is certainly not the time to bring yo' ass in here."

"Leo, you can't make me leave. According to this, it's not your call. It's my call," Robert announced, and all eyes were directed toward us.

"Fuck those papers!"

"Leo, I'm not here to stop anything that you have already started. I just wanted a chance to put this on her and tell her the truth while there's a chance that she might still hear me."

I stepped to the side and allowed him to do as he pleased.

Robert took out a diamond apple necklace and pendant and placed it around Anneka. He then began to speak. "Anneka, you met me as Mr. Martin, but I'm your biological father. I've loved you from the first time I heard about you growing in Eva's belly. Each year, I would wait for pictures and a full-written report about what you loved, your hopes, and dreams. It wasn't that I was out of your life because I wanted to be, but out of respect for your mother's wishes and marriage, I supported financially from afar. Every day for the last nineteen years, I've waited and wanted you. I wish I could have told you everything when you came to my office, but that wasn't the plan that I made with Eva. I love you, my sweet daughter. You are the apple of my eye."

He wrapped and secured the necklace around her as tears spilled from his eyes. He sat at the side of the bed and laid his head on her shoulder as he cried like a newborn baby. Looking around the room, there wasn't a dry eye in sight. I knew I told him to go away and never show his face because he was the man that Eva had an affair with only after her finding out about my many affairs. Eva knew how much that hurt me, and I probably still wouldn't have found out, but she wanted me to hurt just as much as I hurt her.

Watching Robert pour out his heart to Anneka made me feel worse because he would have been a much better father to her than I'd ever been. I guess you could say that I treated my daughter like shit because I knew deep down she wasn't mine, and I resented her and her mom for that.

The doctor explained to us all what was going to happen. We gathered around Anneka's bed as the doctor slowly began unhooking things and turning off her machines. It was time for the last machine to be turned off, and Robert bent down, kissed her cheek, and then…

"Aaaahhhh!"

Chapter 36- Anneka

5 Months Later

As I sit here in a much better headspace, I'm excited that my mom taught me forgiveness. Forgiveness simply put is just letting go. I knew my story wasn't going to be pretty, but the things that I went through made me a stronger and wiser woman today.

Being in that coma caused me to really see things as they were. I finally got everything that I'd ever wanted, and my natural products are sold in many major retail stores, and I can't be happier with it. I also have one of the best health and fitness studios that Manhattan has ever seen, and pretty soon, I'll be opening up another one in the Bronx.

In the beginning of my tale, I told you that I liked to think of myself as the fairest of them all. I've always tried to see the good in people, and I'm sure that's part of the reason why I'm so successful.

The day I woke up, I woke up to a world that existed with new hope, new beginnings, and everlasting love. As hard as it was for me to forgive my father for taking my beautiful mom away from me, I had to really soul search and find a way to forgive him because I knew that was what my mom would have wanted. Who would have thought my father, Leopold Snow, a man who was once green with envy, now has a heart of gold.

I found a wonderful friend in Regina, who is constantly teaching me the way of the hood, and every day, there's something new to learn.

Mrs. Charming has become more of a mentor to me and a true mother figure in my eyes.

I've met my biological father, who I like to think of as my angel because he provided me with my true love's kiss.

I may not be Snow White, but throughout my journey, I was met with seven men who became my protectors. They may have been strange to me at first, but the bond that they shared amongst each other was like nothing I'd ever seen, and in their own way, each of the men taught me something different to add to the life skills that was taught by my mother.

Bernard, bashful, and sweet. He taught me that there are some genuinely kind people in this world full of greed and chaos. Sebastian, with his sneezy self, taught me that people are full of surprises, and just because a person does bad things doesn't mean that they are bad person. Dakota, I like to call him Doc, taught me that you may stumble over your words, but if you take a moment to collect your thoughts, you can be heard loud and clear.

Then there's Seth, he taught me that sometimes, we need to take a break to just relax and unwind. Drake, even though he was a dope head, he taught me how to have fun and not take life so seriously. Harper, always so happy. He taught me to always find positivity in even the most negative situations. Geovanni. What can I say about his grumpy ass? He taught me that even the coldest of hearts can soften at times, and through all the hate, there's love.

Finally, there's Pierre, a very charming but wise young man—a prince in his own right. He taught me many lessons, but the main lesson I learned from him is to stop running, be brave, and fight for what you want.

These men gave me the tools that I needed to move forward with my life, and for that, I will forever be grateful; but my story hasn't really ended. This is only the beginning. Pardon me as I take a walk down the aisle to accept my true love's hand in marriage.

…

As I walked down the corridor of the beautifully decorated St. Patrick's Cathedral in my mother's redesigned wedding gown, I was met by both of my fathers. Leo, stood at my right, and Robert stood at my left. They each wrapped their arm around mine as I held on to the apple-shaped red, blue, and yellow bouquet of gorgeous flowers.

"You look as lovely as your mother did on our wedding day," Leo complimented as he placed a kiss on my cheek.

"I have to agree with Leo. You look simply amazing, darling, and I'm grateful that you let me be a part of your special day," Robert said before planting a kiss on my other cheek.

"Of course. You are my father. I feel like the luckiest girl in the world. I have two dads who love me unconditionally, and for that, I'm more than grateful," I stated as tears started to form in my eyes. Leo and Robert both took out their handkerchiefs and started dabbing the tears away.

Eric Benet's "Spend My Life with You" started playing, and that was my cue that it was time for me to make my entrance.

"Are you ready?" Leo asked. I nodded my head, and both my dads opened the doors and led me down the aisle to take the hand of my very own Prince Charming.

Into the Hood: Pierre & Anneka

Epilogue

Anneka

"I invite you all to stand," I heard the pastor say as the doors opened for me to make my entrance.

Butterflies began to dance in the pit of my stomach. I closed my eyes and took in a deep breath to calm my nerves. I opened my eyes and was taken by surprise as everyone rose to their feet and stared at me with so much love and admiration. It was such a loving and emotional moment. It was almost impossible to keep myself together. I began to tremble as I held the attention of everyone in the church.

Am I moving too fast? Am I too young for this? What the hell am I doing? I internally asked myself.

Standing at the door and waiting to start my march, my father Leo spoke. "You'll be fine."

I looked at him for comfort, and then Daddy Robert spoke. "Do you remember that other recording I was supposed to give you?"

I quickly shook my head, and he pointed in the direction of the pastor. When Daddy Robert nodded, a monitor scrolled down, and my mother appeared.

"Anneka, my sweet darling. You better not get your makeup all messed up. You're such a beautiful bride, and I know this because you were always a beautiful young lady. I'm watching over you and know that your father more than likely did the right thing. Leo, thank you for accepting our princess, and Robert, you are such an amazing man. Neka Pooh, on this day, do not dwell on the fact that I'm not standing at your side. Celebrate this day, and take the hand of your prince. Young man, whoever you are, take care of my Neka Pooh. Love her, honor her, respect her, and make sure she's the apple of your eye. I love you forever, darling. Wipe your eyes, and I'll be waiting on you on the other side."

The monitor went off, and there wasn't a dry eye in the cathedral. My daddy Robert took out his handkerchief and dabbed at my eyes and kissed my cheek. After we all collected ourselves, I had the answers to all of my questions and was ready to take the hand of my prince.

Looking straight forward, I spotted Regina and Laquanda standing at the end of the aisle with tears in their eyes and smiles plastered on their faces. Laquanda curled my tresses to perfection, and I marveled at how gorgeous she and Regina looked as my bridesmaids.

Into the Hood: Pierre & Anneka

With my fathers by my side, I began to march down the aisle right at the crescendo of the song. You would have thought I was in a marching band as fast as I got to my prince. As I took the hand of the man that I fell for the moment I laid eyes on him, my heart started beating at a rapid pace.

"You look stunning, simply stunning," Pierre mouthed as he stood before me dressed in an all-white tux trimmed in gold, looking as handsome as ever. Waiting for the song to end, we stood silently, looking at each other, holding hands, and trying our hardest not break down. The music stopped, and the pastor began the ceremony.

"You may all be seated," he announced and waited for everyone to take their seats.

"We have come together at the invitation of Anneka and Pierre to celebrate their union and their hearts in love. To the bride and groom, as you enter into this holy estate, remember that no other human ties or vows are more sacred than these that you are about to assume. Your lives are not united by this ceremony but only by the power, love, and grace of God. May you continue to grow in love, respect, and faith. Now, who gives this woman's hand in marriage to this man?"

Both of my fathers stepped forward. “We do,” they said; then they both gave me a kiss on the cheek and took their seats in the front row.

The pastor acknowledged their declaration then announced that Pierre and I had written our own vows. As Pierre started reciting his vows, our ceremony was interrupted.

“Stop!” Bernard shouted from the crowd.

Pierre and I stared at him with confusion written on our faces as Bernard started to approach the alter.

“I’m sorry to interrupt, but I can’t let this happen unless I know for sure,” he stated as Pierre walked up on him.

“What the hell are you doing, Bernard?” he questioned through clenched teeth, trying his best to remain calm.

“I’m sorry, Pierre. I have to know.” Bernard gazed deeply into my eyes.

“Anneka, you know how I feel about you. I love you, and I want to be the man you marry. We shared a connection, and I know you have feelings for me. If it’s any chance for us, you can’t marry him.” His eyes started to fill with tears.

My heart was pounding. I cared a lot about Bernard, and I didn't want to see his feelings hurt, but I had to be honest with him.

I took a step down and stood by Pierre's side, "Bernard, you're right. We did share a connection, but I think you have mistaken the nature of our relationship. I love you, yes, just as I love all of you. I will forever be grateful for all you did for me, but I'm sorry Bernard. Pierre and I connected on a different level, and it's him who holds my heart and my love, so yes, as a dear friend, I love you, but I'm in love with Pierre."

My soon to be mother-in-law stood and shouted, "That's right, daughter! Confess your heart to my son and your man."

The crowd chuckled, and that lightened the mood and eased the dagger that I'd just tossed into Bernard's heart. With empathy in my eyes, I simply said, "I'm sorry, Bernard."

Bernard nodded his head. "Very well," he stated as he took my hand and placed into Pierre's hand.

"Anneka, all I want is for you to be happy, and if it's Pierre who makes you happy, then I'll be happy for the both of you and give you both my blessing."

Turning to Pierre, Bernard reached out his hand and extended it for a handshake.

"I'm sorry. I had to know, but now that I do, I can live with it. It seems as if you have taken another woman from me. You have won, my brother," Bernard said to Pierre.

Pierre shook his head, "Naw, we all won. You once told me that I will meet a woman that would make me change my ways, and I laughed in yo' face. Well, for me, Anneka is that woman. She makes me want to be a better man and an overall better person. I think she does that to us all. We are all blessed to have her as a part of our lives."

Bernard nodded in agreement; then he gave Pierre a brotherly hug. "I'm sorry for the interruption, everyone. Pastor, please continue the ceremony," Bernard stated as he stood in line with the other groomsmen.

After Pierre and I shared our vows, thc pastor announced us as husband and wife. We jumped the broom and walked hand and hand down the aisle and out of the church to start our new lives as Mr. and Mrs. Pierre Charming. I loved the sound of that.

...

Into the Hood: Pierre & Anneka

Wedding night

I stood at the foot of the bed, dressed in a sexy white lingerie set that Regina bought me. I was nervous, and my body showed. All of the things that Regina and Laquanda coached me on went out of the window. My husband was lying there just as sexy as he wanted to be, and I was nervous as hell, trying not to make a mistake and mess up our night.

"Damn, wife. You look sexy as hell. Come here. You can't make me wait anymore," Pierre said in a low voice as his lust-filled eyes scanned the length of my body.

I was feeling embarrassed and somewhat uncomfortable, but the soothing tone of Pierre's voice and the gentleness of his touch somehow made me feel a bit more at ease. Pierre kissed me with so much passion than I'd ever felt from him before. I made him wait this entire time, and now it was time to give my husband a gift that I'd never given to another man.

When Pierre entered me, I felt as if the breath was leaving out of my body. He taught me how to please him, and I found out things that I loved him doing to me. The range of feelings that took over my body was something that I wasn't sure that I could possibly explain.

That night, I made love for the very first time. It was everything I ever imagined it to be, and it was with my husband as I always intended it to be. Pierre was gentle and passionate, he took his time with me, and he made sure that I was comfortable during every moment, and as we lay in each other's arms, I knew that I had made the right choice. Pierre was my forever, and I was certain that I'd found my happily ever after.

"I love you, Mrs. Charming."

"And me you, Mr. Charming."

Pierre was still inside me as he held me close to him. The sound of our hearts beating as one was something more than delightful. It was enchanting.

"Will you be mine forever, Mrs. Charming?"

"Forever and a day, Mr. Charming."

The End

Into the Hood: Pierre & Anneka

From Author Ms. T. Nicole

There are so many emotions that are going through my head when I look at the catalogue of books that I have. When it comes to the **readers**, you all are amazing. Without readers there's no need for my pen to keep moving, but you all have shown me so much love and I appreciate each and every last one of you who like, share, read and review my work. I wish I could thank you all individually, but out of fear of leaving someone out, I would simply say thank you to any and all of my readers. **Bookies**, my new favorite group on Facebook who make me want to bring my A game each time I put pen to paper. I thank you all for your support and love and accepting me and my pen. My mom always said that my gift would make room for me and I'm excited to see where this will take me. **Treasure**, not only are you an amazing author, but you are a great publisher, I thank you for this platform so that I'm able to get my work out to the masses. **TP family**, you ladies are amazing and I'm overjoyed with the amount of support that comes from our team. Continued blessings to you all. **Bianca, Sunny Giovanni, Dee Ann, Ms Brii, Hadiya** you ladies rock and I thank you all for your undying love and support for my pen. Several times I wanted to give up but you all wrapped your sisterly love around me and helped me to continue my journey and I'm forever grateful. **Reign, and Annitia** I just want to thank you both for always having your inbox and phone opened to me whenever I need you. Reign it's been a bit over a year and you're still rocking with me and I love and appreciate you. Annitia, God knew exactly what he was doing when he placed you in my life and I'm thankful for your support and friendship.

Love you Auntie (inside joke) **Ty Leese Javeh**, where do I began when it's so easy to say thank you and move on? This collab has been a long time coming but outside of this collab I want to thank you as my sister, friend, counselor, shoulder, and motivator. This past year has been trying for me and through it all you were right there not just for moral support, but you were there for me in ways that I could never repay you. The many nights that you sat on the phone with me and listened to me cry over my personal situation I thank you. I thank you for taking the time to talk to my daughter whenever she picks up the phone and calls her auntie Ty. When I felt that I'd lost everything, it was you that pulled me out of that rut I was in and made me realize that God took it to replace it with more and made room for me to receive greater. Thank you for not allowing me to give up when it seemed as if that was the easiest option. I love and appreciate you as my sister and my friend and I'm looking forward to us working on so much more together. This series might be over, but we have material for days that I think the world need to read. Love you to the moon and back.

Please check out my other titles listed on Amazon and Barnes & Noble:

I had to do it (1 and 2)

Love VS Trust (1 and 2)

Cold Case Love

Daddy Issues

No Loyalty in the Hood

True Undying Love-A Twisted Love Story

Fell In Love with a Bad Guy (1 and 2)

So Gone Over You (1, 2, 3)

It Hurts Me to Love You (1, 2, and 3)

Giving My Heart to a Savage: Who Could Love You Like I Do (1 and 2)

This Thug Turned My Heart Cold (1 and 2)

Your Love Was Breaking the Law- Broken Promises, Shattered Dreams: A Scary Thing Called Love

Into The Hood: Pierre & Anneka

CPSIA information can be obtained
at www.ICGtesting.com
Printed in the USA
LVOW13s1741230218
567697LV00010B/465/P